Letters From Greenview

by

Margaret Groh

Publisher's Note:

This is a work of fiction. All names, characters, places, and
events are the work of the author's imagination.

Any resemblance to real persons, places, or events is
coincidental.

Solstice Publishing - www.solsticepublishing.com

To my late mother, Lena M. Yacenda, who showed us all how to put one foot in front of the other and to keep going.

Excerpt From the Greenview Times

April 30, 2010

Construction for the Greenview Interchange at the site of the Old Heidelberg Hotel has been halted due to the discovery of human remains found under the hotel foundation. The remains, thought to be a female approximately 25 years of age, have been entombed under the hotel since the foundation was poured on October 15, 1945. A preliminary search of police records indicate that no missing persons have been reported either before or after that date, leading investigators to believe the victim might have been from out of town. Anyone with information that may lead to the identification of the remains is asked to call the Greenview Police.

Chapter One

June 20th

Laura Hunter caught her first glimpse of the darkening sky as she pulled into the parking lot of the Tre Pane restaurant. She was about five hundred feet from the entrance, not exactly sprinting distance given that she was wearing high heels and a pencil thin skirt. If she didn't hurry, she'd get soaked. Maybe it wasn't such a bright idea to pull her favorite business suit out of the closet. She was only meeting Dave Schubert, a lowly summer intern trying to become an investigative reporter. Like most college seniors, he'd probably wonder why she wasn't wearing jeans and a tee shirt.

Why? Laura asked herself. Why had she agreed to her editor's request to meet with Dave? Talk about lousy timing. She was still reeling from her mother's sudden death late last month and even though summer vacation for her three young children was only a few days old, she was already pulling her hair out.

Laura sighed. She had no doubt that Sandy Watters meant well. "Look, Laura," Sandy had said. "I know how hard these past few weeks have been for you but we need you back as much as you need us and I have the perfect distraction. His name is Dave Schubert. He's a bright kid. He's first in his class and will probably be a great reporter some day but he actually thinks he can identify the remains found under that hotel in Greenview. I don't want to stymie him but I think he's wasting his time. Maybe you can guide him. You love cold cases and this is right up your alley. I've already told him that you'd love to be his mentor."

All things considered, Laura had been flattered by Sandy's request. She was proud of her reputation as a tenacious investigative reporter and knew the awards that she had won opened doors for her that were closed to newbies. She liked to think that she had great instincts but in an honest moment, she couldn't discount the role that luck played in her success. *Luck*, Laura mused. Given everything Sandy had told her about Greenview, Laura figured she would need more than luck to get through this one. Somehow she would have to steer Dave onto another project, but how? He didn't sound like someone who would be easily distracted. No doubt she could be in for a long evening but then again, on a personal level, all was not lost. She'd get to enjoy a quiet dinner and in the process, learn more about Greenview, the town where her mother grew up.

The first raindrop from the approaching storm splattered on Laura's windshield. It was large and loud. Estimating that she had all of 10 seconds to traverse the parking lot, Laura flung her car door open and ran as fast as her skirt and heels would allow. She reached the restaurant's protective canopy just ahead of a deafening wall of water. Congratulating herself for her masterful timing, she stepped inside dry as a bone.

The crowd was thin for a Thursday night but Dave was nowhere to be found. *Not again*, Laura fretted. Did she have the wrong night, the wrong time or possibly the wrong restaurant? Prior to her mother's death she had been able to manage her packed schedule down to a nanosecond. How comforting it had been to know her mother was always there, always ready to lend a hand. Laura hadn't expected the transition to be easy but she hadn't expected to feel so lost. Defeated, she started over to the hostess desk. She didn't see the young man coming in from the back room until he called her name.

Laura spun around, her eyes locking onto the walking version of Dave's Facebook picture. A good ten pounds underweight, his dark curly hair complemented his bright greenish hazel eyes. His complexion was clear and creamy, making it all but impossible to hide his five o'clock shadow. He was wearing a jacket and a tie and spoke with a distinct confidence. His handshake was firm and his warmth seemed genuine. Laura couldn't help but wonder why someone this impressive would waste time on an investigation that stood little chance of going anywhere.

Sheets of water were now pouring from the sky. Dave led Laura to the back room. "Sorry to bring you out in such miserable weather. It's an honor to finally meet you."

Laura smiled a thank you as Dave pulled out her chair. He sat her on his right, giving her a great view of a lovely outdoor garden, now more like the view from a submarine. To the left of his plate, Laura noticed a half empty glass of wine as well as a large accordion envelope. She was intrigued.

"I hope you don't mind that I've started without you. I've been in Greenview. Came directly from there. I headed out early so I could stay ahead of this storm and got here with time to spare. By the way, the house merlot's pretty good. Would you care for one?"

Dave flagged down their server, who returned a short time later with Laura's drink. A rumble of thunder shook the room. The lights flickered. "Greenview," Laura said, trying to ignore the storm. "I probably should have mentioned that my mother grew up in Greenview."

"No kidding! That's really awesome. Whereabouts?"

Laura shrugged. "I'm not really sure. She never talked about it much. Kind of a sore spot for her. When she was sixteen, her mother died and about a year later, their house burned to the ground. My mother was the only survivor. She made it out unharmed but had to listen to her father and brother scream for help. High-tailed it out of town right after the funerals. I don't blame her for refusing to take me back there but I've always been curious. What's the place like?"

"Oppressively boring, at least until several weeks ago. My grandmother lives in Greenview and as a kid I spent many a visit trying desperately to amuse myself. Who knew sixty-five years ago someone planted a body? Really got the place jumping."

"I can imagine. The police—what are they saying?"

"Not much. They've given up on the case, small town, no budget. Too bad for them. Here's the cool part. The Jane Doe was wearing a solid gold ring which is surprisingly well preserved. There's a design on the face of the ring that looks like a family crest. I've done tons of research in this area and I think I can track it down."

"A family crest as in a coat of arms?"

"I'm hoping. So far, the closest I've gotten to this ring is a grainy photograph, but the shape of the crest suggests European heritage."

"Hold that thought," Laura replied, her eyes peeled on the bowl of salad and the basket of garlic bread that their approaching server was carrying. "I know nothing about family crests but having waited tables in college I know how annoying it is when people aren't ready to order. She opened her menu. "We'd better figure out what we want."

Wanting to shorten the interruption, Dave picked the first chicken dish that he saw but he soon realized he could have studied the entire menu for the amount of time Laura was chit chatting with their server. "About that crest," he said the minute the intruder walked away. I'm guessing Germany."

Laura tossed the salad. "Germany?" she asked, filling her own dish and then handing the bowl to Dave. "Why Germany?"

"The police report. There was an altercation in the cemetery on October 14, 1945. That, by the way was the day before the foundation for the Old Heidelberg Hotel was poured and most likely the day someone dumped Jane's body. The groundskeeper reported a scuffle between a man and a woman. He was busy preparing for a large funeral and figured it was just a lover's spat. He saw the man try to grab the woman, but she broke free and started to run. He claimed she was yelling in German. By the time the guy jumped into his car, she was running across the street. Picture this. That street was all that separated the cemetery from the construction site."

"Wow," Laura replied. "You might actually be onto something. If I'm following you correctly, the concrete was poured the next day. Any description of the car?"

"Nothing about the car or the license plate. At the time, the police believed the incident was a domestic quarrel, a quarrel that just might have ended at that construction site."

"Any chance the groundskeeper knew the woman?"

Dave broke off a piece of garlic bread. "Doesn't appear that way. Poor guy thought he'd seen her at a recent funeral but couldn't remember which one. Promised to review his records and give the police a name. Was killed in a hit-and-run the next day. No investigation into the hit-and-run, or into locating the woman."

"Nice."

"Well, they figured the victim was from out of town since none of the locals reported her missing. To them it was a dead end."

"Unlikely," Laura replied. "You said that this woman was seen at a funeral and then at the cemetery a couple of days later. That means she couldn't have been a total stranger. Someone had to know her. Odd they didn't report her missing. Too bad you don't know what gravesite she might have been visiting."

Dave pushed the bread and salad bowls aside. "Actually, I think I've figured that out." He pulled several charts from his folder and then placed them on the table. "Here. Take a look."

Between tiny bites of salad, Laura studied chart after chart. "Wow! So this is what the cemetery looked like on October 14, 1945? How'd you do this?"

"Time and patience. Check this one out. It's the only gravesite Jane Doe could have been visiting, the only newly dug grave that the groundskeeper could have seen from where he said he was standing."

"I'm impressed," Laura replied. "You've really put a lot of time into this. Did you find the family?"

"Yeah, but they're all gone. The last surviving member of this family died several weeks ago."

"That stinks," Laura replied. "What about friends, neighbors?"

Dave shrugged. "Been working on a neighbor but she's not very cooperative. Turns out the lone survivor was a male who lived by himself in Greenview, on a huge farmstead, a little off the beaten path. I've been told the farmstead was once a beautiful place but now it's a falling down dump. I managed to get inside but it was a total waste of time."

"What were you looking for?"

"Anything that might confirm his connection to the Jane Doe. Unfortunately, I got there too late. Looters took everything that wasn't nailed down but there is a glimmer of hope. The man had a daughter. She ran away years ago and hasn't been heard from since. The township is still trying to find her even though they don't know if she's alive or dead. Turns out, the farmhouse is a death trap and Public Safety wants it torn down asap. Naturally they don't want to pay for it and were hoping to stick the daughter with the bill."

"That's about right." Laura replied. "As long as money's involved, they'll keep looking for her. Good for you, bad for her."

"Not necessarily. The cost of the tear down is a fraction of what that property's worth. If they find that woman, they'll be doing her a favor. Hey, I have an idea. Your mother might know the family. Could you ask her?"

"Wish I could. She passed away late last month."

Dave cringed. "Oh, I didn't know. I'm so sorry."

"Thanks. It's been rough. My husband was killed in a freak car accident shortly after my youngest was born and my mother came to live with me. She was everything to me and my kids. To be perfectly honest, she was the reason I agreed to help. Like I said, she never talked much about Greenview and frankly, I was nostalgic to learn a little more."

And there it was, Dave mused, the reason someone of Laura's stature would agree to help a lowly intern. Somewhat deflated, Dave took out his phone. Hoping to keep Laura interested, he tapped the photo icon and then swiped the screen several times. He handed the phone to Laura. "Maybe this'll help. It's a little taste of Greenview. This is the tombstone I was telling you about. Not one hundred percent sure how but this family is connected in some way to Jane Doe."

Laura took the phone but as she studied the picture, she could feel the color drain from her face. *Can't be. Can't possibly be.* She forced the lump down her throat. "Abbott? The family's name is Abbott?"

Surprised by Laura's reaction, Dave hesitated. "Yeah. John and Ethel were the parents. They had three kids, Amelia, George and Mary. The mother and one of the daughters died years ago. The father passed away almost three months ago and the son about four years ago. Mary's the daughter who ran away. They figure if she's still alive, she's in her sixties. Be a real coup to find her. She's the only member of this family who might know something about Jane Doe. Would love to pick her brain."

Laura sighed. "So would I but I'm afraid that'll never happen. Mary Abbott was my mother and you've just described her family."

"What?" Dave whispered. "Are you sure? You said her family was killed in a fire years ago."

Laura sighed. "That was the story I grew up believing. Clearly it wasn't true. Wow! I can't believe my mother's father and brother were alive all these years."

Dave was speechless. "Geez, Mrs. H. I'm really sorry."

Laura shrugged. "So am I. I often wondered about that fire and why my mother was so reticent to talk about it. Now I know." She placed the phone on the table. "I figured it would be interesting to learn something about Greenview but I wasn't expecting this."

Their server appeared, carrying a large tray. He waited for Dave to remove his charts and then he placed one dish in front of Laura, the other in front of Dave. "Portabella mushroom ravioli, chicken parmesan. The plates are hot. Please be careful. Need anything else?"

Shaking her head, Laura waved the server away. She turned to Dave. "You sure about that gravesite?"

"I was, but a second set of eyes couldn't hurt. Let me take you up there. I can show you how I did it; show you the actual gravesite and even the house where your mother grew up. How 'bout next week? You available?"

"You gotta be kidding. I barely made it here tonight and the last time I looked Greenview was four hours up and four hours back. As much as I'd love to see the farmhouse, that's a huge chuck of time I just don't have right now. Can it wait?"

"Not if you really want to see the house. One good wind and its gone. The place is amazing. The house is an absolute disaster but it sits on eighty acres of what is now prime real estate. It's worth a small fortune. When did you say your mother passed away?"

"Late last month."

"Then you're in luck. If my timeline is correct, your mother passed away after John Abbott, so the farmstead would have gone to her. As her heir, it should go to you."

Laura bristled. "Are you kidding? I just found out that my mother, who didn't have a deceitful bone in her body, spent a lifetime fabricating a godawful lie. What's lucky about that?"

Dave gestured surrender. "Sorry. Poor choice of words. I was referring to the farmstead. Everyone's been talking about what will happen to it. It's yours for the asking."

"I wouldn't bet on that. My mother had no contact with her family from age seventeen which means that if her father had a will, he probably wrote her out. Besides, you've potentially linked the victim of a sixty-five year old murder to my mother's family. I need to know exactly how my mother's family was involved before I stick my foot in that pond."

"What do you mean?"

"Well, think about it. Sixty-five years ago, someone dumped a woman's body at a construction site and got away with it. How did that happen? Who was this woman? What was her connection to my mother's family? It's a little creepy."

"Really, Mrs. H. Creepy never stopped you before. I've seen some of the stories you've covered and Sandy went on and on about how fearless you were."

"*Were* is the operative word. Things change. To be honest, I'm not in a very good place right now. I've already lost two people who meant the world to me so I know bad things can happen for no good reason. I'm a single mother with three great kids and I'm not going to take any unnecessary chances. I'll help in any way I can but at this point, I want no part of the Abbott farmstead, or the Abbott family for that matter. In my mind, they've all been dead for years."

Dave hesitated. "I gotta say, Mrs. H. After six weeks, tons of media coverage that even included a photo of the ring found on the body I haven't gotten very far. If you decide to claim the farmstead, who knows, it might get the ball rolling again. What do you say?"

"No, no, and no. I'm not sticking my neck out until I know who this Jane Doe is and how she wound up under that hotel. I know in my gut that if that farmstead was a good thing, my mother wouldn't have done all that she did to keep me away. Maybe I'll see things differently after I've had some time to absorb all this. Besides, we leave for vacation in eight days. I'll touch base with you after we get back."

No way, Dave mused. He wasn't going to wait that long. "Eight days?" he asked, searching for a distraction. "Where are you going?"

"The Outer Banks. It's been a family tradition for years. Was my mother's idea. She'd gone down with friends and came back in love with the place. We started going after our first child was born, a three generation vacation. Got a lot of good memories. I wanted to cancel that first summer after my husband died but my mother insisted we go. She was right. It was hard being there without him but it was very healing. Life goes on. Same deal this year although I know it's going to take a lot more energy. Don't want to start out on an empty tank."

"I understand," Dave replied, knowing full well that this was his last shot. "I'm going back to Greenview on Monday. I'll drive. You pick the time. Like I said, I'm not sure how much longer that house will be standing. Wait till after your vacation and it might not be there."

"Ouch," Laura replied, shaking her head. "You really know how to tighten the screws." She hesitated. Her thoughts were racing. This morning she had no idea her mother's childhood home still existed and now she had the chance to see it for herself. She took a deep breath. "I probably should have my head examined but guess I can squeeze out a few hours. Two conditions: we see the house first and then the cemetery, but if you so much as mention me claiming the Abbott farmstead, all bets are off."

Dave laughed. "No problem, Mrs. H. What about your mother's neighbor? You gotta meet her. She's a tough nut to crack and I'm telling you, she knows more than she'll admit. Lives a stone's throw from the farmhouse. Had to know your mother. If anyone can get her to open up, you can."

"We'll see." Laura raised her wine glass in a silent toast of approval and then took a long, slow sip. She tasted her ravioli. It was surprisingly delicious. She sighed. All in all, the evening had been reasonably pleasant but she had just mortgaged time she didn't have not only to please her editor but to dissect a secret that her mother had spent a lifetime trying to keep from her, a secret that might have something to do with a sixty-five year old unsolved murder. Wise decision or stupid mistake? Only time would tell.

Chapter Two

June 24th

"What?" Dave said, pressing the phone against his ear. "Friday night? This happened three days ago? How'd you find out?

Dave's grandmother took a deep breath. "It was in this morning's paper. A group of teens were partying at the Abbott Farmhouse. It got pretty cold so someone had the bright idea to build a bonfire in the fireplace. Most of the bricks in the chimney were long gone so it didn't take long for the walls to catch fire. Everyone got out okay but by the time they managed to call for help, the fire was out of control. The house is gone. Totally gone. I'm really sorry."

"Not your fault, Gram. Thanks for the heads up. I'll talk to you later."

Not good, Dave told himself, staring at his phone. How was he supposed to break the news to Laura? In exactly one hour, he would pick her up for their trek to Greenview. Maybe it hadn't been such a bright idea to use the farmhouse as bait, but knowing Laura's reluctance to take the trip, what else was he supposed to do? He weighed his options. He could call Laura and let her know the house was gone but why give her an excuse to bail? If he waited to tell her in person, she might feel compelled to stick with the plan. Then again, she'd probably have a few choice words. Taking a deep breath, he made the call. To his surprise, Laura not only doubled down but insisted that they leave asap.

The ride to Greenview was long, punctuated by lively conversations and pensive silences. "Three days,"

Laura sighed. "I missed seeing my mother's house by three days. What lousy timing."

"No kidding," Dave replied. "You missed seeing the house by a matter of days and I missed interviewing John by about a week. Sure wish I made the connection between him and Jane Doe sooner. No telling what I could have learned."

"Well, don't beat yourself up. After sixty-five years, there's no guarantee John could have told you anything. Besides, just because Jane Doe might have been accosted at the Abbott gravesite doesn't mean they had an actual connection. Any idea how John died?"

"Fell down his steps. Rotted there for two weeks. No autopsy. The place was a real dump. Warped steps, loose banister. Easy to understand why they said it was an accident."

"Easy to understand?" Laura repeated. "That's not exactly a ringing endorsement."

"I know, but at this point I just don't have enough information to write anything off."

Laura smiled. "I like your approach. Always good to keep an open mind. So tell me: what was the house like? How big was it?"

"Glad you asked," Dave said, taking his phone out of his pocket. Holding the phone and the steering wheel with one hand, he keyed in his password, found the photos from May 20th and then handed the phone to Laura. "The Abbott Farmhouse. Unfortunately, I didn't get there until after the house was boarded up. Went in through the basement window. The lighting's awful but you'll still get an idea of what it was like. Remember this was a showplace when your mother lived here."

Laura held the phone at eye level. "I can't believe you have pictures. This is awesome."

The first picture, taken approximately half way up the driveway, caught Laura by surprise. "You're kidding!"

She stared in disbelief. The first floor windows had been covered with thick wooden boards into which rectangular holes had been cut. The holes were centered in such a way that the windows looked like gigantic light-switch plates. "Are those boards someone's idea of a joke?"

"Not exactly. They make those holes small enough to keep the human element out but big enough to let some light in. The light is supposed to keep the rodents away. Love to know who came up with that one. You should have heard it in there. It was like a rodent rodeo."

Laura studied the next shot, a close up of the crumbling front porch. A crooked beam meant to support the roof looked to be detaching from the house. A "DANGER: KEEP OUT" sign hung on the front door. "What were those kids thinking? I'll betcha there were rats in there the size of gophers."

"Not just the rats, Mrs. H. The place reeked." Dave glanced at his phone. "That's the living room. Kinda dark. The flash was worthless. Not that much to see in there anyway. All the furniture was gone except for that floor lamp and that broken chair."

Laura swiped to the next picture. It was a shot of a darkened area at the bottom of the steps. "My God. What's this?"

"That's where they found John. It was pretty gross. I don't know how those kids could stand the smell. The authorities cleaned up after they removed the body but those fluids had plenty of time to seep between the cracks in the floor. In terms of sanitation, burning that place down was the best thing that could have happened. The next shot is the kitchen."

Tucking a loose strand of hair behind her ear, Laura stared at a crooked wooden table, cabinets with no doors, gouged out counters, warped floor tiles, a pockmarked stove and a missing refrigerator. "Who lives like this?"

Laura demanded, not really expecting an answer. "No wonder my mother wanted to keep me away."

Dave just shrugged. "The next three shots are the steps. Almost killed myself on the third step from the top. Didn't know how loose it was until I stepped on it. I'm guessing John fell from there. Poor guy. Don't know if he died right away or if he lay there calling for help. The neighbor I was telling you about. Her husband found the body. They'd known each other for a long time. Had to be tough."

"You said they didn't do an autopsy. Any reason why?"

"Can't say for sure but remember that heat wave the first week or so of May? Even though it might have been a few degrees cooler in Greenview, it was plenty warm. Two weeks in that heat, you gotta think that body was so badly decomposed that there wasn't much left to autopsy. Sorry to be so graphic."

"Don't be. For some reason, my mother set out on her own when she was only seventeen. What kind of father would let something like that happen? This may sound cruel but it's kinda hard for me to have any feeling for John whatsoever."

"I understand," Dave replied. He glanced at his phone. "Now you're on the second floor. There were three bedrooms and a bath. The stench up there was almost as bad as the first floor. The last shot is your mother's bedroom. If you enlarge what's left of the curtains, you can see how frilly they once were. That room was in the worst shape. The plaster on the side wall was rotted all the way down to the studs. It was pretty bad."

Laura studied the ruins of her mother's old bedroom and then placed Dave's phone on the center console. "I'm almost glad my mother isn't around to see this, although I'd love to know why she made up that fire story. Any chance you can send me those pictures? Oddly enough, just looking at them kind of takes the sting out of my mother's crazy story."

They drove the rest of the way in silence. The sun was directly overhead by the time Dave pulled onto the long and winding driveway that led to the Abbott Farmhouse. Given the crumbling asphalt, he stopped a good distance from where the house once stood and parked under a gigantic old oak tree. Laura stared straight ahead. "Wow! This is so strange. It's only been like this for a couple of days and yet, and yet it's exactly the way my mother described it."

They got out of the car. All was quiet. The smell of burned wood permeated the air. Dried leaves and old twigs crunched underfoot as they walked toward the charred remains. Looking around, Laura shook her head. "This is nothing like I imagined." She made a visor with her right hand and peered beyond the rubble where she saw a barn, choked by overgrown weeds, its roof long gone. "I get that the neglect here was years in the making but it's hard to believe this was ever a showplace. Do I hear water?" she asked, suddenly aware of a gurgling sound.

"There's a stream behind the house. When your grandfather farmed the land, he dammed it up and used it as an irrigation pond. There's a great picture of it in the Greenview library. A winter scene, kids ice skating. People say this was a happy place but after your grandmother died, your grandfather went into a tailspin and never recovered."

Laura sighed. "That was about a year before the alleged fire. What about my uncle?"

Dave chose his words carefully. He hadn't heard one kind word about George Abbott. "He was a loner, worked on the farm. No wife, no children."

They wandered aimlessly. It was uncomfortably warm. Laura was disturbed by the overgrown fields and what might lay behind them. She found herself gravitating toward a stand of trees that stretched from where the house once stood to the two lane road that ran in front of it. She sighed. "Meg was right."

"Who's Meg?"

"My best friend. We met on an interview about five years ago. I was doing a piece on the plight of battered women and she was trying to open a shelter for women and children. She's a psychologist. Really knows her stuff. She warned me about what I might find up here. There's a lot of anger in the story my mother fabricated: her father and brother burning to death, screaming for help. Things that might account for that anger aren't very pretty. It's curious to me that you say this was once a happy place but I'm getting really bad vibes."

Dave wasn't sure how to reply. "You look very warm. We can cut through these woods. It'll bring us out to the road right across from your mother's neighbor."

They stepped onto the path. Laura jumped as a covey of quail burst from the underbrush. "It's okay, Mrs. H. With John gone I guess no one uses this trail anymore. We'll be ok. Just follow me."

Several minutes later they reached the road. Laura welcomed the sunshine.

"Well, look at that, Mrs. H. We're in luck." Dave pointed to the neat garden in front of the house. "There's Neeka. Brace yourself. I seem to bring out her inner pit bull and I think I made things worse by telling her that the Abbotts might be connected in some way to Jane Doe. Figured if she knew, she'd open up. Wrong. You shoulda heard her. Feisty lady. She's old but she's sharp."

They crossed the road. "The flowers she's cutting," Laura whispered as they quietly approached. They look like peonies. That was my mother's favorite flower. I can practically smell them from here."

Neeka was so engrossed in what she was doing that she wasn't aware she had company until she heard Dave call her name. "Go away," she said without even turning around. "I have nothing more to say to you. Stop wasting my time."

Laura stepped closer. "Please," she said. "We don't mean to bother you."

Neeka turned slowly. She ignored Dave and stared at Laura. Something about her seemed familiar but she didn't know what. "Who are you?" she demanded.

"My name is Laura Hunter. I'm an investigative reporter. Dave and I would like to ask you a few questions. We think you might have known my mother. Her house burned to the ground just a couple of days ago. Her name was Mary, Mary Abbott."

"Mary?" Neeka whispered. "No wonder you seem familiar. Your voice. You sound so much like her." She hesitated. A slow smile crossed her lips. She wiped her hands on her apron and then reached for Laura. "Dear Lord, I don't believe this. After all these years. Let me look at you." She squeezed Laura's hands.

"This takes me back, way back. I was in my twenties when we moved here, shortly after John and Ethel. Your mother was only two. Such a sweetie." She hesitated. "This must be a sign. Not too long ago, we found something that belonged to her but couldn't decide what to do with it. Please. You should take it. Come inside while I get it."

Dave and Laura exchanged glances as Neeka began inching her way up the long front sidewalk. "You're my lucky charm," Dave whispered to Laura. "You've gotten further with that woman in five minutes than I got in five hours."

"Don't kid yourself," Laura replied. "I haven't gotten anywhere. This isn't about me; it's about a lady who wants to offload something that belonged to my mother, something she's kept for half a century, something she clearly can't wait to get rid of."

Dave shrugged. "So what? You said you wanted to learn more about your mother. Now's your chance."

"I know, I know, but for the record, I was hoping to get a sense of what her life was like. Simple stuff, her favorite color, the friends she hung out with. Certainly not this. Maybe I'm on edge. It's not every day you learn your family might be connected to a sixty-five year old murder victim. This is just a hunch, based on years of experience and maybe a bit of paranoia but it wouldn't surprise me one bit if whatever that sweet old woman wants to get rid of turns out to be radioactive."

Chapter Three

June 24th

Neeka held the front door open. As she waited for Laura and Dave to catch up, she couldn't take her eyes off Laura. She was beautiful like her mother but taller and she seemed friendly even though she said she was an investigative reporter; hopefully nothing like that bothersome kid who brought her here. Neeka sighed. All things considered this had to be a sign. Finally, after all these years, she would be able to keep the promise she had made so long ago. "The kitchen," she said, gesturing for Laura and Dave to follow. "I just need to spritz these flowers. Won't take more than a minute."

Laura stepped in front of Dave and then followed Neeka down the long hallway into a bright and spacious kitchen. "This is beautiful," Laura exclaimed, looking all around. "You said you moved in the same time as my grandparents but your house looks so new."

"It is," Neeka replied. She placed the peonies in the sink, turned the water on and gently sprayed the flowers until they glistened. "I don't know if you noticed the houses behind ours. That was our land. We sold out to a developer who built this house next to where our old one was." Neeka wiped her hands on her apron and then poured two glasses of iced tea. "Come. Let me show you to my sunroom. It's my favorite place, my absolute favorite."

They reached a bright open room with huge glass windows. "Wow!" Laura exclaimed. "I can see why you love this room. What an awesome view."

"Thank you," Neeka replied. "She gestured toward a round oak table. "Have a seat. I'll be right back."

Several steps later, Neeka stopped to catch her breath. Her heart was pounding. She walked into her bedroom. Taking a deep breath, she sat down at her vanity and removed a tiny box from the back of the top drawer. Closing the drawer, she glanced at the photo of her late husband. Their last moments together still haunted her. How she wished he was still here.

Sensing she was about to lose her nerve, Neeka hurried back to her sunroom. She placed what looked like a miniature treasure chest on the table in front of Laura. "Sorry about the scratches. The box was locked and we didn't have the key. My husband pried the hasp off so that we could see what was inside. Go ahead. Open it."

Not sure what to expect, Laura lifted the lid. "Oh, my," she whispered, staring at two platinum barrettes shaped to look like a Scottie dog. She took one out and ran her finger over the eyes and nose which were made of onyx, the collar which was made of rubies and the fur which was made of sparkling diamonds. She turned to Neeka. "I've seen pins like these in antique shops, but never barrettes. These stones look real. You say these belonged to my mother?"

"I've had them for years but had forgotten about them until recently. Ethel gave them to me when she found out she had cancer. Made me promise to give them to your mother when she turned twenty-one. Never happened. Ethel died when your mother was sixteen. Things changed radically after that and your mother left home a year later. I felt so bad. Please, could you give them to her for me? Help me keep that promise?"

Laura put the barrette back in the box. "I wish I could, but my mother passed away several weeks ago. I'm hoping you can help me. I grew up believing that my mother's father and brother were killed in a raging fire from which my mother barely escaped. I learned just a few days ago that wasn't true. Do you know what really happened?"

Neeka reached for Laura's hand. "Oh, I'm so sorry about your mother. I was very fond of her and always hoped she'd come back. I wanted to apologize for not doing more after Ethel died. George was such a nightmare. She had to leave."

"George? Do you mean her brother?" Laura replied. "She left because of him?"

"Partly." Neeka hesitated. "After Ethel died, George started making advances toward your mother. John was pathetic. He was drinking so much, that he couldn't control himself much less his son. One night, George tried to rape your mother, in the woods across the street. My husband and I were away but my daughter heard her screaming. She got there just in time. Your mother was hysterical. She stayed at our house for a while and then one morning she went out for a walk and didn't come back. Hours passed. My daughter was beside herself. Finally your mother called to say that she was fine. Wouldn't say where she was or how she got there. She thanked my daughter for her help and said goodbye. That was the last we heard from her."

Laura was incredulous. "My poor mother. Her own brother?"

Again Neeka hesitated. Although the room was cool, she could feel her palms sweating. "Your mother and George may have grown up together but they were not actually brother and sister. You see, your mother was not an Abbott. Her real mother brought her to Greenview just after her second birthday."

"Her real mother?" Laura repeated. "I thought Ethel Abbott was her real mother."

"I did too, until Ethel gave me that box. At that point, I'd known Ethel and your mother for fourteen years. I was shocked."

Laura nodded. "I know the feeling. Tell me. If Ethel Abbott wasn't my mother's mother, who was?"

"A woman named Linda, Ferina, Ferona, something like that. I never met Linda. By the time we moved in, Linda had disappeared. Given the circumstances, John and Ethel felt it best to keep your mother and let everyone think she was theirs."

"Circumstances? What circumstances? What could possibly make someone keep a child that wasn't theirs?"

Laura's challenge caught Neeka by surprise. She often rehearsed this conversation, tried to prepare herself for what Mary Abbott would say, how she would react. Instead, she now had to explain it all to Mary's daughter, a woman she'd never met. She took a deep breath. "You may not approve of what John and Ethel did but they felt they had no choice. They were determined to keep your mother safe."

"From whom?" Laura demanded.

Neeka gestured patience. "Please. Let me explain. Ethel and Linda met at the train station in Philadelphia. Little Amelia Abbott had just been discharged from the Children's Hospital. She was very sick but the minute Amelia and your mother met, they started laughing and giggling. After all Amelia had been through, it was music to Ethel's ears so she invited Linda and your mother to come stay with them. Linda was more than happy to accept. Turns out she was running from a wealthy, powerful but abusive husband and was looking for a place to hide.

"For a while things were working out. Linda managed to get a letter off to her sister and was waiting for a response. Then one morning, Amelia didn't wake up. Ethel was crushed. Linda stayed around to help but a short time later, she disappeared. John and Ethel were sure her disappearance had something to do with her rotten husband and they feared for your mother's safety. Since they were new in town, it made sense for them to tell everyone that

Mary was Amelia's twin. Understand all they wanted to do was to protect your mother from her own father, a man who had allegedly tried to kill Linda and your mother."

"My poor mother," Laura whispered. "Did she know any of this?"

Neeka shrugged. "Ethel wanted to wait until your mother was twenty-one but who knows what John might have said." Neeka patted Laura's hand. "I know how hard this must be for you but your mother was happy here, until Ethel died. John changed after that. He was never the same. Drink, drink, drink. Your mother was right to leave."

Laura sighed. "I always thought it was odd that my mother never talked about John or George. Now I know why."

Neeka nodded. "John got even worse after George died. These past four years, John being all by himself. He was miserable. We tried to help but he was rarely sober. We realized just how bad he was after they discovered those remains. Honestly, I wish we never bothered." She shrugged. "Truthfully, I'm still trying to sort it all out."

Laura waited. *Here it comes*, she mused. The real reason Neeka was so reluctant to talk to Dave. "Sort what out?" she asked.

Neeka took a deep breath. "When it first happened, them finding the remains, we didn't pay much attention. Then one day we saw an article about Jane Doe in the Greenview Times. It even had a picture of the ring she was wearing. What struck us was the date they thought she had been buried. October 14, 1945. That was the same day Linda disappeared."

Laura squinted. "Wow. You remember that, all these years later."

"Not that hard. October 14, 1945 was Ethel's twenty-fifth birthday. It was a terrible day for her. The only thing she wanted to do on that day was to bring flowers to her daughter's grave but she was too sick. Linda brought them for her but she never came back. Ethel felt responsible. She and John assumed Linda's husband had found her but unlike before, she didn't get away. One bad decision: sending Linda out on her own had changed everything."

"Are you sure about that date?"

"Absolutely. October 14th is no ordinary day. Every year Ethel and I would bring flowers to the cemetery. I still go. I bring a bunch for Amelia and a bunch for Ethel. Rain or shine. Not a date I'd ever forget. You can imagine how we felt when we saw that article, October 14th, the skeletal remains. It hit us pretty hard."

Laura could barely hear above the pulsing in her ears. "So you think those remains are Linda's, the woman who brought my mother to Greenview. Linda, my mother's real mother, my real grandmother."

Flooded with relief, Neeka patted Laura's hand. "I do. I wasn't sure how to tell you. I'm very sorry. I know this must come as a terrible shock."

Laura's head was spinning. She glanced at Dave who looked just as surprised as she was. "Dave's been working this story for several weeks and this is the first we're hearing something like this. Does anyone else know?"

Neeka shook her head. "We probably should have gone to the police, but we were so worried about John. He was the last person to see Linda alive and if those bones really are hers the police would want to know why he didn't report her missing. We brought the picture of the ring over to see if he would recognize it. It was like talking to the wall. He didn't remember Linda and he didn't even remember your mother. He got very angry. Thought we were trying to trick him. My husband managed to calm him down and just like that, he had forgotten why we came. Just as well. We decided to drop the issue and not discuss it again. I mean, with the little we knew about Linda, we wouldn't be much help. Besides, we were about to leave for vacation. I couldn't wait.

"The day before our trip, my husband went to check on John. He was pathetic. Ranting, raving, stuff strewn all over the place. My husband brought him here to sober him up and get him something to eat. Since we were going to be away for a while, I made several meals for him to take home. We washed his clothes and helped put his place back in order. In the morning we left for our trip.

"My husband drove me crazy the whole time we were gone. He worried about John. Didn't think he should be alone. As best I could, I closed my ears.

"Two weeks later, we came home. John was dead. They say he fell down his steps. No big surprise. Some days that man could barely walk a straight line. All the meals I made were still in the refrigerator so we figured John died shortly after we left. My husband made the funeral arrangements. It was sad. No one came. For several days after that my husband hardly said boo. It was so annoying. I knew something was bothering him but he wouldn't say what."

The phone on the credenza rang, loud and shrill. Neeka froze. She knew it would be either her daughter or one of a half dozen realtors trying to get her to list her house. She waited for the answering machine and then hearing a man's voice, she waved her hand in dismissal. "My daughter means well. Doesn't want me living here by myself. Thinks she can get me to change my mind by asking all these real estate people to make nice to me. In the days before he died, her father really got to her. Convinced her we were no longer safe here; that John's death was no accident and that the man who went after him might come after us. I loved my husband but I never fully understood his relationship to John. He was loyal to that man to a fault. No way would I ever give up my garden or my sunroom for my husband's crazy ideas."

Several minutes later, Dave and Laura began their trek back to Dave's car. "I'm really sorry about your grandmother, Mrs. H. I knew Neeka was hiding something but I never expected this."

"Neither did I. It always bothered me that I never got to meet Ethel Abbott. My mother always spoke so highly of her. I'm not sure which is worse. That Ethel's not my grandmother or that my real grandmother's been lying under that hotel all this time. Gonna take a while for everything to sink in. I feel like I've been hit by a tidal wave."

"Yeah," Dave agreed. "Neeka really offloaded. She didn't hold anything back. I've sort of changed my mind about her. Now I get why she was so uncooperative."

Laura sighed. "That was quite a story. Imagine her husband not telling the police that he thought John's house had been ransacked. Then again, it was kind of sweet of him to put everything back before calling 911. Poor guy was afraid the police would think John went off on another one of his benders and he wanted to protect him from all the unpleasant gossip."

"Not sure about sweet, Mrs. H. John's death may or may not be related to the discovery of Linda's remains and if Neeka's husband suspected that the place had been ransacked but straightened up to protect his friend then he obstructed justice. He hid evidence."

"Hid evidence? That's a little harsh. I get that the timing of John's death is a little suspect but he was a falling down drunk, living in a falling down dump. Give me one good reason why someone would ransack that place."

"Your mother's barrettes?"

Laura stopped dead in her tracks. "My mother's barrettes! You can't be serious. The only one who would even know about them is my grandfather, a guy who must be ninety or more by now if he's even alive."

"True," Dave replied, "but those cute little Scotties are unique. For all we know, everyone in your mother's family knew about them."

"My mother's family," Laura sighed. "It really stinks that we have no idea who they are, where they're from or what they're capable of. If someone really did ransack John's house because of those barrettes, it means they're way ahead of us. Never good not to know what you don't know."

They walked in silence for several seconds, cautiously navigating the overgrown trail. "I just thought of something," Dave said as he helped Laura over a hollowed out log. "Scratch what I said about those barrettes. I mean it really would be a giant leap to think John still had them after all this time."

Laura agreed wholeheartedly. An odd sense of relief began to wash over her until she noticed the pensive look on Dave's face. "What?" she demanded. "What?"

Dave gestured surrender. "No need to kill the messenger, Mrs. H but let's say the house really was ransacked. The place was a dump. No reason to think there was anything worthwhile in there. Agreed?"

"Makes sense."

"Well, what if it wasn't a thing? What if it was a person, your mother to be exact? Someone could be looking for her to see if she has any idea who she really is."

Laura stared at Dave. "Is that supposed to make me feel better?"

"Well, it's a reasonable possibility."

"Really?" Laura challenged. "May I remind you that mother was only two when Linda disappeared. Even if she were alive, what could she possibly tell them?"

"She might not have to tell them anything. Unless Neeka was exaggerating, your grandfather wanted your mother dead. You gotta wonder why anyone would want to kill a two year old."

"I'm not sure I like where this is going," Laura replied.

"I'm not sure I like it either but you've gotta remember that your mother was supposedly the daughter of a rich and powerful man, a man who got away with murder all these years. I'm guessing he wasn't all that happy when his crime was uncovered but as long as no one can identify those remains, it's all good."

Laura sighed. In her heart she knew Dave was right. "And if I'm following you correctly, my mother could be the missing link."

"Exactly. Her very existence could have the potential to bring down a powerful dynasty. Picture this. Linda's body is discovered and your mother comes up as a potential problem. Someone comes to the Abbott Farmstead hoping to talk to her. He gets there. Is pissed that there's no Mary and freaks when he realizes John can't manage more than a blank stare. Rips the place apart looking for clues as to her whereabouts."

Laura sighed. "I like your barrette theory better. At least I can hide them."

"And maybe you should. Those barrettes are valuable in two ways. They're worth a lot of money to be sure, but they may also be the only way we can find out who your mother really was."

They walked in silence. As they neared the clearing, they caught a whiff of the burnt out farmhouse. The air was oppressive and the odor grew stronger as they approached the blackened rubble. All of a sudden they heard a disturbance in the woods behind them.

"Hello?" Laura called, spinning around. She waited. "Hello," she called again. Seeing how frightened Laura looked, Dave grabbed her arm. She jumped.

"It's okay, Mrs. H. It's just a doe and her fawn."

"Sorry," Laura replied. "I guess all this nonsense about someone looking for my mother is getting to me.

Thing is if someone really is looking for her, who's to say they won't come after me? It's way too close for comfort."

Dave shrugged. "Maybe not that close. Remember. Greenview's been looking for your mother for weeks now and haven't gotten anywhere."

"Not yet. What about Neeka? All she has to do is tell one person."

"She won't. Look how guarded she was with you. She clearly wants to stay under the radar. Besides, in a couple of days, you'll be on the Outer Banks. No one's gonna look for you there and by the time you come home, I'll have this thing wrapped up."

Sure you will, Laura mused.

They headed down the rutted driveway. Just before they reached the car, Laura turned around to take one last look at the house where her mother grew up. She couldn't decide if its destruction was a sign that she needed to let the past go or if it was an ominous warning of the danger that lay ahead. In any event, she understood why her mother never wanted to come back here, and in that regard they were actually on the same page. It was little consolation.

Chapter Four

June 25th

"The county crime lab?" Laura said as they pulled away from the farmstead. "We're going to the crime lab? What for?"

"The ring Jane Doe was wearing. It's a key piece of evidence. Don't you want to see it?"

"Of course I do but isn't the crime lab a restricted facility? You can't just waltz in there and ask to see evidence from an ongoing murder investigation."

"Don't worry, Mrs. H. I don't plan to waltz in anywhere. Greenview's my second home. I've known the lab director since I was a kid. He's an FBI grad. I already talked to him about this. He was impressed with my family crest theory. Said he'd clear the way for me to see the ring. I just have to mention his name when we get there. Our timing's perfect. The ring came back from the state lab yesterday."

"The state lab?" Laura asked. "What was it doing there?"

"County didn't have the resources to do DNA so they sent the hand to state so that state could extract whatever tissue they needed. State agreed to return the ring as soon as possible. I've been dying to see this thing, actually hold it, examine it. The photograph they released was impossible. No detail. Pathetic, actually. Just about every reporter who covered this story was stuck printing this copy in their newspapers. Makes me wonder if that's why no one got any hits."

"Might not be the quality of the picture. Sixty-five years is an awfully long time."

"Yeah, yeah, I know but the man who killed Linda was a real bad ass and we're going to need all the help we can get to figure out who he is. A decent photograph would be nice."

They came to a red light. In Dave's mind this was one of the most annoying intersections in all of Greenview and he knew it would be a long wait. He tapped his steering wheel impatiently. "We gotta get this guy, Mrs. H. We really do. He not only killed an innocent woman, he may have buried her alive."

Laura cringed. "Buried alive? How do you know that?"

"Coroner's report. Her right hand was encased in cement. Picture this. Her entire body was covered with several inches of dirt and the concrete was poured over it. Only two ways her hand could have come in contact with that cement: the killer was careless and didn't see her hand sticking out, or she managed to move after he left her there."

"That's enormously creepy."

"Yeah but on the plus side, the hand and the ring were well preserved. If we're lucky, that should give us two more clues: DNA and a potential family crest."

"It's still creepy."

The light finally changed. Two blocks later Dave pointed to his right. "That red brick building. That's the crime lab. Listen. I'll understand if you don't want to see the ring. It being your grandmother's and all, makes it kind of personal. The building's got a halfway decent lobby. You can wait in there."

"Are you kidding? Yeah, it's personal but there's no way I'm waiting outside. Besides, when I think of my grandmother, I think of Ethel Abbott and not Linda Ferina. It's okay."

Dave parked his car under the only shade tree he could find and then led Laura up the worn marble steps.

"Shouldn't take us long, Mrs. H. Helps to have friends in high places." He gave his name to the sign-in officer and then squinted in disbelief when they were denied admission. "What?" he asked, trying to be patient. "There must be some mistake. Please. Double check with Dr. Ferris. I'm sure this is just a simple oversight. We'll wait."

"Don't," Laura advised the minute Dave began apologizing. "Things like this happen all the time." She pointed to a row of nearby chairs. "Come on. Let's go sit down. We can use the time to Google Linda Ferina, Linda Ferona. See what we can find."

"Good idea, Mrs. H. Sorry I didn't think of it."

Laura chuckled. Almost a half hour later, she couldn't decide who was more disappointed. "I don't believe this," she said. "Not one credible hit; either too old or too young. We must be missing something."

Dave was all set to complain about their long wait when he saw the guard approach. He nudged Laura. "This oughtta be good," he whispered, disquieted by the man's stone faced expression.

"Sorry for the delay," the guard said in an indifferent monotone. "Dr. Ferris is a busy man and he's got a new secretary. Took her forever to fax this approval letter. Follow me."

Laura tried to ignore the high pitched squeal of the guard's gum soled shoes on the newly polished linoleum floor. The walk was a long one and Laura was greatly relieved when the guard introduced them to the evidence technician who led them into a locked but blissfully quiet room and then handed Dave a clear plastic bag along with two sets of cotton gloves. "You can remove the ring as long as you wear the gloves," she advised. "Fifteen minutes. I'll be back in fifteen minutes."

Dave waited until the technician left the room. He put his gloves on and removed the ring from the bag. "Wow, Mrs. H. Check this out. I'm guessing this is 14 K gold. A flat rectangular face. Wish it was a little bigger. Approximately one-quarter inch in length by one-eighth inch in width isn't much to go on. Gonna need a magnifying glass." He held the ring between his thumb and index finger. "I'm not surprised at how small this thing is. They figure Jane wasn't quite five feet tall and that she weighed all of ninety pounds."

"Really?" Laura replied, her thoughts racing. At 5'7" she felt an immediate disconnect. Was the body found under that hotel really her grandmother or had Dave made an innocent mistake? Could be. His drawings were impressive but what if they were wrong? Had she been so taken by Dave's academic credentials that she had missed something she should have noticed? "What about the design?" she finally asked. "Do you recognize it?"

"Well, nothing's jumping out at me, but based on the shape of the design, I'm still thinking family crest. I'll know better after I have some time to study this thing. One little detail can make all the difference."

No kidding, Laura mused. "What about the inside? Any inscriptions, dates, initials?"

Dave held the ring up to the light. "There's a date. 2/10/43. Mean anything to you?"

"Maybe a wedding date, although my mother was born just seven months later."

"Well, I gotta say. Whoever killed Jane must be kicking himself for not removing this ring. Family crest or not, this design's unique. Listen." Dave whispered. "I saw two no smoking signs on the way in here but nothing about taking pictures." He took out his phone. "I need my own copy. Their photographer sucks. Everyone else has gone digital but he still uses film and film just doesn't cut it. I need detail." He handed the ring to Laura. "Here. Would you hold this for me? I need just the right angle."

"You need to have your head examined. This is a government facility. I assume that any picture you take in here becomes government property."

"So, who's gonna know? Will you help? If I don't get more detail, I'll never know if this is a crest or not."

Reluctantly Laura took the ring. She was getting antsy. They had a four hour ride ahead of them and it was already well past lunch time. "Okay, but make it quick."

Dave finished just as the door opened. He calmly slipped his phone into his pocket, took the ring and then zipped it into the bag. Dave and Laura were casually removing their gloves when the technician approached. Dave smiled, held out the bag and the gloves and then thanked her for her help.

"Well, that was interesting," Laura said as they walked out of the building. "Any more bright ideas?"

"Yeah, let's eat. I'm starving."

"Me too. Any decent restaurants around here?"

Dave checked the time. "A few but they all close between lunch and dinner. It's after two. I'm afraid Mickey D's is the only game in town."

Not much of a fast food junkie, Laura resigned herself as Dave drove to a nearby McDonald's. The smell of french fries hung in the air, whetting their appetites. "I have no idea what they use to cook those fries but there ought to be a law," Laura complained as they walked across the newly paved parking lot. "I haven't had fries in ages but now I'm salivating."

Laura's first stop was the ladies' room. By the time she joined Dave at the counter, he had already ordered for both of them: two Big Mac Meals for him and one for Laura. Although Laura would have preferred a salad, she placed twenty-five dollars on the counter. "Hope that covers it," she whispered and then grabbed several napkins, selected a sun drenched booth and sat down. She called her babysitter just to make sure everyone was okay, and by the time Dave joined her she realized just how hungry she was.

"It's not the Ironmaster but it will have to do," Dave said, taking his food off the tray.

"The Ironmaster?"

"Yeah. It was my favorite restaurant when I was a kid. Your boys would love it. They have great corn and mushroom fritters, magic potions to drink and best of all, the walls are covered with the implements of medieval torture. You should see some of the things they have in that place. It's fascinating. Unfortunately, they close between lunch and dinner. You'll have to remember that if you ever bring your kids up here."

"Are you kidding? You're talking an eight hour round trip. I'm not sure any restaurant is worth having to listen to *are we there yet* every two minutes. Then again, corn and mushroom fritters do sound good."

"Don't forget medieval torture. They'll have plenty to talk about on the ride home."

Laura chuckled. She opened a packet of ketchup, poured a dollop onto her wrapping paper and then swirled a french fry through the ketchup. "You know, it's funny. When I was little, I used to beg my mother to bring me up here but somewhere along the way I realized how uncomfortable she was even talking about Greenview, so I stopped nagging."

"That was thoughtful of you," Dave replied. "Sorry you gave up?"

"Who says I gave up? I simply waited until I got my license."

Dave dumped his fries onto his wrapper. "Your driver's license? Don't tell me. You tried to find the place?"

"My first driving adventure. What a disaster. My friend and I got hopelessly lost. We missed curfew and were both grounded for two weeks. I never told my mother what I was trying to do. I guess that was when I figured Greenview was out of reach. That said, I wish I knew two months ago what I know now."

Dave poured a packet of salt onto his fries. "What's your gut feeling, Mrs. H? Do you think your mother knew the Abbotts weren't her real parents?"

"I don't know. I'd like to think that if she did, she would have told me, but then again she clearly had her own agenda. You know, it's so strange. I grew up thinking Greenview was a wonderful place and I felt so sad about what allegedly happened. That fire story was brilliant. It was meant to keep me away and it did. Just think. If they hadn't dug for that interchange, I wouldn't be here. I'd still think my mother left Greenview after a devastating fire and those Scottie dog barrettes would still be sitting on some shelf in Neeka's house."

Dave popped a few fries into his mouth. "Yeah, Mrs. H, about those barrettes. Been thinking. Expensive ring, expensive barrettes, maybe made by the same jeweler? Mind if I took a look? My girlfriend loves antique jewelry. Says you can learn a lot about the pieces if they have special markings."

"She's right." Laura reached for her purse, removed the box and then pushed it across the table. "But I'm afraid these don't. Already looked. Here. See for yourself."

Dave shoved a few more fries into his mouth, wiped his hands and then took one of the barrettes out of the box. He turned it several different ways, held it up to the light, returned it to the box and then studied the second one. "Geez, Mrs. H. You're right. Nothing." He took out his phone. "Mind if I take a few shots? Just think. If I find the right jeweler, if he's still in business, if he kept good receipts…"

"Yeah just think," Laura replied. She admired Dave's intractable optimism even though she didn't share it. "Any idea where you'd find such a guy?"

"New York. I've been told it's the jewelry capital of the world. Don't get me wrong. My main focus is still the ring, but those barrettes might come in handy. Think about it. Diamonds and rubies for a little kid? Only someone with mucho bucks and a few loose screws would pour all that money into something guaranteed to get lost. I'd bet on New York. It's a magnet for flakes like that."

Laura reached for a french fry. "Don't say that too loud but let's say New York is your place. Shops close, jewelers retire. Where would you begin?"

"Don't know yet but I'll figure it out. Least it'll give me a good excuse to get away from Greenview for a few days. I could use the break."

"Word of advice: before you go traipsing all over with pictures of my mother's barrettes you might want to establish whether or not Jane Doe really is my grandmother."

"What? I thought we already did."

"Almost. You had me convinced until you showed me that ring. It is a tad small. I'd be lucky to get it on my pinky. It might not mean anything but I want to be sure. DNA won't take that long and once we get confirmation you can stop looking for other families."

"I haven't been looking for other families."

"Too bad. Investigative reporting 101: never put all your eggs in one basket. Your cemetery drawings are impressive but given how long ago that was, there's always a chance you miscalculated. Believe me. You don't want to build a case around the wrong family. It could take you forever to walk it back."

"No worries. That police report. I went over it so many times, I've got it memorized. The witness reported a late model car near the cemetery entrance which was just a few feet from the gravesite. Given that there was only one entrance, the Abbott gravesite was the only one Jane could have been visiting when she was accosted. We'll get a match, I'm sure."

Laura just shrugged. "We'll see."

Dave squirmed. *'We'll see'* wasn't the affirmation he wanted to hear. "I gotta say, Mrs. H. I'll be shocked if the DNA's not a match but now you've made me a little nervous. How long do you think it will take?"

"Talk to our editor. She can probably get it expedited. Just remember, I'm leaving for North Carolina at the end of the week."

Dave wolfed down his first sandwich while Laura daintily nibbled on her french fries. For several seconds neither of them spoke. It was Dave who broke the silence. "I have another question. Now you've got me thinking. What if it turns out Jane Doe is not your grandmother?"

Laura shrugged. She arranged her sandwich so that the top bun and the bottom bun were in perfect alignment. "Everything points to her being the woman who brought my mother to Greenview, the woman who saved my mother from the man who tried to kill her. In my mind, she's a hero. I guess I'd be disappointed."

Dave just nodded. "Tell me, Mrs. H. If this was your story, what would you do next?"

Laura thought for a moment. "I guess I'd get as much information from as many people as possible. Neeka's off the list. I'm pretty sure she's told you everything she knows. That leaves the cops who responded to the 911 call at the Abbott farmhouse. I'd interview them. It's absolutely key to know for sure whether John's death was just an unfortunate accident or something more."

"I agree, but I gotta tell you, I read their report. We're not exactly dealing with the best and the brightest."

"You don't have to be. Let them know John might have had some connection to those remains. Who knows? They might remember something they didn't put in the report. Five minutes. You'll know in five minutes if you've jarred their memory and if you play your cards right, they may even buy you a donut."

"This is really important to you, isn't it?"

"Well, yeah. Think about it. What if someone really did ransack John's house because they were looking for my mother? You gotta admit that's way too close to home. On the other hand, if you get assurances that his death was an accident and nothing more, I'll sleep a lot better."

Dave nodded. "Gotcha."

"One more thing," Laura replied. If someone really did go after John you may want to be a little more judicious about your updates. No sense giving the enemy a road map."

"A roadmap?" Dave repeated. "I'd love it if the enemy was following my updates. It might be the perfect way to pull this guy out of the weeds."

Laura's silence spoke volumes.

"Okay, okay," Dave replied, keenly aware that Laura was not amused. "About that interview. You win. The cops. I'll get on it as soon as I can."

Laura smiled. In some ways Dave was like a bull in a china shop. Then again, he seemed smart enough to know when to be discrete. "Thank you," she replied, squeezing her empty wrapper into a tight ball. "You have my cell. Let me know what happens."

"Will do," Dave replied. Sensing that Laura was in a hurry, he checked his watch. "We should probably get going. The cemetery closes at five."

Laura hesitated. "Hold on," she replied. "If you don't mind, I'd rather pass on the cemetery. I know you wanted me to second the link between my mother's family and Jane Doe but for now, your word is good enough. I've already seen a picture of the Abbott gravesite and given how horrible George and John were, I'd rather keep my distance. Besides, it's been an awfully long day."

Dave was disappointed. As confident as he was in his cemetery diagrams, he had been looking forward to Laura's stamp of approval. Then again, he really couldn't complain. Thanks to Laura, he had made as much progress in one day as he had in the past two months. "I understand, Mrs. H. We really did cover a lot of ground today. Thanks for all your help and for lunch."

Laura smiled. "You're welcome."

The car was hot and it took forever for Dave's air conditioner to cool it off. Exhausted, all Laura wanted to do was to get home and put as much distance as possible between herself and Greenview. For the first time since her mother's death, she was actually looking forward to their trip to the Outer Banks. Grateful that Meg had agreed to come with them; she couldn't wait to get away. The change of scenery would do her good and with any luck, she'd find a way to put Greenview and all the disturbing possibilities out of her mind.

Chapter Five

June 25th

Laura was annoyed but not terribly surprised when a jackknifed tractor trailer lengthened their already long ride home. As they inched their way though miles of backed up traffic, Dave made a valiant effort to be entertaining. Laura tried to reciprocate but with so much on her mind, she found it difficult to engage in small talk and it certainly didn't help that she was tired, hungry and a little sick to her stomach. Why? she asked herself. Why, with traffic sensors everywhere was there no warning about that accident? Had she and Dave been aware of the situation, they might have been able to find an alternate route.

The fourth full day of summer was winding down by the time Dave dropped Laura off. After sitting in an air conditioned car for hours on end, Laura welcomed the fresh night air. Under a three-quarter moon she walked from her driveway to the back door. Cicadas in full song were loud enough to soften the drone of the air conditioner. Like the weather in Greenview, the day here had been uncomfortably humid and a haze was thickening in response to the dropping temperature. The overnight low was predicted to be in the low 70's with record breaking heat on the way for tomorrow. The beaches of North Carolina couldn't come soon enough.

The smell of freshly brewed coffee greeted Laura the minute she opened her back door. A dish containing a barbecued chicken breast, a slice of cantaloupe and several strawberries sat atop of a single placemat. The house was unusually quiet except for the footsteps coming in from the foyer. "Ah, you're home," Meg said as she walked into the kitchen. "The last of the Mohicans just went down. The other two are sound asleep."

"Sorry I'm so late. Traffic was awful. Let me go up and say good night."

"Take your time. I'll be here. Not going anywhere till I hear all about Greenview."

"It was interesting, that's for sure," Laura replied. She started out of the kitchen and then spun around. "Hey, what's that smell?"

"Aloe vera. We were at the swim club all day. I lathered on the sunscreen that you keep in your beach bag but obviously SPF 30 doesn't work for redheads. I'm going to need a higher SPF for North Carolina."

Laura turned on the overhead light. "No kidding. The higher the SPF the better. Although I gotta say, the color does you good. Your hair's more blonde than strawberry and your freckles have disappeared."

Meg touched her cheek. "I'm glad you're amused. I feel like I'm on fire. I'll probably be peeling like a dried up onion by the time we leave."

"Four more days. I can't believe how fast it's coming. I'll be right down."

Meg had fixed two mugs of coffee by the time Laura returned. "We made brownies for dessert. It was fun. Then again given how ungodly hot it was today, any excuse to be in an air conditioned house and out of direct sunlight felt like heaven."

Laura smiled. "For whatever it's worth, I don't know what I would have done without you today. Stressful as it was, at least I didn't have to worry about the kids. Plain and simple, Greenview was a nightmare. Given your sunburn, you may not want to hear this but I can't wait for North Carolina. The more distance I put between us and Greenview, the happier I'll be."

Meg grabbed a brownie to go with her coffee. She could hear the angst in Laura's voice. "So what happened? Was Dave bugging you about claiming the farmstead?"

Laura cut a piece of chicken. "No. Believe it or not, the farmstead is the least of my worries. It was exactly the way Dave described it: eighty acres of prime real estate, a burnt out farmhouse, neglected fields and developers chomping at the bit to get their hands on it. Wow! This chicken's good."

"Thank Flying Feather. What a great place. Got the cantaloupe and strawberries there too. Wish I had a place like that near me. Developers? What's the deal? Eighty acres in a prime market has to be worth a small fortune."

"Apparently."

"That's so strange. Your mother worked so hard and all this time her own father was sitting on a gold mine."

Laura took a deep breath. "About her father…."

Through dinner, dessert and two cups of coffee, Laura haltingly recapped the entire Greenview saga. She was missing her mother terribly and welcomed the chance to share her feelings with Meg, her closest friend, a great listener who wouldn't judge her. Some of those feelings were positive, some negative and some she didn't even want to admit to herself. They laughed, they cried, and they worried.

"I don't know about you," Meg finally said, toying with one of the barrettes that Laura brought home, "but I need a glass of wine. How about you?"

"Nicest thing I've heard all day. Forget the glass. Just bring me a straw."

Meg ducked into the dining room, took two wine glasses out of the china cabinet, grabbed an opened bottle of Merlot and then filled both glasses. "And I thought I was having a bad day because of a little sunburn."

Laura took a long slow sip of her wine. It went down warm and calming. She held the stem of the glass with her left hand and began running her right index finger around the rim. She sighed. "There were times today when I thought my head was going to explode. The hits just kept on coming. I don't know what bothers me more: why my mother was forced to leave Greenview or that she never told me. I would have understood and I wouldn't be sitting here right now with a hundred questions I'll never get answers to. I feel bad that she had to go through all that crap but I'm also angry. One minute I'm pissed because she betrayed me and the next I'm feeling guilty as hell for being so harsh. Does this make any sense?"

"Of course it does. You and your mother had a very close relationship and it hurts that she deceived you about her family. That said, I'm sure her intentions were good. She clearly wanted to protect to you and to protect herself. For what it's worth, I never questioned her fire story either, although the part about John and George screaming for help was always a bit worrisome to me. At least now we know. Your mother was a tough lady. She saw a better way. She left Greenview and all its horrors and started over. On her own at age seventeen—hadn't finished high school, couldn't even vote. That took guts, but she did it. Made a good life for herself and for you."

Laura could feel the muscles in her neck relax ever so slightly. She sipped her wine. "I know, and I get that she was only trying to protect me but the thing is, the whole time we were at the farmhouse, I kept thinking how different things might have been if Dave had linked those remains to the Abbotts when John and my mother were still alive. Imagine getting them together? I know John was a hopeless drunk but maybe seeing my mother might have sobered him up. We know nothing about Linda, my own grandmother. It's such an empty feeling. We don't know where she came from, how old she was, or even her real name."

"Her real name?" Meg asked.

"Yeah, think about it. We didn't get one credible hit using Linda Ferina, Linda Ferona or tons of variations. We're pretty sure my lovely grandmother used an alias. Bottom line: all we have is a name and it's not even the right one. That said, my grandmother must have been pretty smart. If I was running from some rich bastard who wanted to kill me and my kid and who probably had plenty of resources to find me, I'd do the same thing."

"Yeah, so would I," Meg replied. "Aliases fascinate me. Isn't there some way to decode those things?"

"Not easily and not without knowing something about the person."

Meg took a long slow sip of her wine. "You might not want to hear this but I used an alias once. I met this guy shortly after my divorce. He seemed nice enough but I just wasn't ready to get involved. Told him my name was Michele Roberts, after my sister and brother. I realized later I was using my own initials."

"You ever hear from him?"

"Not intentionally. Ran into him at a gas station. He wasn't very happy."

Laura smiled. "I wonder why. L.F. Now you've got me wondering if those are Linda's real initials. People do that, you know. They use names that have some kind of link to their past. I probably could have figured out that you were Michele Roberts because I know something about you but we know squat about Linda. Only thing we've got is that she might have had a sister who lived in New York. It's an awfully big place."

Meg picked up one of the barrettes. "That's not the only thing. What about these? I know they don't have any special markings but they are certainly unique. You can tell they're custom made just by the clasp, nothing like the flimsy ones you find on most little girl barrettes. I don't know how but if you could find the jeweler who made them."

Laura chuckled. Shaking her head, she picked up the other barrette. "You and Dave must be drinking from the same cooler. I see a black hole and you two see rays of sunshine." She held up the barrette. "Wonder what my mother would say if she saw this. She'd probably have a few choice words. When I was little, our next door neighbor had a Scottie. Yapped all the time. Drove her crazy."

Meg studied the barrette. "I'll betcha there's a reason why her parents chose this particular dog. For all you know your mother once loved Scotties. Maybe even had one of her own. I can just picture her all dressed up, proudly pinning these things in her hair. She had such a flare for fashion. I loved the way she accessorized. Beautiful as her clothes were, it was the cool things she wore with them that made her outfits. I'll betcha your daughter goes crazy over these barrettes. You know how she loves anything that sparkles. That dark, beautiful, silky hair—these barrettes, they'll really stand out. She won't be able to get her face out of the mirror."

Smiling, Laura brought her finger to her lips. "Shhh," she whispered. "Sara's not gonna see these things until after I get them appraised and then some. You realize this is all I have of my mother's early childhood. Musta been some childhood. I'm guessing she didn't start out as a poor little farm girl. Can't help but wonder what her life was like before Greenview."

Meg studied the barrette. "Privileged, definitely privileged, but if her parents hated each other, not very happy. Poor little rich girl."

Laura took a deep breath. "I can't stop thinking about something Neeka said. When she found out my mother wasn't an Abbott, she wasn't terribly surprised. She talked about how different my mother was. How she really didn't belong up there."

"I can see that," Meg replied. "Your mother had an inbred grace. She was a classy lady but the way you describe John and George, not so much. I doubt that grace came from her Greenview family. Nature vs nurture."

No one spoke for several seconds. "A poor little rich girl," Laura sighed. "What if my mother was more than that?"

Meg shrugged. "What do you mean?"

"Expensive barrettes, my mother's demeanor. What kind of family did she actually come from? Supposedly my grandfather was rich and to have gotten away with murder all these years, I'd say he had some power. How would identifying Jane Doe impact him, his family? Would it turn out to be nothing of consequence or complete ruin?"

Meg squinted. "Where are you going with this?"

Laura took a deep breath. "If identifying Jane Doe could ruin my grandfather or whatever family he has, don't you think they would be desperate to make sure that didn't happen? I'm a little nervous. John Abbott is dead. His death was ruled an unfortunate accident, but what if it wasn't? What if someone actually went after him and at this very moment, is looking for my mother, looking for me?"

"Stop!" Meg replied. Until now she thought they had addressed each and every possible concern and then some. "Look. You've already managed to convince Dave to interview the cops who responded to the call at the farmhouse. That's impressive, very proactive, but before you write your obituary, why don't you wait and see what he finds out?"

"I'd like to, Meg but in this business, a lot can happen in a couple of days."

Meg hesitated. "Please, don't take this the wrong way. I'm not an investigative reporter but I am a psychologist. You've had a terrible shock. You've had the rug ripped out from under you. I understand your anxiety but you've got to be careful not to make things worse than they are. Keep in mind that sixty-five years is a lifetime. If your grandfather is still alive and has the stamina to go looking for your mother, God bless him."

"I thought about that, but who says it has to be my grandfather? Someone else could know how Linda died. Powerful family, powerful secrets. Don't forget, the discovery of those remains got national coverage. Imagine a family member picking up the newspaper and realizing that some idiot reporter thinks he can identify the poor lady my grandfather planted all those years ago. Their secret's been uncovered. They go back to Greenview and John becomes their first target. That was several weeks ago. We may be running out of time."

Meg didn't know what to say. She took a deep breath. "Look, in a couple of days you'll be in North Carolina for an entire week. If by some very remote chance, someone is looking for you, they'll never find you there. I'm not discounting any of your concerns, but truthfully I'm more worried about how that week will go. If you keep stressing over this, it's not gonna be much fun for any of us. You gotta relax."

Laura kneaded her forehead. "Easier said than done."

A car pulled onto the driveway casting a bright flash of light across the back window. "Not necessarily," Meg replied. "I think the solution has just arrived. I probably should have told you this sooner but Mike's been calling all day, asking how you were, when you'd be home. He was hell bent on seeing you tonight and if those lights are his, I'd say his timing was impeccable."

"Mike! Now you tell me? It was so hot in Greenview and I probably smell as bad as I look. I could have jumped into the shower."

"Too late now." Meg got up from the table. She put her glass and dish into the dishwasher, walked into the dining room and returned with a clean wine glass. "Then again, the kids are asleep and I'm leaving. No one to chaperone. The night is yours and it's still relatively young." She grabbed her purse and headed for the front door. "Tell Mike I said hello. I'll talk to you tomorrow and this time you don't necessarily have to tell me everything."

Chapter Six

June 26th

Halfway though his morning shave, Dave Schubert wiped the mirror for the third time. Even with the window open, and the loud and noisy vent running, the mirror kept fogging up. Dave knew his apartment was a dump but he didn't expect much more from inner city student housing, at least not until he met Julie, now the love of his life. It had been an eye opener to see how the other half lived, something he might have learned sooner had he not had his nose buried in his books these past few years.

Thinking of Julie made Dave smile. It didn't bother him that they were a study in contrasts. She came from a wealthy Main Line family while he came from a hardworking middle class one. She wore designer clothes. He wore off the rack specials. Both were students at the University of Pennsylvania, having bumped into each other on Locust Walk last November on a cold, snowy day. She was a third year Wharton undergrad while he was a senior at the Annenberg School for Communication. They loved the Beatles, the beach, tennis, concerts and just being together.

Dave considered Penn his reach school, Julie his reach girlfriend, with one major difference. From the get go, Dave felt right at home in his classes and with his professors, but he had yet to reach that comfort level with Julie's family. Dave loved her mother. She was a terrific cook who always made him feel welcome but her father's chill sucked all her mother's warmth right out of the room. Dave got it. He didn't come from the Main Line, didn't have a trust fund, and worst of all, he wanted to become an investigative reporter. Like he'd ever be able to support the man's daughter in the style to which she was accustomed.

Above the noise of the fan, Dave heard his front door open. "Damn," he blurted, checking the time. Julie was early and it could only mean one thing. She wanted to do breakfast before they headed to NY. Not a horrible idea but not the best one either.

It had been Julie's idea to take the 9:40 Acela from 30th Street in Philadelphia to Penn Station in New York. Even though she loved to be fashionably late and he loved to be annoyingly early, Dave allowed Julie to convince him that the 9:40 would be perfect. He leaned over the sink and ran his hand over his face. *Smooth enough*, he decided. He wiped off any leftover shaving crème with the same towel he'd been using to wipe the mirror, tossed it onto the sink, adjusted the towel he was wearing around his waist and then hurried to greet his girlfriend. There were better ways to kill time than to waste it on breakfast.

They were way behind schedule by the time their server brought their food. Dave kept checking his watch. Julie was amused. "Wasn't my idea to get this late a start but you gotta admit we did work up an appetite. Don't worry. We won't miss the train."

"You hope. Imagine explaining why we did to your father? I still can't believe he hooked me up with his jeweler friend, a real live expert in family crests. The guy's leaving in two days for a ten day cruise to Alaska and yet he agreed to see us at 11:30. That's pretty impressive. Know what the last thing your father said to me? 'Don't keep him waiting.'"

Julie chuckled. "Okay, okay," she said, wrapping the last of her corn muffin in a napkin. "I can take this with me. Let's go."

They arrived at the station with just enough time to board the train and get the last two side by side seats.

"See," Julie said, squeezing Dave's arm. "I told you we would make it."

Dave tried to relax and for the first hour he enjoyed the changing landscape. "Are you kidding me?" he asked when the train started to slow down. "What's going on?"

Julie patted his hand. "Don't worry. We're approaching the station. Not the brightest idea to pull in at full speed."

Dave stared out the window. The landmarks that once appeared to be flying by now seemed stationary. All of a sudden the sun disappeared. Eerie yellow lights lined the tunnel walls. Dave checked the time. Could this tin can go any slower?

Unfazed, Julie had no doubt they could find a cab, go approximately twenty blocks and make it to their destination on time. "Told you," she said as they emerged from the station. Pulling Dave by the hand, she hurried over to a long line of taxis. "That Crown Victoria. Looks good. Let's take it." She tipped the driver as she got into the car and hinted that there was more where that came from depending on how quickly he got them to their destination. Smiling at Dave, she leaned back in her seat. "Brace yourself," she whispered as she buckled her seatbelt.

No one spoke. The driver wove in and out of traffic, squeezing between cars at breakneck speed with only inches to spare. Several times during the ride, he jammed on his brakes and then immediately gunned the accelerator. "Proof you don't have to be in an accident to get whiplash," Dave whispered to Julie. He was green by the time they finally stepped out of the cab. Not only were they a few minutes ahead of schedule, he was only seconds away from tasting his breakfast for the second time.

Aaron Jankowitz was sitting at a desk behind a glass showcase. He looked up the minute Dave and Julie opened the door. "Ah, you're right on time," he called, taking his glasses off and hurrying across the squeaky hardwood floor. He extended his hand to Julie and waited for her to introduce him to Dave. "It was so good to hear from your father. Please. Come on back. I remember how much you love New York bagels," he said to Julie. "I just put on a fresh pot of coffee. Can't wait to hear all about this family crest."

Dave and Julie had decided that it was best to tell Aaron the whole story. They hoped it would give him a sense of urgency and maybe whet his appetite to help. At first Aaron listened with rapt attention but he became stone faced when Dave began showing him the pictures he had taken at the crime lab. He squinted through a magnifying glass, studying each and every picture from all possible angles. He put the magnifying glass down, placed his glasses on top of his head and then handed the pictures back to Dave. "So, what makes you think this is a crest?"

Dave selected his most detailed shot and then pointed to several characteristics that originally brought him to that conclusion. As he explained his findings, Aaron nodded in agreement and Dave could feel his confidence grow. "I've been studying crests for years and although I'm no expert in this area, I think the design might be unique enough to lead us to the family who commissioned the ring. That, in turn, might help us identify Jane Doe."

Aaron looked at Julie and then winked. "You picked yourself a pretty smart one." He gestured for Dave to put the picture on the desk and then turned it in such a way that the design was facing Dave and Julie. He clicked on a laser pen and began pointing to certain characteristics. "Aside from the crest, the most prominent features are the laurel leaves and the chaplet. Now, while the laurel leaves look like random designs, they're actually not. Look closely inside that chaplet," Aaron said, pointing to what appeared to be a circular wreath. "As best as I can tell, the laurel leaves are actually two combinations of letters, possibly initials. One appears to be FCP and the other

GRB. Notice, depending on which way you look at it, one set of initials is upside down, and the other is right side up. They're intertwined so that unless you know what you're looking for, you wouldn't be able to interpret it."

Dave was encouraged. "A crest with initials—wouldn't that be relatively easy to trace?"

"Technically, I can't call this a crest, at least not one that I recognize, and as for the initials, they're always a double-edged sword. There's never any way to know what order they're meant to be in. They could be linear initials, backward initials or totally random. But all is not lost. Your ace in the hole is the design itself. I can tell you it was not done here. The lines on this appear to be incredibly fine. You mentioned an inscription of 2/10/43, so I'm assuming the ring was commissioned around that time and I can tell you we weren't equipped to do such an intricate design until August of that year. That was a good six months later."

"Wow!" Dave replied. "That ought to narrow the field. Any idea who might have had that capability?"

"Let me see." Aaron walked over to a file cabinet and pulled out a folder marked "February 1943." "My father always had one eye on his competitors so he kept impeccable records on them: their successes, failures, new lines, upcoming products. Give me a minute."

Dave squeezed Julie's hand as Aaron flipped through the file, scribbling several notes to himself. He returned to his desk and then picked up his rolodex. "Good news. There were several shops with this capability in 1943. Four are out of business and the three remaining have changed hands but I do have their updated information. I don't know how helpful the current owners would be, but it certainly wouldn't hurt to ask around." He scribbled their names on a sheet of paper and handed it to Dave. "Is there anything else I can help you with?"

Dave tried to swallow his disappointment. Clearly the route to identifying Jane Doe via the design on her ring was more circuitous than he had hoped. Although he felt a bit foolish, he decided to show Aaron the picture of Laura's barrettes. He took his phone from his pocket. "Would you mind taking a look at these pictures? I'm sorry I didn't print them up for you. They're barrettes, Scottie dogs. I'm wondering if the same jeweler who did the ring, might have done the barrettes."

Aaron's mouth hung open as he looked at the picture. He scratched his head, a slow smile appearing on his face. "I haven't seen the Scottie dog for years. Where'd you get this?"

Dave sat a little straighter. Aaron's reaction made him think he was onto something. "A friend of mine believes these once belonged to her mother. Have you seen them before?"

"As pins but not barrettes. There was a period in the early 50's when the Scottie dog was the craze, at least around here. The post war economy was booming and people wanted to spend their money. Most of the shops were selling dog pins but it was all costume stuff. My father's partner decided to go a step further and make the pins out of platinum and then decorate them with real gemstones: diamonds for the fur, rubies for the collar, onyx for the eyes."

"Wow!" Dave replied. "You've just described my friend's barrette to a t. Could this be something you would have sold?"

Aaron shook his head. "I'm afraid not." He turned to Julie. "I don't know how much your parents told you about us, but we used to be Jankowitz-Feldman Jewelers. Jerry Feldman and my grandfather set up shop in the early twenties. By the time the market crashed, they were well established and managed to ride out the bad times. In the mid-40's my grandfather and Jerry decided to turn the business over to their sons. Unfortunately the Steve Jankowitz-Robert Feldman partnership was a shaky one and it was eventually done in by the Scottie dog."

Intrigued, Dave glanced at Julie. "How so?" he asked.

"Foresight or lack of it. Robert and my father knew they were taking a chance when Robert designed his Scottie dog pin. Despite slow pre-sales Robert decided that in addition to offering pins in three different sizes, they should include barrettes. My mother went nuts. Who would pay a fortune for a hair ornament that even the most responsible little girl could easily misplace? But to Robert, it was all or nothing, and needless to say, things got ugly. After several heated arguments, Robert took his prototypes as well as his share of the business and left.

"To my father's dismay, Robert's idea took off like wildfire. The barrettes were replicas of the pins and I understand he produced several different styles and sizes but in limited quantities. He was a shrewd businessman who realized it was only a matter of time before imitations of his work would flood the market and in that vein, he engraved every piece of work with a number series as well as his very own trademark. An authentic Feldman would not only have his trademark, RMF, it would also have a sequence of numbers. For example, if an item was the first in a series of let's say, twenty-five, it would have a 1/25. The second would be a two and so on. Naturally the lower the first number, the greater its value. Do you know if these barrettes have any markings?"

Disheartened, Dave shook his head. "None that we can see but if they did, would we be able to trace it back?"

"Possibly, but even with markings, it wouldn't guarantee that you have an original. As intricate as Robert's trademark was, it wasn't counterfeit proof and the only way to know for sure would be to get it appraised."

"By whom? Can you do it?"

"I'm afraid not. To be perfectly honest, Feldman would be your best bet but he passed away a good ten years ago."

"What happened to his business?" Dave asked hopefully.

Aaron shrugged. "Gone. Robert retired almost twenty-five years ago. Thanks to his remarkable talents, he was filthy rich. He had hoped his daughter would take over but she wanted no part. Essentially he was forced to hand the business over to his lawyers and I understand they divided it into sections and then sold it off to several different investors."

"What about his daughter? Might she be able to help?"

"I doubt she'd be much help even if you could find her. She married and divorced several times so I'm not sure what name she's using. Her first name is Sally. I can ask around for you, see if anyone knows where she is, but I can't promise anything until I get back from vacation. I've got a new assistant who will be taking over in my absence and there are numerous issues that I've got to go over before I can leave. I wish I had more time to give you."

"That's okay," Dave replied. "You've been very helpful."

Just as Aaron was about to say his goodbyes, he caught the subdued look on Julie's normally bright face. Her parents were important clients of his. Maybe he could make a more convincing effort. Turning to Dave, he took out a pad and pencil. "Here. Give me your name and any contact information. I'll try to make some calls and at least get this thing rolling for you. No guarantees."

"Good enough." Dave replied. He scribbled his contact information and as an afterthought, decided to include Laura's as well. "I'd really appreciate that."

Aaron nodded. "Sorry I couldn't be of more help."

Julie got up from her chair. "You've been very kind to see us on such short notice. My parents wanted me to wish you bon voyage."

Aaron smiled. "Give them my thanks." He stood up and then offered his hand to Dave. "You've got a good eye, young man." He winked at Julie. "In more ways than one. Good luck with those addresses. Feel free to mention my name." He led Dave and Julie out into the showroom and then walked over to the front door. "One word of advice. Be careful with those barrettes. If by some chance they really are Feldman originals, they're worth a small fortune."

Julie slipped her arm through Dave's as they stepped out onto the street. "That was incredibly helpful, don't you think?"

Dave shrugged. "Not really. I had so much hope for that ring. I really thought I could nail this down."

Julie stopped dead in her tracks. "So who says you can't? That ring could still lead somewhere and besides, that's not your only option. What about those barrettes?"

"What about them? They don't have any special markings."

"How do you know they don't? How carefully did you look at them?"

"Very. Believe me. If there was anything on those barrettes, we would have seen it."

"Maybe, maybe not. Maybe the markings are only obvious to someone who knows what he or she is looking for, and in that vein, I'd pursue Feldman's daughter."

"To what end? You heard Aaron. Even if we could find her, he doesn't think she'll know anything. Face it, Jules. I'm up to strike two."

"So you strike out. Who says this is a one inning game? Look at how far you've gotten already. Now, where's that paper Aaron gave you. The way I see it, any one of these three jewelers might recognize that ring. Three more potential leads, three more chances to grab the prize."

Dave handed the paper to Julie. "You actually know how to get to these places?"

Julie studied the paper for several seconds. "Perfect," she finally said, pointing to the second shop on the list. "This one isn't that far from here, so I say we visit that one first. Then we can grab ourselves a fabulous lunch before going to number one and then to number three. Number three will bring us closest to Penn Station and we can hop on the train from there."

She held his arm tightly as they crossed the street. "Isn't this exciting? Some of my friends bitch that New York is just a huge, unfriendly place, but just think. Almost seventy years ago, some jeweler engraved a rather unusual gold ring. Now, thanks to a bit of luck and some incredible detective work, you might find him and for all you know, he may have the original purchase order. Translation: you get to identify that skeleton. All this without the internet, without computers. Where else but New York?"

Chapter Seven

June 28th

Meg Richards stepped onto her patio and sat down in her favorite lounge chair. Wrapping her hands around a mug of tea, she stared at the soft purple sky. She loved this time of year. It was almost 9PM and the sun was just setting. She sipped her tea. In the morning, she would take off for an eight day vacation with Laura Hunter and her kids. *Unbelievable*, she decided, not because she was going to spend a week hiding from the sun but because she was actually taking a vacation. It had been years, not since her divorce and then some. No wonder she felt so ill prepared.

Meg sighed. Maybe it hadn't been such a good idea to have spent the past five years living in a self-imposed cocoon. Then again, how else was she supposed to get all those painful memories to fade from the rear view mirror? Would she ever be ready to fall in love again or more importantly would she ever find someone she could trust? In some ways Meg envied Laura. She and Mike were perfect together. If Laura had any sense she would have asked Mike to come along. The guy was a gem. In any event, it was sure to be an interesting week.

Destiny, Meg mused, having met Laura at a time when their careers were at a crossroads. Meg, childless and newly divorced was trying to establish a shelter for battered women and children while Laura, a married at home mother, was trying to establish herself as a freelance investigative reporter. Meg smiled. No doubt their instant friendship, challenged by great joys and devastating losses, had strengthened over the years.

Meg sipped her tea and then rested the half empty mug in her lap. Absently she ran her finger around the rim. This was definitely her favorite mug, not so much because it somehow kept her tea hot but because it had been a gift from Laura. Meg often wondered how different her life might be had she not agreed to Laura's interview. A lot had happened since that hot summer day but Meg could recall it in vivid detail. She didn't know it then but she knew it now—without Laura's help, Jill's Place might never have come to fruition.

Meg sighed. Laura's request for an interview couldn't have come at a worse time. With all she had to get done, the last thing she wanted to do was to sit and chat with some annoying reporter. When Meg realized Laura would not take no for an answer, she took the easy way out. She invited Laura to the house she was trying to fix up to use as a shelter.

Meg could still recall that day and the relentless early summer heat. She was on a ladder trying to scrape wallpaper off a nine foot wall when the doorbell rang. Having forgotten all about Laura, Meg went to the door and was surprised to find a stranger standing on her doorstep. Not only was this broad strikingly beautiful, she appeared to be immune to the godawful heat and humidity.

Laura introduced herself. "May I come in?" she asked, handing Meg a large white bag. Looking all around, Laura followed Meg into the living room. "Oh my," she said, stopping dead in her tracks. "Where'd they ever get that wallpaper?"

Totally disarmed, Meg chuckled. "I don't know but there are several layers under that, each one uglier than the last. Not only that I think they used some space age adhesive. This paper does not want to come off." She held up the white bag. "What's in here?"

"Lunch. There's a diner near me. They're known for their salads but their bread basket is to die for. I brought bottled water. I hope you don't mind."

"Mind? Are you kidding? This is the nicest thing to happen to me in weeks. I've been living on peanut butter and jelly sandwiches. This house. I don't know what I was thinking. I want my residents to feel comfortable, but if I don't get rid of this paper, I'm afraid I'll have to hide all the sharp knives. Those colors, that print, it's enough to make even the sanest person want to slash their wrists."

Nodding, Laura looked around. "You got that right. I tried stripping wallpaper once. It was a disaster. Took me forever. Luckily I found a painter who did in one day what would have taken me three weeks. Listen," she said, knowing from an earlier conversation that Meg was on a very tight budget, "why don't you let me give him a call? He's big on community service and what he doesn't do gratis, I'll cover. Consider it your first donation."

Meg had been stunned not just by the offer but by how easy it had been to talk to Laura. Smiling, she recalled the hectic weeks that had followed that first meeting. With Laura's help she not only had the shelter up and running by her target date, she was also the beneficiary of widespread publicity thanks to Laura's award winning series on the plight of battered women. They'd been best friends ever since.

The purple sky was now turning a smoky shade of blue. Meg wiggled her toes. The brick patio that had trapped the heat of the day was beginning to cool. Lightening bugs, flickering in the nearby woods, added to the peaceful ambiance. Soon it would be dark. It was time to pack.

Meg finished her tea and then went inside. If the ten day weather forecast for the Outer Banks proved to be accurate, it would be sunny and hot for most of the vacation. A cold front was possible toward the end of vacation but as usual, computer models were in total disagreement. Meg began tossing shorts, tops, sundresses and bathing suits onto her bed. In the event that cold front did materialize, she added a pair of slacks, two long sleeved tops and a sweatshirt. She had just pulled her suitcase out of her closet when her phone rang. Seeing that it was Laura, she plopped down on her bed and took the call.

"Just checking in," Laura said. "You packed?"

"Just about. Is our EDT still the same?"

"Theoretically. Moving my kids *en masse* is always an adventure. Speaking of which, do us both a favor and get yourself a good night sleep. You should have heard the kids at dinner tonight. If they get any higher, we'll be peeling them off the ceiling."

"Sounds like fun."

"Hope so," Laura replied.

"What's the matter?" Meg asked. She knew Laura was still stressing over her trip to Greenview. "I hope you're not having second thoughts. You need this vacation and after all that has happened, you gotta admit that it couldn't come at a better time."

"I know that but there's a fly in the ointment. Mike took us out to dinner tonight. He had the kids so revved up. Went on and on about the beach and all the fun they were going to have. Told them stories about what he did when he was little. I admit he was very amusing and the kids really love him."

"So what's the problem?"

"We were all having a lot of fun until, out of the blue, Jon asked Mike if he's his daddy."

"Awkward. What he say?"

"No, but he'd like to be."

Meg was at a loss for words. She knew Mike had proposed more than once and that Laura was not quite ready to accept. She understood her reasoning, flawed as it was. "Not the worst thing in the world, you know."

"Don't start. Please. You sound like my mother."

"Well, you gotta admit, 'No, but I'd like to be' is a fair answer."

"I don't need any more pressure, Meg. Greenview's got me frazzled. Taking this trip without my mother."

"So what did you expect Mike to say? Jon's a little young for a biology lesson."

"It was so uncomfortable. Mike was staring at me, waiting to see what I would say."

"What did you say?"

"Nothing. Fortunately, dessert came. Good thing little kids are so easily distracted."

Meg sighed. "I know. I know it kills you that Jon never knew Dan. He was a wonderful father. He loved you and he loved his kids. He wouldn't begrudge them being happy, or you, for that matter."

"If he loved us, why did he go out that night?"

"It was a freak ice storm. No one predicted it. No one could stop. It wasn't his fault. It happened. It was horrible but you can't keep reliving it. Answer me this: If you knew Dan would be taken from you so young, would you still have married him?"

"Of course I would."

"Well, you've got a second chance at something just as special. Not many people get that lucky even once. Believe me, I know. You gotta stop beating yourself up, dragging around all that extra baggage. I get tired just watching it. I can't imagine how Mike feels."

Laura hesitated. "He asked me again, Meg and I have a feeling this was his last and final proposal. Says he'll wait until we get back."

"I would say, good, if his timing didn't suck. Now I get to spend a whole week trying to protect myself from those UV rays and watching you second guess yourself the entire time. I guess it'll be worth it if at some point, you finally realize that Mike Romano is a problem few people would mind having."

"You sorry you agreed to come on this vacation?"

"Not yet, but you are pushing the envelope."

"At least you're honest."

"I have no choice. You'd see right through me. You know, sometimes you remind me of the shoemaker. He can make beautiful shoes for everyone, everyone but himself."

"What are you talking about?"

"Laura, you can interview a rock and come away with valuable information but you can't look in the mirror and see what's going on."

"What's that supposed to mean?"

Meg rolled her eyes. "A gorgeous, loving man just proposed to you for the umpteenth time but instead of being happy, you're beating yourself up. None of us knows what tomorrow will bring and I get you've gotten a raw deal or two but think about what you might be throwing away. Yeah, yeah, I know. It's better that you throw it away than it gets taken from you."

Laura hesitated. She needed to change the subject. "Have you seen the extended forecast?"

"Yeah. Except for tomorrow, it looks pretty nice. Should be a good week."

"Glad to hear. Truth to tell, this next week…This next week. I'll be happy just to get through it."

"Well, don't set the bar too high."

"Come on, you know what I mean."

"Yeah, I do, but how about forcing yourself to look forward to this next week, to making new memories, good ones. Think of it as a self-fulfilling prophesy. Look. I have to admit, I have my concerns about this trip but for rather vacuous reasons. I'm still peeling from the other day and can't imagine what I'm going to look like after a week in the sun. That said. I'm hoping to come away with enough good memories to make it all worthwhile. Believe me, I'll need them to get me through those first few nights after we come back. I'll be alone. No kids, no lover. It'll be so quiet."

"Okay, okay," Laura replied. "I get it."

"Good. Try not to worry. One day at a time. I'm sure you'll figure it all out. Besides, you need your beauty sleep. It's a long ride and traffic tends to make you impossibly cranky."

Laura chuckled. "You psychologists. You think you have all the answers."

"I wish. If I could get you figured out, I could write a bestseller."

"And if you do, I promise to come to your book signing. See you in the morning… Meg…thanks…thanks for everything. I promise. I promise to do whatever it takes to make this vacation worth your while. You have my word."

Chapter Eight

June 29th

Laura woke with a start. No big surprise. She never slept particularly well the night before a vacation. Too much to think about. She made lists to be sure she remembered everything she had to do before she left home and everything she had to do once she arrived at her destination but they never seemed to help. Meg claimed to have figured it out. Laura hated change. Plain and simple. Laura loved routine and change knocked her off balance.

Laura shrugged. This time, Meg was only half right. This vacation wasn't about a change in routine. It was about a change in lifestyle. It would be her first trip to the Outer Banks without her mother, and although her mother was totally useless when it came to navigating, she was wonderful with everything else. Tears welled in Laura's dark brown eyes. It was her mother who had gotten Laura through that first year without her husband; her mother, a young widow herself who taught Laura to put one foot in front of the other and to keep going; her mother who saw joy in the little things, who didn't care if they got lost, who didn't care if they walked into a restaurant and had to wait. In her own quiet way, her mother had been her rudder. Now she would have to sail alone. No wonder she couldn't sleep.

On the plus side, Laura was enormously grateful that Meg had agreed to accompany them. Meg was a great navigator with an enviable sense of direction. She was a quiet observer who could assess any situation with almost one hundred percent accuracy. Best of all, she was as flexible as Laura was rigid. She knew how to jettison routine for new adventures, had a ready laugh and despite all the knocks she had taken in her own life, she still saw the glass half full.

Rolling over in the predawn darkness, Laura checked the time. All was quiet, and tempted as she was to start her day, she saw no advantage in getting up any earlier than she had to. In a matter of hours, she would be behind the wheel, making the six hour drive to Virginia where they would spend the night. Laura smiled. It had been her husband's idea all those years ago to break up the trip, by stopping at a hotel. That allowed them to get up in the morning, enjoy a leisurely breakfast and then complete the two hour drive to their final destination well ahead of the crushing traffic. It had been a solid plan, one that worked to this day.

Laura sighed. Although she tried, she worried that vacations for her kids were not as much fun without their father as they had been with him. That first summer, she forced herself to learn how to bait fishing lines and how to gut the fish they sometimes caught. She honed her tennis skills and endured lengthy bike rides. She didn't freak out when one of the crabs they caught escaped from the bucket and nipped at their feet. In time she learned how to kayak and how to use a wave runner. She could pack the car almost as efficiently as her husband once did and she even learned to control her lead foot when driving through areas known for their speed traps. Her mother was right. Life goes on.

Slowly but surely the birds began making their early morning chatter. Energized by the growing racket, Laura decided to get up, to go downstairs, to make some coffee and to enjoy some quiet time. She donned her robe and then slipped out into the hallway. As she always did, she tiptoed past her kids' bedrooms, taking several seconds at each doorway to sneak a peek at their angelic faces. All in all, she felt blessed.

Laura wended her way into her kitchen. Almost every morning since her mother had passed away, she wondered why she didn't make use of the timer on her gourmet coffeemaker. Even though her mother didn't drink coffee, she always prepared it the night before. Maybe coming down and not smelling the coffee was Laura's way of accepting the fact that her mother was no longer with her, a subtle way to force herself to move on. Then again, maybe she was just too tired at night to care.

Whether it was a smart thing to do or not, Laura kept the coffee in an airtight container in the refrigerator. She opened the door, took out the container and then walked over to the sink. She checked the time. Meg was like clockwork. When she said she would arrive at a certain time, she usually did, so in anticipation of her arrival, Laura made two extra cups.

At some point between filling the carafe with water and pouring it into the coffeemaker, Laura glanced out the kitchen window. Although the flood lights that went on at dusk and off at dawn were still burning, Laura's eyes were drawn past her back porch to the distant tree line. The sun rose in front of the house but it often brightened the tops of the trees behind the house and made for a breathtaking view. Laura had often tried to capture the scene on her I-phone but could never do it justice. It annoyed her that although she could do many things well, photography wasn't one of them.

Laura was about to return the coffee container to the refrigerator when she realized there was a package on the picnic table, something that wasn't there when she went to bed. She made sure the coffeemaker was on and then walked over to the sliding glass door that let out onto the patio. Curious, she stepped outside to investigate.

Thanks to the flood light streaming through the overhead skylights, Laura could see that the wicker basket sitting on the table was filled with beach toys, baseball caps, kid sunglasses and a rather impressive long tailed kite. Despite the dim light, she was able to read the note taped to the basket. "Meant to leave this last night. Hope the kids have a great time."

Next to the basket was a bag of bagels. The bag was warm indicating it hadn't been on the table very long. A note was also attached to this one. "Sorry I can't be with you. Enjoy. Awaiting your answer."

Laura gasped. Intuitively she looked around. She listened hopefully for footsteps, for the close of a car door, the awakening of a car engine, the roll of tires passing down the street. All was quiet. Clearly Dr. Mike Romano had left the neighborhood.

Sitting down on one of the benches, Laura sighed. How strange it felt to have known Mike longer than her late husband. They met in high school when everyone called him Mikey, a nickname that once fit him in so many ways. Mikey was enormously cute but incredibly immature and there was no way Laura could take him seriously. She was both shocked and annoyed when he asked her to their Junior Prom. Too kind to refuse, she agreed to go only if she could call him Michael. By the time they graduated from high school, Mikey had not only matured, he had become as awesome as his given name.

Somewhere between their first and second years of college, they quietly separated. Mike's family moved out of the area and they lost touch. Although Laura's days were filled with new friends and new interests, she sometimes wondered what had happened to the first boy who turned her head. That question was answered a little over two years ago when her oldest child broke his arm. Terrified, she was sitting in the emergency room waiting for the orthopedic surgeon, when Mike passed through. At first she didn't recognize him. He was dressed in scrubs over which he was wearing a starched white doctor's coat. He was clearly in a hurry and as he raced past her she caught a glimpse of the red lettering on his chest pocket. Michael C Romano, MD. Cardiology. She froze, just as he stopped dead in his tracks. Several nights later, when he came to pick her up for their first date, it was her mother who quipped, "See, I told you, there's a silver lining in every cloud."

Grabbing the bagels, Laura went inside. She placed the bag on the counter and then grabbed her cell phone. Mike answered on the first ring. "Where are you?" Laura asked.

"Just pulled out of your neighborhood. I was hoping to catch you but got beeped for a heart rescue. Promise me you'll drive carefully."

"Always do."

"When are you leaving?"

"Well, the kids should be up in about an hour, so not too long after that. It's so quiet right now. I'm pouring my coffee as we speak. The bagels are still warm. Crunchy on the outside, soft on the inside, just the way I like them. I'll be thinking of you the whole way there."

"That was the plan. Hope the ride's not too bad. They've doubled down on that nasty weather forecast. If you're lucky those storms will hold off till you get to Virginia, although I wouldn't count on it. It's a huge system. Probably no escaping. After that, the weather looks good. I'm jealous. Would love to be there. Maybe next year."

Laura hesitated, grateful for the sudden loud and annoying screech of Mike's beeper. "Are you being paged again?"

"Unfortunately. I'd better take this. Call me when you get to Virginia."

Smiling to herself, Laura poured some half and half into her coffee and then stirred in a little sugar. She didn't really need Meg or her mother to tell her that Mike Romano was one of the best things to happen to her. She'd known that for a long time. She knew it and her kids knew it. Maybe it was time to stop being stupid and let Mike know it too.

By the time Meg arrived, Laura was on the driveway, trying to shove the basket Mike had left into her packed suburban. "Whatcha doing?" Meg asked.

"Last minute item. Mike dropped it off this morning. I don't want the kids to see it, at least not yet."

"Here. Put my overnight bag over it. That should hide it."

"Good. I saved a spot for your suitcase. One more overnight bag and then we're ready to go." Laura closed the tailgate and began walking toward the house. "Hope you're hungry. Mike also left a dozen bagels, butter and cream cheese. The coffee's fresh and the kids are still sleeping. Our last quiet time."

Laura could feel her excitement grow as each of the kids came down. In addition to the bagels, she made scrambled eggs, insisting that everyone have some protein for their long ride. Breakfast and last minute chores went smoother than Laura expected, and under copious sunshine, everyone climbed into the car. Checking her rear view mirror, Laura started the engine. She couldn't believe that for the first time in recorded history, the Hunter family was actually leaving home several minutes ahead of schedule.

The ride on the interstate was uneventful at least for the first hour. A disabled vehicle was blocking the left lane and had traffic, including the tow truck, backed up for almost two miles. As they inched their way through the slowdown, the bright, clear sky began to morph into a monochromatic gray. Storm clouds amassed in the distance and the rain began a short time later. It was not a gentle rain, but an angry deluge and it continued as they arrived in Virginia. The noise on the car roof was loud and constant, and by the time they arrived at their hotel, Laura could barely hear herself think.

A large screen TV was the first thing Laura saw when they walked into the lobby to check in. She could feel the kink in her neck tighten as she read the bright red print scrolling across the bottom of the screen. "SEVERE THUNDERSTORM WARNING FOR THE FOLLOWING COUNTIES....TORNADO WATCH UNTIL 11PM."

Laura stared dumfounded as she tried to read the list of counties and/or towns in the warned areas but it was all Greek to her. All she knew was that she was in Chesapeake, Virginia. Despite all the times she had come to the Outer Banks, it had never occurred to her that she would need to know their exact geographic location. She gave her name to the clerk at the reception desk, pointed to the TV and then asked what county they were in.

The clerk glanced knowingly at the TV screen. "Figures. The only time anyone ever asks what county we're in is when there's a severe weather warning. We are in the warned area but I wouldn't worry. Seen hundreds of those warnings but nothing ever happens here. You'll be fine...although if you need to go out for dinner, I'd do it sooner rather than later...you know, just in case." She handed Laura the keys to adjoining rooms on the ground floor. "Oh, and by the way. Both pools will be closed tonight. Have to close any time there are thunderstorms in the area."

Less than thrilled, Laura rounded up Meg and the kids. Swimming was half the charm for this part of the journey and not surprisingly the kids were disappointed. "Maybe in the morning," Laura promised, "depending on the weather."

As they wended their way through several corridors, the kids complained that their rooms were on the first floor and that they would have no excuse to ride the elevator. A few minutes later, Meg and Sara opened the door to room 156 while Laura and the boys took the adjoining room. Laura placed the overnight bag onto the luggage caddy and opened the drapes. She cringed as she took in the tall grasses behind the hotel and the expansive, dark, ominous sky. "Okay," Laura announced. "Who's hungry?"

Despite the severe weather threat, the rain let up just long enough for Laura to make the short drive over to the restaurant and to get inside. Their wait was a short one and *Pirates of the Caribbean* was playing on the nearby TV monitor. "So far, so good," Meg commented as everyone settled in. "Nothing like a six hour drive to work up an appetite."

Laura smiled as the waitress placed two dishes of salsa and a basket of chips on the table. "I have to admit, this is going better than I thought it would."

"Better than you thought it would? A short time ago, you were complaining about not being able to hear yourself think, them closing the pools and that tornado watch. What gives?"

"Being here, I guess. I didn't realize until now just how much I needed to get away."

"Glad to hear that. What's that noise? Is that your phone?"

Laura hesitated and then reached for her purse. "Thanks. It's so loud in here I'm amazed you heard it. It's probably Mike. He wanted me to call him as soon as we got to Virginia."

"Nice. You're a good half hour late. Hard to know why he puts up with you."

The call lasted less than fifteen seconds but it was enough to dampen Laura's mood. "That wasn't Mike. It was the security company, false alarm, or so they say. It's also storming back home. Lots of wind and lightning. They sent someone over to the house. Everything was okay but if it happens again during the storm, they don't plan to send anyone out. They're getting too many false alarms."

"Your alarm? I've known you for years and I've never seen you use it. Since when?"

Laura shrugged. "Since Greenview. Since I started hearing all kinds of noises at night. Had to do something. I just can't get John's death out of my head; John's death, Linda Ferina. Not knowing what I don't know is really getting to me. Dave should be interviewing those cops soon and I've got my fingers crossed that he comes away convinced that John's death was just an unfortunate accident. One less variable."

A gust of wind rattled the restaurant windows. Meg looked around. "I think our server's on the way over. Any idea what the kids will want?"

By the time their dinner arrived, there were no empty seats to be had. The food was good but the atmosphere was growing more and more frenzied. In the middle of dessert, the lights went out and a hush fell over the huge room crowded with diners. The sudden quiet was immediately replaced with sounds of hail pounding the roof and wind rattling the windows. For several seconds, it felt as though they were in a wind tunnel, then as suddenly as it started, it stopped. The lights came back on and conversations resumed. Meg and Laura exchanged glances. "I hope that wasn't an omen," they both said at the same time. Half a second later, they were chuckling and locking pinkies. "Great minds do think alike," Laura joked.

Back at the hotel, they passed the evening playing card games. Hoping that the storms were dying down, Laura checked the radar one more time before they all went to bed. Shades of red and yellow covered the viewing area and Laura slept fitfully, this time thanks to the sirens that blared until the wee hours of the morning. She was deep in REM sleep when the storm finally pulled away. Her dreams were disjointed and haunting, but she awoke too tired to remember any of them. *Just as well*, Laura mused, knowing her propensity to look for hidden meanings. Her imagination certainly didn't need any more fuel. Thanks to her mother's seemingly innocent secret, it was already running overtime.

Chapter Nine

June 30th

It wasn't the rain pounding against the glass that woke Laura up. It was the peace and quiet. She slipped out of bed and then tiptoed over to the floor length drapery covering the large sliding door. Not wanting to wake her boys, she slowly, quietly, inched the door open and then stepped out onto the tiny patio. There she was surprised not only to find brightening skies, but also to see Meg sitting on the adjacent patio. "What are you doing up so early?"

"I promised myself I would watch every single sunrise on this vacation."

"Your idea of a vacation is to drag yourself out of bed so you can watch the sunrise?"

"And the sunsets. It's like bookmarking your vacation."

Laura shrugged. She slipped through the bushes separating the patios and sat down. "We should try to be on the road in about an hour, hour and a half. That'll give us just enough time for a dip in the pool and a decent breakfast."

"The pool? That water's going to be freezing."

"I certainly hope so. We'll see the blue lips sooner rather than later. Dan and I had this rule that once the lips get blue, the kids get out. Keeps complaining to a minimum and we'll be on the road well ahead of the heavy traffic, no sweat."

"Blue lips, brilliant."

Laura sighed. "Wish I could take credit but it was Dan's idea. He had such a way with the kids. Knew how to get them to do things that always seemed fair. It makes me so sad that Jon is too young to remember, even Sara."

"Well, you gotta admit, even though Dan isn't here, he got your kids off to a great start. They're beautiful, smart, resourceful and determined, especially your daughter."

"What's that supposed to mean? Don't tell me. What did Sara do now?"

Meg hesitated. "Your mother's barrettes, any idea where they are?"

"Home. On my dresser, in my jewelry box."

"And you showed them to Sara?"

"Not exactly. She found them when she was rifling through my jewelry box. I told her they were her grandmother's and that I'd think about letting her wear them when we got back."

"Good. That's the same story I got. Problem is: to a six year old, when we get back and right now mean the same thing."

"What? Sara has my mother's barrettes? How'd she sneak them past me?"

"I told you she's resourceful. Why do you think she insisted on bringing her American Girl doll? You know; the one that looks just like her, the one with all the dresses, pinafores and bonnets that your mother made?"

Laura shrugged. "She said all those outfits reminded her of my mother and that if she brought her doll, it would be like bringing my mother with us."

"Boy, does she have your number. The doll just happened to be the perfect way for her to hide your mother's barrettes. When your daughter's not admiring the barrettes in her own hair, she lets her doll wear them, under any one of those cute little bonnets. The reason you haven't seen them is because Sara's smart enough not to take the bonnet off whenever you're around."

"That's my girl," Laura chuckled. "How did you find out?"

"Last night Sara was taking forever to brush her teeth so I went to check on her. There she was standing at the mirror, turning her head every which way and just loving the way the barrettes were catching the light. I shoulda taken a video. She was adorable."

Smiling, Laura just shook her head. "So where are they now?"

"Back under the bonnet. I offered to keep them for her. Told her how important they were to you but she made a good point. Said someone might steal my purse but no one would bother with her doll."

Laura shrugged. "She's probably right. Between you and me, I don't mind that she has them. They're hers after I get them appraised. I just don't want her to lose them in the meantime."

"She won't. Sara takes better care of that doll than some mothers take care of their babies. She has no idea that she did anything wrong, but I did suggest that at some point she tell you she has them. Try not to flip out when she does."

"Don't worry. I'm not that upset. In her own little way, she's brought my mother with her. It's kind of sweet."

The sunrise was beautiful, the pool water freezing and the breakfast decent. By the time Laura and company headed out, traffic was light but building. After a brief stint on a major highway, Laura pulled onto the road that would lead directly to the Outer Banks. When they passed a sign welcoming them to North Carolina, everyone cheered.

They entered farmers' market territory and for the next several miles, everyone was captivated by the clever billboards: corn stalks dressed in overalls and topped with round melon faces, smiling doe-eyed peaches wearing straw hats and waving. Laura slowed down after they passed a cluster of signs displaying a happy family of bright red smiling tomatoes. A short time later they pulled into their favorite market.

The parking lot was packed. As Laura searched for a spot big enough to accommodate her suburban, she lowered her window. "Listen to that. I just love that sound; all those tiny pebbles crunching under the tires."

A car finally pulled out. Laura pulled in. As they walked toward the entrance, Laura grabbed her youngest's hand, not only to keep him safe but to keep him from stomping in the puddles left over from yesterday's storm. Once inside, the kids made a b-line past the fruit stands and past the freshly baked goods. "Walk," Laura called as they charged to the back of the store to an oasis packed with wall to wall toys, trinkets and just about anything onto which the North Carolina logo could be printed.

A woman, pushing a rack of freshly baked items, excused herself. Backing out of the way, Meg grabbed Laura's arm. "That smell. I knew it. Peach pies. I'll bet they're still warm. A slice of that with a scoop of vanilla ice cream: heaven."

As Meg followed the cart lady, Laura caught up with her kids. She couldn't help but smile as she watched them pick out cute but totally useless trinkets. Before going to the cash register, she grabbed an Outer Banks cookbook for Meg and selected a new mug for her collection. They met up with Meg on the way to the car. She was juggling two bakery boxes and two brown shopping bags, one filled with peaches and the other with melons. Laura grabbed the boxes. "Wow! You don't mess around."

"This place is awesome. I couldn't decide between the peach pie and the peach cobbler so I bought one of each. They're still warm."

They got into the car. As Laura checked the kids' seatbelts, Meg read the latest text on her I-phone. She keyed in a response. "Your GPS says another 40 minutes. Is that about right?"

"Give or take. Depends on traffic." She pointed to the screen on her GPS. "That blue blob is the bay. It's only a stone's throw from here. We've got a breathtaking ride over the bridge, turn left and then we're at Southern Shores. This year we're renting a house called Gatekeeper. It was empty last week so we can have an early check in. That'll save us a ton of time. We can get the grocery store run out of the way, pick up the key and then head to the house."

"The grocery store run?" Meg repeated, sending another text. "Before going to the house?"

"Yeah, sorry to have to do that. That's the worst part of this vacation. Don't ask me why but I can't relax until we get that over with."

"You gotta be kidding. We've been on the road for two days. Can't we at least see the house first, make a pit stop, have a little snack? Vacation. This is vacation, not boot camp."

Laura chuckled. She checked the time. "Okay, okay, but we'll have to be quick about it. The shopping will go a whole lot quicker if we stay ahead of the crowds."

Meg stared at Laura. "Who knew?" she asked, repressing a smile. "Under that beautiful, calm exterior lies the heart of a drill sergeant."

They began their trek across the bay. "Check it out," Laura said. "The bridge to our left— at one time that was the only way in or out. Traffic would back up something awful if they had to open for a tall boat and every Saturday from 7AM till noon, they would they would reroute the traffic: two lanes for departing vehicles and one for arriving. At noon, they would reverse the flow. If they had to evacuate, all lanes went outbound. You were out of luck if you wanted to get onto the island once the order was imposed."

They turned onto Southern Shores. Laura opened the windows so everyone could enjoy the salty air. "That pier," Laura said, pointing to her right, "was one of Dan's favorite spots. Never caught anything he could keep, but that didn't stop him."

Traffic was slow but moving. They drove past normal looking houses on either side of the road but soon the landscape gave way to vacation homes and resort enclaves. Eventually they came to the largest resort town on the Outer Banks. Here bikers and sunbathers from the bay side of the road were carting their umbrellas and beach chairs across to the ocean side.

Laura pointed to a bright yellow building. "See that? That's the real estate office where we used to go to get our key. I can't pass that place without thinking about the year we came down here to an approaching hurricane. I'll never forget walking in to get our envelope. Everyone was gawking at the TV. A hurricane watch had just been issued for the Outer Banks. We arrived on Saturday and the hurricane hit on Sunday. They issued a voluntary evacuation and since it was voluntary, I wasn't too worried. Then I found out they wanted to make it mandatory but couldn't because there wasn't enough time to get everyone safely off the island."

"And there went your comfort level."

"No kidding. I wanted to leave but got outvoted. Dan and my mother figured it was safer to stay than to be out on the road, even though were uncomfortably close to the ocean. It turned into a category 3, but staying was the right decision. Took those who did leave hours and hours just to get over the bridge."

"You stayed for a Category 3? I'm impressed that Dan managed to talk you into that."

Laura chuckled. "It wasn't easy. That hurricane was making me crazy until he reminded me that hurricanes often follow the Gulf Stream which is about fifty miles offshore. Even better, its worst winds are on its eastern side. Dan convinced me that the storm would probably track far enough offshore so that the most destructive part would stay out to sea. He didn't mention that if the storm changed tracks and came right at us, we would have been in big trouble. A land falling Category 3 hurricane can cause a deadly surge and we were about seven hundred feet from the ocean."

"Wow! You lucked out. You've been in a major hurricane, several major blizzards, and an earthquake. All you need to complete the cycle is a tornado."

"No thanks. I'll pass."

They were nearing their destination when they passed a sprawling shopping center. "Well, there it is, one of the biggest grocery stores you'll ever be in. You can get your ten thousand steps just trying to find milk. Talk about a mad house."

They passed a second complex on the left. "Tim Buck II? What a neat name."

"We have to go there. They have some really interesting shops, restaurants, miniature golf, paddle boats. At least once, on every vacation, my mother insisted on babysitting the kids so Dan and I could dine at one of the fancier restaurants."

Further down the road, Laura pointed to an indoor sports complex on her left. "One of the reasons we picked this place. Even if the weather's awful, the kids have the indoor pool. Truthfully we've never used it but it's nice to know it's there."

After a brief stop at the real estate office to pick up the key, Laura turned into the sprawling resort development known as Corolla Light. She drove slowly, giving everyone a chance to enjoy the fountains on either side of the road, spewing bubbles of white water. Several hundred feet later, she made a left onto Lighthouse Court. Gatekeeper was the fifth and last house on the street. The cleaning crew was just pulling out of the driveway. "Wow!" Laura cried. "Did we time that perfectly or what?"

The minute Laura stopped the car, the kids jumped out. Although her first impulse was to make everyone bring something inside, she decided not to kill the moment. Carrying just the goodies from the farmer's market, they entered the house on ground level where the kids ran into the rec room. "Wow!" Laura sighed. She immediately felt at home. The room was warm and welcoming with something for everyone. Even better, it put more distance between her and Greenview. "Okay," Laura called a few minutes later. "Let's head upstairs. Time to choose the bedrooms."

Although Laura had braced herself for an argument, there was none. Even more surprising, the kids claimed the bedrooms that she would have assigned. They headed to the third floor of the upside down house, the floor which housed the living room, dining room, kitchen and the second master bedroom where Meg would sleep. Halfway up, Laura stopped dead in her tracks. "I must be hallucinating. I could swear I smell coffee."

Giggling, the kids darted in front of Laura and Meg and hurried to the kitchen. Laura glanced at Meg, who just shrugged. "They can't be hungry. We had breakfast not too long ago."

By the time Laura and Meg arrived, the two younger ones were sitting around the table waiting for their brother to fill their glasses with the milk he had just taken out of the refrigerator. "Hold it," Laura cried. "You can't drink that. God only knows how long it's been in there."

Meg checked her watch. "About about two hours," she said, pointing to the coffee maker. "They can have their milk and we can have our coffee."

Laura stared as the last of the coffee dripped into the carafe. "How'd you do that?"

"Easy. Mike was tracking you on your I-phone. When he saw how close we were, he called the real estate office to see if someone could set the pot for us. The cleaning crew was still here, so they did it."

"How do you know that?"

Meg tapped her phone. "We've been texting."

"You said those were from the shelter."

"No, I didn't. You just assumed it was the shelter and I saw no reason to correct you."

Laura stood dumfounded as Meg walked over to the pantry and opened the double doors. "Look at that. We're freshly stocked and ready to go."

Laura stared in disbelief. "That's enough food to feed an army. How'd you do that?"

"All I did was make a few suggestions. Your mother and Mike did the rest."

"My mother?"

"Yeah. These plans have been in the works for a long time. Your mother didn't want to hear you bitch about the grocery shopping and about having to carry the bags up three flights of steps. Once she booked Gatekeeper, she found someone to do the shopping for you. Full disclosure: your mother hated squeezing down the crowded isles just as much as you did. Mike took over after she died. It was hard to rein him in. He showed me the order before he placed it. I wanted him to trim it down but he wouldn't listen. I doubt we'll starve."

Covering a smile, Laura walked over to the refrigerator. It was stocked. She checked out the freezer. Same scenario. As Laura was gushing her appreciation, Meg opened the cabinet on the far left. "Well, Mike nailed it. Look at all this wine."

Laura closed her eyes. "That coffee smells so good. Kind of like old times. The first thing my mother did after we got back from the grocery store was to put the coffee on and then lecture us about too much caffeine. Caffeine and sugar."

Meg opened the pastry boxes. She looked at the cobbler and then at the pie. "I miss those lectures. Your mother had such a nice way of letting you know you were quietly killing yourself."

Laura chuckled. "She did, didn't she? I used to love the way she and Dan would go at it. She was always trying to get him to improve his diet and he always had some crazy remark that made her break out laughing. It's ironic. His diet didn't kill him and her diet didn't save her."

"Well, her influence lives on. Truthfully, your mother she was the reason I got the cobbler. More fruit, less lard."

Laura smiled as she pulled her phone out of her pocket. "Fix us all a huge chunk of cobbler with a nice scoop of ice cream and then pour some coffee into the biggest mugs you can find. I'll be right back. I have to call Mike."

The milk and ice cream were cold, the coffee was hot and the cobbler was delicious. "Okay," Laura said as they finished. "Let's leave the dishes and show Meg the beach."

A few minutes later, Laura and Meg followed the kids as they bonked down the shaded path that led from the back of the house to a narrow two lane road. "Head's up," Laura said. "In the heat of the day this road gets ungodly hot. If you're barefooting it, be prepared to run."

The kids sprinted down a long boardwalk, built to carry beachgoers over the dunes and onto the beach. "Stop at the gazebo," Laura called.

"Wow!" Meg said as they walked along. "These dunes. They don't mess around down here, do they? They're huge."

"Have to be. High enough and deep enough to protect the development from hurricanes. You'll see when we get to the gazebo. About twenty steps from the top to the beach. It's a nice security blanket."

Meg looked to her right. "How many gazebos are there?"

"Five altogether. Five gazebos and five boardwalks. You're outta luck if you hate climbing steps but the views are awesome. Nice breeze, plenty of seating."

Laura and Meg were only halfway down the boardwalk when the kids reached the gazebo. Not surprisingly, they turned around to wave and then ran down the steps. Laura sighed. "Funny the way vacation gives a different meaning to the word stop."

By the time Laura and Meg reached the gazebo, the kids were challenging each other to wait for an approaching wave and then trying to outrun it. "At least the tide's going out," Laura said. "Better than even chance their shoes will stay dry."

"Yeah, right," Meg replied. "I may not have kids but even I know that's a pipe dream."

"Speaking of dreams, you're going to love the swim club. Don't know if you can see it from here but it's the last gazebo all the way down on the right. Leads from the beach to the club. Not quite as many steps. A restaurant, four swimming pools and a great bar."

"Sounds wonderful. I can see why you like this place so much. Tell me, though. Why is our house named Gatekeeper? Gatekeeper to what?"

"Whalehead. Whalehead was one of the first estates down here and at one time this entire subdivision was part of the estate. They sold their land up to the tree line just outside our house and made the developer promise not to touch any of the trees. Since our house is the closest one to Whalehead, the owners named it Gatekeeper."

"Cool. Are we supposed to keep the interlopers out?"

"I don't know but if we are, I want a discount."

"Well, either way, it's a beautiful house."

"Thank my mother. She picked it out. She would have loved being this close to Whalehead. That place fascinated her. Said it reminded her of the house where she grew up. Don't ask me why. When we have time we can walk down the path by the bay. Given the way it curves, there's one spot in particular where you can see the entire house. Tourists are always down there taking pictures. Must drive the people who live there nuts."

"How many people live there?'

"I'm not really sure. The woman who owns it is a widow and she's in her eighties. She's kind of a recluse. Can't really blame her. She's had a tragic life."

"A tragic life?" Meg repeated. "She owns half this island. How tragic could it be?"

"Tragic enough. Her husband, her daughter and her daughter's governess were all killed when her husband's yacht exploded as they were leaving the island, end of summer, 1945. No one saw the explosion but parts of the yacht washed ashore several months later. Between the explosion and the ensuing fire, none of the bodies was ever found. Come on. We'd better move it. I don't see the kids anymore and if they've inherited my mother's sense of direction, we could be in big trouble."

"Your mother's sense of direction? Look who's talking. At least she knew how to get from point A to point B without a GPS."

"Yeah, by way of Antarctica. You know, I've been thinking. I'll betcha the real reason she never took me to Greenview is that she knew she'd never find it."

"Like you did? You and your friend?"

"I was a brand new driver. I probably would have found it eventually. Oh, my God, look! The kids. They're in the water. God, I hope they took their shoes off. I have a terrible feeling I forgot to pack their beach shoes."

Meg burst out laughing. "Their beach shoes? Seriously? Look at them. You honestly think they care if they have dry shoes, and if they don't care, neither should we. Come on. Let's show them they're not the only ones who can outrun the waves. Last one in's a rotten egg."

Chapter Ten

June 30th

Catherine Preston peered out the window of her bayside estate. It was Saturday, turnover day. For the next several hours, the local roads would be clogged with vacationers—those who were leaving and those who were coming. The walking trail along the sound would be empty and no one would be trying to get pictures of her or her house. It wasn't that Catherine begrudged them. She envied them: people with families, scrimping and saving for a special week together. On those occasions when she dressed down and walked the trail, she could see it on their faces: pleasure, enjoyment, and most of all, love. There were times when she overheard talk about herself, talk about the old lady with all that money, the old lady who lives at Whalehead. Many were awed by her wealth. Few had any idea how difficult it was to be in her twilight years with no husband, no children or grandchildren.

Catherine sighed. This was certainly not the life she had hoped for and she often wondered how different things might have been had she not become Mrs. Charles Preston. To this day she regretted her decision to marry so young, but she had come to understand why she did what she did so many years ago.

As the only child of wealthy, doting parents, Catherine had mastered the art of pretending to be older than she was. Not only had she convinced the admissions committee at George Washington University that she was more than ready to compete with students two or three years her senior, she had also managed to convince her parents to let her go.

Catherine knew she had an unfair advantage. Andrew and Marie Ferarra often praised their daughter for having a quick mind, a beautiful face and an irrepressible spirit of adventure. They were not surprised when Catherine finished her freshman year at the top of her class and were waiting for her to join them at the Dorchester Hotel to celebrate when a fire broke out. Catherine's parents, along with twenty-nine others, perished.

All these years later, Catherine could still taste the bitterness of her loss. As an only child who had lived a life of wealth and privilege, she couldn't believe something this awful would happen to her. For hours she wandered near the hotel ruins hoping to find her parents. By the time she bumped into Charles Preston, the reality that she was all alone was just sinking in.

Catherine couldn't deny that Charles was just what she needed, at least at first glance. A good ten years older, he was better equipped to deal with the tragedy and the loss of his own father and stepmother. For a time, Charles' guidance and empathy filled the crushing void. They married six months later. By the time the whirlwind began to slow down, Catherine was pregnant with their first child. Marney Preston was almost two years old when a man showed up at Whalehead, a man who would alter their destiny.

Catherine first laid eyes on Tad Quigley on a warm sunny day. She was stunned to learn that this gorgeous man was Charles' stepbrother, a man her husband had never mentioned. She had no idea that Tad's mother had once been married to Edward Preston, her husband's father, the man responsible for the Preston fortune. She also had no idea that Tad, by virtue of his mother's ten year marriage to Edward had come to lay claim to what he believed was rightfully his. Tad had his issues, to be sure, but given his childhood, Catherine understood.

Tad first came to Whalehead as a curious nine year old. Having grown up dirt poor, Tad embraced their fresh start. His stepfather made it easy. He was a kind and generous man. His stepbrother, an insufferable know-it-all a good ten years older, made it difficult.

Tad might have accepted his unpleasant relationship with Charles had he not treated Tad's mother with the same disdain. "Ignore Charles," his mother used to say. "Edward is the only one we need to answer to. Be good and be patient. Some day it will all be worth it."

The years passed quickly. When Tad received his draft notice, Edward offered to pull strings to keep him home but the eighteen year old proudly went off to serve his country. He was preparing for deployment to Germany when he was notified of his mother's sudden illness. Edward, wanting to comfort his wife, arranged to get her son home as soon as possible but his efforts were for naught. Tad arrived a half hour after she died.

Edward took great pains to comfort his stepson. After the funeral, he encouraged Tad to return to duty and promised to resolve any inheritance issues that might arise in Tad's favor. He even hinted that with Charles' approval, he would find a place for Tad at Whalehead when his tour of duty was over. In a speech reminiscent of the one Tad often heard from his mother, Edward advised Tad to be patient.

Patience became a relative concept. Several months after he arrived in Germany, Tad received a much belated letter from Charles, informing him that Edward Preston had died in the Dorchester Hotel fire. He enclosed a copy of Edward's will and made no apologies that Tad was not mentioned. He also advised Tad that all his mother's possessions had been sent to her sister's house and that he could retrieve them there when he returned. His message was clear. He never wanted to see his stepbrother again.

Tad had been reluctant to return to Whalehead but did so because of his mother's sister and her constant nagging. 'Your mother was a Preston, for God's sake. You're entitled to something and if you had any balls, you'd fight for it.'

Dreading another confrontation with his stepbrother, Tad had expected his visit to Whalehead to be a short one. He walked slowly toward the front door, trying to decide if he should knock or walk right in. A beautiful young woman carrying a basket of colorful flowers made the decision for him. "Hello, there. Can I help you?"

For Tad it was love at first sight. He had never met anyone so beautiful and so welcoming but his heart dropped when she introduced herself as his stepbrother's wife. In an instant, on that warm, sunny day, Tad's mission changed. He no longer wanted Whalehead. He wanted Mrs. Catherine Preston.

Had Catherine not intervened, Tad's stay at Whalehead would have been shorter than a winter's day. Horrified by the animosity her husband showed toward his stepbrother, Catherine reminded him how important family was to her. She made it clear that she could not abide a man who would turn his back on his own brother, step or otherwise. Sensing the wisdom in appeasing his wife, Charles reluctantly gave Tad a job as estate caretaker and allowed him to live in the caretaker's cottage. In a rare generous moment, he even acquiesced to Catherine's request that Tad take his meals at the big house, with the family.

Tad turned out to be a natural caretaker. He had a green thumb and could fix anything that needed to be fixed. He worked harder than anyone on the estate. In his spare time, he built a spectacular doll house for little Marney Preston and was never too busy to push her on the swing set that he had constructed.

Although the relationship between Tad and Charles remained strained throughout that fateful summer, it flourished between Tad and Catherine. Tad was warm and attentive while Charles was cold and distant. Tad shared Catherine's pleasure in little things while Charles scoffed at anything that did not improve his bottom line. Tad treated Catherine like a treasure. Charles treated her like a possession.

As the summer deepened, Catherine, bored by her husband's predictable behavior, found herself mesmerized by Tad. She came to love the way his mischievous eyes would sparkle whenever he looked at her, the cologne he wore, his oozing masculinity. Increasingly her fantasies included time alone with Tad, a dream that was realized the day he followed her to the lighthouse.

It had been a comfortable June day courtesy of a cold front that had passed through the area the night before. Having had another disagreement with Charles, Catherine had been hoping her morning walk would calm her nerves but her heart began to pound when she realized Tad was following her. She walked deeper and deeper into the woods, toward the lighthouse, purposely stopping at the most secluded area. She acted surprised when Tad called her name but he seemed to know what her plan had been even before she did. They made love with a passion she had never known before. That day everything changed.

Although her spirits soared, Catherine tried to maintain a somber demeanor. Despite her best efforts, she suspected her husband knew what was happening. Charles berated Tad every chance he got and as the summer wound down, he doubled his list of chores. When Catherine missed her period, she reluctantly sought her husband's affections. After weeks of being turned down, Charles obliged with a vengeance that caught them both by surprise. Catherine sensed she had made a terrible mistake and that Charles saw through her ruse. She was alarmed by his icy silence and fully expected him to get even. She just didn't know how.

Closing Whalehead for the season was a complicated process and as he always did, Charles waited until 5PM on their last full day there to post the final schedule for his family and his staff. As usual, Catherine, her daughter and the governess would leave in the morning and ride to the winter estate with the chauffeur. The head cook and the chambermaids would leave as soon as everything was in order. At noon, Charles would set sail in his yacht for his season ending trek across the bay. Tad would do the final walkthrough and then depart the estate in time to meet Charles at the marina where the yacht would be stored for the winter. Tad would then drive Charles to the winter estate.

Tad balked when he saw the schedule. He went to Charles with a simple request: delay his launch for a mere two hours. When Charles refused, an argument ensued. Both men said things they shouldn't have but it was Charles who crossed that invisible line by berating not only Tad but Catherine as well. For Tad, it was the final straw.

Tad worked through the night and managed to arrive at the marina a bit ahead of schedule. It was 1:40. His heart was thumping. He hurried to the dock where Charles was scheduled to pull in. For once, he welcomed his stepbrother's obsession with punctuality. He held his breath. At any moment, he expected his shiny white craft to appear on the horizon. The bay was choppy, the skies bright and clear. Tad squinted. He checked his watch. "Hurry," he whispered, anticipating the best moment of his life. At exactly 1:50, in plain view for all to see, Charles and his precious yacht would blow sky high for no discernible reason.

Minutes passed, a half hour, an hour. Nothing. Tad waited, trying to tamp down his agitation. With the wind to his back, he searched the clear sky for signs of an explosion. Again, nothing. Finally, he tried to reach Charles by radio. Silence. Then came the moment that haunted him till his final day: a worried call from Catherine.

Tad listened to Catherine's concern that Charles hadn't called her like he always did when he pulled into port. Tad was confused and even a bit jealous by Catherine's sudden concern for Charles. "I wouldn't worry. Charles knows what he's doing."

"I know that," Catherine had said, "but it's not him I'm worried about. It's Marney and Rosa. Didn't you know? Marney kicked up such a fuss about wanting to go on the boat that I gave in. Rosa assured me she'd watch her like a hawk, but, well…"

Things were never the same. The bodies were never recovered. There were no known witnesses to the explosion and by the time debris was discovered, it was too late to determine a cause for the accident. Catherine never stopped mourning her loss and Tad often wondered about the little girl who, for almost three short months, so lovingly called him uncle.

Catherine was grateful that she couldn't remember those days and weeks after the explosion. She miscarried shortly after learning that her daughter was lost and drifted in and out of consciousness. It was her doctor who informed her, when she finally came round, that she had lost so much blood that he expected to lose her as well. He praised Tad for his vigilance and credited him with saving her life, a life that would be filled with intractable guilt. Together Catherine and Tad mourned the loss of little Marney and all the wonderful things that might have been.

Catherine walked into her kitchen. Today was exactly eight weeks since the man she once loved passed away. Eight weeks and counting since Tad Quigley's sudden death. After a lifetime of loves and losses, all Catherine had left was Tad's grandson, a young man now in his thirties. This time she would do things right. In about an hour she would meet with her lawyer to discuss Keith Quigley's future.

Catherine knew exactly what Henry Weinstein would say. As her late husband's best friend, Henry had spent a lifetime trying to protect Catherine from both herself and anyone who might prey on the once young and beautiful widow. Ill health had forced him to turn many aspects of the Preston Estate over to his associates but he occasionally donned his three piece suit and returned to his office. Catherine had been expecting his call ever since she made it known that she wanted to leave Whalehead to Tad's grandson.

It annoyed Catherine to have to defend her position, but as she stared at her reflection in the mirror, she could feel her resolve weaken. Henry not only seemed to know all Catherine's secrets, he seemed to know how to use them against her. Tad Quigley had always been one of his favorite targets. Catherine often wondered whether Henry hated Tad simply out of loyalty or if he knew something she didn't. In any event, she wanted to be prepared.

Catherine expected Henry to arrive inconveniently early. Although time was short, she decided to shower and wash her hair. She dried her shiny white curls and then applied enough makeup to look half her age. She chose a red dress, wanting to send a message of strength rather than weakness. When she caught the expression on Henry's face, she knew she had made the right call.

Henry greeted Catherine with his usual charm. He poured a glass of sherry for her and a glass of Black Label for himself. He waited until she sat down before taking his seat. "Thank you for seeing me on such short notice."

Catherine nodded her acknowledgment. An uncomfortable silence filled the room. Several seconds passed. Catherine was growing impatient. "You said it was important."

Henry cleared his throat. "The estate looks pristine. I have to hand it to Tad. He trained the grounds crew well."

Catherine took a long sip of sherry. Henry looked sincere, but she knew he was snowing her. "How odd to hear you say that. You've never, ever said anything nice about Tad."

"That's harsh."

"Please, Henry. We both know why you're here. Get to the point. I don't have all day."

"It's not that simple, my dear. There are things you need to understand."

"I understand perfectly. You found out that I want to leave Whalehead to Tad's grandson and there's no way you will allow any part of this estate to go to a Quigley."

"That's unfair. If Keith worked as hard as his grandfather, I'd consider it. He'll run this place into the ground. Surely you realize that."

"Oh, please. You know nothing about Keith. You've never even met him. For your information, Tad trained him well. There's nothing on this estate that he can't do. It's a shame Charles was long gone when Tad's son dumped Keith on our doorstep. Vindictive as Charles was toward Tad, I'm sure he would have found a place in his heart for Keith. He's family."

"Family? The Quigley's aren't family. They're part of a very raw deal that your late husband was saddled with and he wasn't the only one who was upset when his father married Blanche Quigley. There wasn't a soul for miles around who wasn't shocked that a man like Edward would marry so far beneath his station. Not only was that woman barely better than a hooker, she brought her bratty nine year old into the family. What was Charles supposed to do?"

"Oh, I don't know," Catherine replied, her voice oozing sarcasm. "Maybe he could have given the boy a chance. Been a guiding big brother. He was ten years older.

Things might have been so much different if Charles hadn't been such a jackass."

"Edward had a responsibility to his son, to his family name, and he abdicated that when he married that woman."

"Get off your high horse. Edward's marriage to Blanche lasted a lot longer than his first marriage. Charles was only five when his mother ran off with another man. You know darn well that Edward was happy with Blanche. Charles had the problem, not because of who they were but because Tad and his mother had a loving relationship, something Charles never had."

"At least Charles never tried to steal another man's wife."

Catherine could feel her face flush. She often wondered how much of their marital woes Charles had shared with Henry. "Why would he? He didn't know how to treat the one he had."

"Oh but he did. For your information, Charles and I had a long talk just before he closed Whalehead. I've held my tongue all these years because your husband wouldn't want me to embarrass you for no good reason. Yet, if he knew you wanted to leave his most prized possession to Tad Quigley's grandson, he would not only give me permission to reveal the story, he'd hand me a megaphone. He told me all about your affair, about the baby. We drew up a proposal, one he intended to slap you with once we got back to the winter estate. Strange the way it worked out. Charles wanted to declare you an unfit mother and to take Marney away. Instead, it was your lover who did just that."

Catherine was both outraged and mortified. She wasn't surprised that her late husband would have shared such intimate details with his best friend but to plot to take her beloved daughter away was too much to bear. "Get out!" she demanded. "I don't need to sit here and listen to this."

"Yes, you do. You need to understand why no Quigley will ever get a morsel of the Preston fortune. You're a reasonable woman. You should hear me out. It's an interesting saga."

"There's nothing you can tell me that I don't already know. For your information, Tad and I had no secrets. He told me everything. I know all about the witch hunt you launched after the accident. I know how much you wanted to blame Tad for the explosion and I know you couldn't prove anything then and I'm sure you can't prove anything now."

Henry sighed. "You're right, my dear. In a court of law, I could prove nothing but in the court of public opinion…I'd hate to have to go that route but I've protected you long enough. I was lucky. Tad made it easy for me to keep my promise to Charles. I was prepared to do anything and everything I could to keep that leech from becoming Mr. Catherine Preston."

Catherine bristled. "That wasn't your call."

"Whether it was or wasn't, Tad made it easy. He turned out to be more of a gentleman than I ever thought possible. Charles was wrong. He believed Tad was using you just to get Whalehead but had he lived, he would have seen the same thing I did. Tad loved you. He didn't give a damn about the Preston fortune."

"I could have told you that."

"Don't make this uglier than it has to be. You've put me in a very at a difficult position."

"Nothing difficult about it. Charles is long gone. He didn't control me then and you don't control me now. My decisions are none of your affair."

"Oh, but they are. Your father and your late husband made brilliant investments. Huntington and Whalehead are just a drop in the bucket. It's my duty to protect the Preston fortune, to protect you. Answer me this. If you say yes, I'll leave knowing I've done everything that

I could. You claim you and Tad had no secrets, but did he tell you about the letter?"

Catherine stared at Henry for several seconds. "What letter?"

Henry smiled. "I thought so. My dear, dear Catherine. We need to talk. Scratch that. I need to talk and you need to listen. Once you hear what I have to say, the ball will be in your court and for Charles' sake as well as for your own, I sincerely hope that you play it wisely."

Chapter Eleven

June 30th

They were sitting in the gazebo tying to brush the sand off their feet. None of the kids wanted to put their wet shoes on nor did they care that their clothes were soaked. Instead, they were begging Laura to take them up to the bike shop so that they could pick up the bikes that they rented every year.

"Okay, Okay," Laura replied. "Grab your shoes, shake the sand off and when we get back to the house put them on the deck to dry. Just be careful walking back. We'll head up to the bike shop as soon as I unpack the suitcases."

"Unpack the suitcases?" Meg asked as the kids raced each other down the boardwalk. "Why?"

"Because their shoes are wet and I'm not letting them go up to the bike shop barefoot. I know I put all the beach things together so it shouldn't take too long to find their flip flops."

"Yeah, right. I know you. Once you start opening suitcases, you won't stop till everything is where it belongs."

"So what's wrong with that?"

"You may think organizing everything is an adventure but I assure you, no one else does."

"Well, for your information, it's not just about organizing. What if I forgot something? Wouldn't it be better to know before we got to the shops?"

"Not necessarily. Do you see how much fun your kids are having? Why not stay in the moment and leave the suitcases till we get back?"

"I'd love to but I can't let the kids walk up to the bike shop barefoot. That's asking for trouble."

"They don't have to go barefoot and you don't have to unpack the suitcases. Just bring in the basket that Mike brought over. I have it on good authority that he might have put several pairs of flip flops in there."

"Yeah, right. Like he would know what sizes to get."

"Hey, don't be so quick to write him off. Do you remember the day you went to Greenview? Mike called while I was getting the kids ready to go to the swim club and since no one could find their flip flops, I might have sounded a bit frazzled. Mike was amused. Said he's been through that drill before and that you had enough mismatched pairs to open your own shop. He mentioned the basket he was putting together and asked me to text him everyone's sizes, including ours."

Laura stopped dead in her tracks. "Enough mismatched pairs to open my own shop?"

Already several steps ahead of Laura, Meg turned around. "Well, you gotta admit it's only a slight exaggeration. You probably do have enough mismatched pairs to open your own shop."

"Very funny. You, Mike, and that damn basket. You're making me crazy."

"Whoa, whoa, whoa. That damn basket? Why are you so freaked out?"

"I'm not freaked out. I just don't want to be reminded."

"Reminded of what?"

Laura took a deep breath. "Don't overanalyze this but Dan used to do the same thing. About a month before vacation, he would buy a big basket and start filling it with all kinds of crazy toys for the kids. It was so much fun, so many great memories. After he died, I gave all the baskets away. I didn't want to be reminded that Dan was gone."

"Oh, Laura," Meg sighed. "I had no idea. I'm so sorry. Does Mike know about the baskets?"

"He does now. Last week, we were all talking about North Carolina and Scott was telling the little ones all about the baskets, how fun it all was and how he used to look forward to it. I know Mike is only trying to help but it feels like he's swooping in and is stealing Dan's thunder. Guess I'm not quite ready to be the only one who remembers him."

They walked in silence for several seconds. Finally Meg spoke up. "Look, for what it's worth, I understand why you feel the way you do. I don't mean to make you sad but I gotta say, you and Dan were perfect for each other. I might be a hopeless romantic but I don't see that very often and when I do, it makes me happy. Gives me hope that one day, I might get as lucky."

Laura sighed. "Your point?"

"Well, they say lightening doesn't strike twice in the same place but in your case, it has. You and Mike. You have something very special. I'm sure he's keenly aware of Dan's shadow and yet he hasn't run for the hills. Gotta give him credit. He probably has no idea that something as innocent as leaving a basket of fun things on your porch would freak you out."

"I told you, I'm not freaked out. It was a nice gesture, the basket, the groceries."

"Yeah but I know the way you think. If something seems too good to be true, it probably is." Meg waited for a response. There was none. "Mike doesn't belong under that umbrella, Laura. Trust me. He's the real deal. I see the way he looks at you, the way he looks at the kids. He knows exactly who you are and for some reason, he loves you anyway."

Laura feigned insult. "For some reason? I beg your pardon."

By the time they crossed the road, the kids were running along the tree covered path that led to the back of the house. Without breaking stride, they started up the outside steps. Meg had to laugh. "Boy would I love to harness that energy."

"You and me both," Laura replied. She made a megaphone with her hands and called up to her kids. "Make sure you wipe your feet. If you need to make a pit stop, do it now. It's a long walk to the bike shop. Meet me in the rec room. I have a…"

Laura threw her hands into the air as her kids ran inside. She turned to Meg. "I love talking to myself. Think any of them will come back and close that door? Mosquitoes will have a field day." She started for the steps.

"I'll do that," Meg said, grabbing Laura's arm. "You get the basket."

Laura hesitated, waiting until Meg was halfway up the steps before heading to the car. She sighed. Both amused and curious, she lifted the tailgate and uncovered the basket. Slowly, carefully she removed three pairs of sunglasses, three red baseball hats with the Philadelphia Phillies logo, a long tailed kite and several beach toys. She couldn't help but smile. There they were—five pairs of flip flops, two adult and three kids. She took the basket from the car and closed the tailgate.

Walking slowing toward the house, Laura looked around. The air on her arms was warm and tingly. A gentle breeze was blowing. She felt oddly content as she recalled all the giggles she and Dan shared once he started buying things for the basket. Wanting everyone to be surprised, he hid his booty all around the house and for weeks, Laura conducted a full court search. She'd lost count of all the times she was certain to have located a stash, only to find a note telling her to look elsewhere. Such fun times.

Smiling, Laura brought Mike's basket into the rec room and called her kids over. As she watched them ooh and aah over its contents, she suddenly realized how lucky she was not only to have such cherished memories but to have the chance to make new ones.

Several minutes later they were on their way to the bike shop. "Look at them," Laura sighed as she and Meg followed several steps behind. "Too bad Mike can't see this. Prancing around in their baseball caps, sunglasses and flip flops. You'd think it was Christmas."

"When you're that age and you're on vacation, every day is Christmas."

Laura chuckled in agreement.

The bike shop was located on ground level in the far right corner of the shopping center. There were approximately thirty stores in all, connected by a maze of boardwalks. Some of the stores were two steps up from the main level and some were two steps down. The shops on the main level saw the most traffic thanks in large part to their access to a large square which was outfitted with park benches, umbrella tables and chairs surrounded by colorful planters.

Laura and company were almost at their destination when someone driving a convertible late model Rolls Royce screeched past. The driver, a young man wearing Wayfarers and a backward baseball cap, stopped just a few feet from the bike shop and killed his engine. He pressed a button, waited until the driver's seat was back as far as it could go and then, without opening the car door, he jumped out. "Don't tell me," Meg whispered to Laura. "They still play the Dukes of Hazzard down here."

"The Dukes drove a Charger," Laura corrected, "it wasn't a convertible and they climbed out the windows. Don't ask. Dan loved to watch the reruns."

Meg watched the man walk across the parking lot. "Hmm. Sweet, except for the body language. That guy has issues."

"Well he just went into the bike store. Why don't you ask him?"

"Maybe I will," Meg replied, following Laura over to the vast array of bikes. Those already reserved were closest to the door. Those still available were parked behind a yellow rope.

"There," Laura said, pointing to a cluster of five bikes. "Those must be ours. Two adult women, three kids. We might be in trouble. When I reserved the bikes, I ordered training wheels for Jon. At the time he didn't seem all that steady."

"So. If they can put training wheels on, they can take them off."

Laura looked around for someone to help them. "This is weird. They're incredibly efficient here. Usually all you have to do is stand by your bikes and they come out to write you up. I'd better go in and let them know we're here."

A few minutes later Laura walked out, carrying a receipt and a socket wrench. Meg laughed. "Don't tell me. They expect you to take the training wheels off."

"Unless I want to wait until the clerk and Mr. Rolls Royce are done. Can't say for sure but I think he's getting his walking papers. Is none too pleased."

"Told you he had issues." Meg took the wrench. "Hopefully this won't take too long. Learned how to whip these things on and off years ago when we only had one bike and were sheltering a mother and her five kids." She knelt down. "On the other hand, this might take a while. These bolts are kind of rusted. Maybe you guys should head out. Jon and I can manage. Just let us know where you're going to be and we'll find you as soon as we're done."

"OK. Let's meet at the swim club. We can grab a bite and maybe a daiquiri. I'm sure Jon can get you there but just in case, turn left out of the parking lot and once you get past the fountains, the path is marked. They have an arcade. If we're not outside, look for us there."

Laura was well out of sight by the time Meg got the second wheel off. Jon did his part to help, all the while trying to understand why his mother thought he would need training wheels. Pleased to have the issue resolved, Jon carried the wheels back to the shop. The clerk was still talking to the man who had been driving the Rolls. Jon got her attention when he dropped the training wheels onto the counter. Startled, the clerk spun around.

"Sorry about that," Meg lied. "Bike order for Hunter. The training wheels. Can you give me a receipt indicating that we're not taking them?"

The clerk seemed rattled. "Give me a minute. I'll be right with you."

As much as she wanted to be on her way, Meg realized right away that the young man was badgering the clerk and she hoped that her presence would help in some way. "Take your time," she replied. "We'll wait here."

The clerk smiled. "Thank you." She turned to the young man. "I'm sorry if you misunderstood but I must ask you to leave…now!"

"Misunderstood my ass."

Meg moved closer to the counter.

"Like I said, I'm sorry."

"Like hell you are," the man muttered. He glared at Meg and even at Jon. He huffed out of the store, banging the screen door as he went.

"Pretend you didn't see that," the clerk said. "I'm sorry for the delay."

Five years listening to all kinds of stories from women trying to free themselves from untenable situations had given Meg a prospective few people had. "Are you being harassed?"

"I don't know. If you call being pursued by one of the most eligible bachelors on this island, I'd have to say no. If you call him not understanding that I have no interest in him or his millions, I'd have to say yes."

"Who is he?"

"Keith Quigley. His grandmother is the richest woman down here and he's her only relative. When she goes, he gets all her money. Look. It could be worse. He's a nice looking guy and seems pretty devoted to his grandmother but he does have issues. His mother abandoned him at birth and he was just a toddler when his father dumped him on his grandfather's doorstep. Can't really blame him for not handling rejection very well."

"Sounds like you've got him psychoanalyzed."

"Sort of. Life's not easy but some people seem to be more resilient than others. Can't help but wonder why. I leave for medical school in a few weeks. I'm thinking maybe Psychiatry. By the way, I'm Jessica Atwood."

Meg smiled and extended her hand. "And I'm Meg Richards. Medical school. I'm impressed. I thought about going that route until I checked out the MCAT. Decided to go for the PhD in psychology instead. Been directing a shelter for abused women and children for the past five years. It's been very rewarding."

"Nice. Bet you're busy. I think I'm pretty savvy but look what just happened. Been keeping that guy at arm's length for weeks and then one false move. Shoulda known better."

"How'd you meet him?"

"The Islander. He's an interesting guy. His grandfather was the estate caretaker at Whalehead. Whalehead's kind of a big deal down here. Have you seen it?"

"Not yet, but I've heard about it."

"Well, this is my sister's shop. Her husband walked out on her the other night. They ran this place together but have been having troubles. Right now she's a basket case. How could I not help? Saturday's her busiest day. I know nothing about bikes and what you need to do to make them safe so I called Keith. He's always bragging that his grandfather trained him so well that he can fix anything. Figured he could give me a hand, show me the ropes. He was really nice until he walked in and saw that I really needed his help. Desperate or not, I shoulda seen that coming."

"Do you think he'll come back?"

"Nah. The second time I pushed him away, I threatened to call the police."

A car pulled up and a party of six got out. Jessica glanced at her watch. "That's about right. People are checking in and they want their bikes. My sister claims she's on her way. I sure hope so. She's stood me up before and this place can turn into a madhouse in a matter of minutes. Do you have your receipt?"

"No. My friend does."

"OK. I'll just mark ours that you returned the training wheels. Where do you work?"

"New Jersey, not too far outside of Philadelphia."

"Really? I'm heading to Philadelphia, Jefferson Med. What's the name of your shelter?"

"Jill's Place."

"I'd love to see it sometime. Maybe we can meet up. Watching my sister these past few years—it's been tough. Might help to pick your brain. Get a few pointers on ways to help."

"Sure. Let's keep in touch."

They were exchanging emails when the boisterous six walked in. "Take care," Meg said. "It was nice talking with you."

"Same here. Enjoy your vacation."

"Will do." Meg took Jon's hand. She leaned down and thanked him for waiting so patiently.

"Why was that man mad at us?"

Meg was taken by surprise. "What man?"

"The man with the sunglasses."

"What makes you think he was mad at us?"

"Because he was talking to that lady and had to leave because of us."

"You're very perceptive."

Jon chuckled. "That's what Mike says. What does it mean?"

"It means you see things most people your age wouldn't even notice."

"Can I tell you a secret?"

"Sure."

"Sometimes Mommy gets mad at Mike but he never gets mad back. I like that. He always makes her smile."

"I like that too," Meg replied. "You know lots of things. Do you know how to get to the swim club?"

"Hills or flat?"

"Which is more fun?"

"Hills."

Meg smiled. "Then hills it is. Lead the way."

Chapter Twelve

June 30th

Keith Quigley stormed into his cottage. He couldn't get the slut from the bike shop out of his mind. He wasn't the crazy one. She had definitely been coming onto him and in typical bitch fashion, slammed the door in his face the minute he made his move. "You'll be sorry," he predicted. "You and the rest of the gold diggers on this island. You'll see. One day soon, I'll be the richest man on the Outer Banks and you'll all come crawling to me. Just wait."

Wiping his brow, Keith walked over to the thermostat. "Dammit," he muttered. Like he really needed some digital display to tell him his air conditioner was busted again. He must have fixed the damn thing at least a dozen times only to have it run for shorter and shorter periods. No wonder he was pissed.

Keith ripped his shirt off and then walked over to the refrigerator to grab a nice cold beer. "What the hell?" he mumbled. The case he'd shoved in there just the other day was almost gone. What lousy timing. His funds were drying up. He had no job, no money, no girl and worst of all, still no confirmation that Catherine Preston was going to name him heir to her fortune.

Holding his beer can, Keith yanked off the tab and then tossed it into the trash. It hit the rim and bounced onto the floor. He left the tab where it landed and then walked over to the window. Pressing the cold can against his cheek, he lifted the sash. The caretaker's cottage was a dump but it did have decent views and at times, was even cooled by an occasional breeze from the water.

Keith stared out the window. The thrill he used to feel whenever he saw the Preston family mansion was fading all because of his goddamned grandfather. Just because the moron was content to live out his life in a dinky caretaker's cottage didn't mean he had to be. It was his right to wake up at the mansion and be surrounded by people hired to wait on him. After all, his grandfather's mother had once been married to Edward Preston, the man who built Whalehead. In his book that counted for something.

Shaking his head, Keith turned from the window. His romance and inheritance issues would have to wait. It was hotter than hell and his friggin' air conditioner needed a new compressor. He'd have to lift one. Having worked at the largest HVAC Company on the Outer Banks for more summers than he cared to remember, he still had access to the somewhat disorganized warehouse. Why pay for something when he could get it for free?

Keith walked over to his grandfather's recliner and sat down. What a relief that the bastard was gone and that he no longer had to listen his mind numbing tirades. Big deal that the prick took him in after his own father abandoned him. He might have been better off with a total stranger. Like he could help that he was reading by age three or that he had an eidetic memory. A little support would have been nice. It wasn't easy to be different; to be uncomfortable with kids his own age. How much better things might have been if the old man tried to understand instead of trying to squeeze Keith into a totally unimaginative mould.

Resting his head on the back of the recliner, Keith closed his eyes. At least he had Catherine, mercurial as she was. Some days she made him feel like the most important person on earth and some days she made him feel like a useless cog. Still, he couldn't imagine what his life would have been like without her. Strange how one good word from her softened his grandfather's resentment. Clearly they had a special relationship. Hard to know why. How could such a beautiful woman stand a man with such a mean streak?

Keith sighed. No doubt his old man was consistent. If Keith was down, he'd kick him harder; always reminding him that despite his brilliance, he was only an average student; despite his good looks, he had no girlfriend; despite his fancy college degree, he could barely pay his bills. Maybe he wasn't where he wanted to be but he had people skills. Everybody liked him, said nice things about him. He had figured it out. All he had to do was to pour on the charm and never let anyone get close enough to know who he really was.

Oil and water. No wonder they never got along. Tad Quigley was a mental midget. He hated books or God forbid thoughtful opinions. If he couldn't hold it in his hand, it wasn't important. At least the prick had one saving grace: he was smart enough to recognize Keith's innate mechanical ability and at times to even praise him for fixing things that had the old man stymied.

Downing the last of his beer, Keith crushed the can with his bare hand. Why couldn't his old man see that there was more to life than manual labor? Why couldn't he understand that becoming a famous historian wasn't like turning a screw or hammering a nail? It took time, time and good luck. Results were all he cared about but how did that justify him calling Keith a dreamer who would never amount to anything? Prick.

Keith flung the empty can across the room. He wasn't proud to be eleven years out of college and to still be waiting for even one of the brilliant articles he had submitted for publication to be accepted. He wasn't happy to have to quit his substitute teaching job before they could fire him. He knew damn well that his options were dwindling.

Keith closed his eyes. How dumb to have returned to Whalehead several weeks ago, expecting the best summer of his life. Could his grandfather have been more disgusting? The old man deserved everything he got that day and more. Unaware that he was clenching his fists, Keith found himself reliving those fateful hours.

It had been a pleasant day, sunny and warm with a gentle breeze blowing. Keith opened the cottage door, surprised by how nice the place smelled. He dumped his things at the door and then plopped onto the sofa. By the time his grandfather walked in, he was feeling good. He had a half empty beer can in one hand and two empty cans at his feet. To think he actually debated getting up and giving his grandfather a hug. The look on the old man's face said it all: "Don't bother." He should have expected what happened next.

"What the hell are you doing here? School's not out for another few weeks. What. They finally see you for the idiot you are. You got fired, didn't you?"

Like Keith was really going to admit to that. Smarter to pour gasoline on a smoldering fire. "I quit. The kids, the idiots I work with. I've had it. I've got better things to do."

"Yeah, like what? Don't tell me you plan to work for Dutch again. If he had any brains he'd tell you to jump in a lake."

"He's too smart for that. I'm the best HVAC tech he's ever had and he knows it. Ask him. Ask him how many new orders I've gotten for him. Between the mark ups on those units and all the incentives, he's made a fortune. He'd take me back in a heartbeat. Too bad for him I don't plan to go."

"Too bad for him? If he ever finds out what you did, he'd rake you over the coals. You are one stupid ass. I found that vial. What the hell'd you put in it? Spilled some of it on my workbench and it burned a hole. Got me thinking. All those order for new heaters that you racked up, all those people thinking they had unacceptable levels of carbon monoxide. I figured it out. You been rigging those damn heaters. I ought to turn you in."

Shit, Keith mused. Even now he wasn't sure if "I ought to turn you in" was an idle threat or a *fait accompli*. In any event, it had him frozen in place. He needed money, he needed a job and he needed a new compressor. Going back to his old job was his only reasonable option but what if Dutch was onto him? Like he needed more trouble. If only his old man hadn't been such a bastard that day, that day and every day for the past thirty-four years.

Maybe it wasn't all that smart to tell the old coot that he was trying to save the environment by getting all the cheap bastards to spring for more efficient units. Tad Quigley, of all people, would know a snow job. "Listen you little prick," Tad had blustered. "If you think you're gonna sit around here all day, you got another think coming. You find yourself a job by week's end or you're outta here."

"Cool your jets," Keith had replied. "I have a plan."

As he expected, Keith's old man began hurling a litany of insults at him highlighting all his failures. Annoying as that was, it paled in comparison to Tad Quigley's lifelong mantra: "I never should have taken you in after your idiot father dumped you on my doorstep."

Keith was still surprised that he managed to stay focused, that he managed to restrain himself from hurling insults back. How well he remembered clenching his teeth as he walked over to his backpack and took out a folded newspaper. "Here," he said, flinging the paper at his grandfather. "Read this. It's about a body they found under a sixty-five year old hotel. I plan to be the one to figure out who she is. Greenview. It's a small town, a half day's ride from here. I'll probably be gone the entire summer, maybe longer. Sixty-five years—it's a lotta ground to cover."

Oddly enough, in a single heartbeat, Tad went from raging bull to dumb mute. There was a pause. He held up the newspaper. "Where the hell'd you get this?" Tad had demanded.

"At a diner on my way home. You know how people are always leaving newspapers behind. The headline fascinated me. Build an interchange, tear down an old hotel and find a female skeleton. This is great stuff. No one knows who she is. Check out that picture. A gold ring. That's all they got. Not a very clear picture. Don't know how they expect anyone to recognize it. Got my work cut out but once I get up there, figure out the lay of the land, see my stuff in print…I may even be able to turn this into a bestseller."

"Don't be an idiot," Tad had replied after an icy silence. "No one gives a damn about anything you write. Don't waste your time, or money you don't have."

That was the moment, Keith recalled. The moment the bastard drew a line in the sand. He ripped the newspaper from the old man's hand. "I'll have plenty of money once I show this to Catherine. She'll gladly fund my project. She has way more faith in me than you do." Keith started for the door. "I'll let you know what she says."

"Sit down, you moron. Sit down, shut up and listen."

As much as Keith wanted to walk out, he froze. Every instinct in his body told him this was not the usual tongue lashing. Reluctantly, he sat down.

Tad hesitated. "If you want anything from Catherine, the worst thing you can do is to show her that newspaper. Do you know who Rosa Berman was?"

Keith shrugged. "Yeah, she was Marney Preston's governess."

"She was more than that. She and Catherine were glued at the hip. They met at some holiday party shortly after Catherine and Charles were married. Rosa was serving drinks. Had no idea what she was doing. Catherine felt sorry for her. Rosa and her sister got sent to the states to escape Nazi Germany. Rosa was fairly bright, not like her stupid sister who never learned to read or write in English. Long story short, Catherine convinced Charles that she'd make a great governess."

Keith could still remember how sick he felt as he listened to his grandfather. It was a moment that changed his life. First he finds out that the skeletal remains discovered under that hotel were those of Rosa Berman and then he finds out how she got there. He was stunned not just because his grandfather had been the only living soul to know that Marney and Rosa were not on the yacht when it exploded, but that for sixty-five years he had gotten away with not one murder, but two.

At first, Keith wondered why his grandfather would make such a confession. Given their contentious relationship, it made no sense for Tad to give Keith information that could get him locked up for good. Looking back, Keith realized the old prick had a trick up his sleeve.

"I never meant to harm Rosa or Marney. My beef wasn't with them. It was with Charles. He was awful to me, to Catherine. He deserved to die. I had it all worked out. Blow him out of the water, wait for as long as necessary and then ask Catherine to marry me. Together we would raise little Marney and give her some brothers and sisters. Had I known Rosa and Marney would be on the yacht, I would have found another way to get rid of Charles."

"You miserable sonofabitch," Keith sneered. "You killed an innocent woman. Dumped her body at a construction site. What did Rosa ever do to you?"

Keith smiled. Looking back, he never remembered his grandfather being as pissed as he was then. The old man started to explain his voice getting louder by the second. "You wanna know? You really wanna know? Look in my desk, middle drawer, in the back. An envelope, a letter

Rosa wrote to her sister. Full of accusations, why I wanted to kill Charles, how I caused the explosion. Written in German. Stupid bitch. All that time in this country and her sister still couldn't read English. I'd forgotten more German than I remembered. Took hours to translate. Wrote the English version between the lines. I'm sure I got it right. Go ahead. Read it."

Strange, Keith mused. All these weeks later, he could still remember taking the letter from the envelope— how it felt, the way it smelled. Wisely he burned the letter after scanning it to his computer but he had it memorized. He could remember their conversation verbatim. "Rosa knew you rigged the yacht but didn't go to the police. Why?"

"She wasn't as bright as everyone thought. Didn't trust anyone other than her sister, her sister and Catherine. Lucky for me her sister never saw that letter. Helga Berman was a sickly girl, a domestic, worked for a family that was friendly with the Prestons. Probably a little mental. Freaked when she learned her sister had been killed. Wouldn't eat, wouldn't drink. Died the day that letter arrived. The people she worked for thought Catherine might want her things. I went to get them. Found that letter. It was still sealed. Rosa was such a dumbass. She was hiding in Greenview waiting for her sister to go to Catherine."

"She wasn't that dumb," Keith had argued, holding up the letter. "Says right here that she didn't want you to know they were alive. What's this crap about Marney's barrette?"

"Look in the envelope. It's a Scottie dog. Altogether Marney had five. Was wearing three of them the day she left Whalehead. The stones are real. The more ways Charles could show how rich he was the better he liked it. Rosa knew Catherine would have demanded proof and that barrette would have done it. You gotta understand I never meant to harm Rosa or Marney and once I found out they were alive, I had every intention of going to Greenview and bringing them home."

Strange, Keith mused. His old man wanted him to think he was a hero, but Keith wasn't fooled. At least the old coot was honest when he described how he found Rosa, kneeling over what he thought was Marney's grave and how he chased her over to the construction site, killed her, buried her body in the newly excavated ground and then waited for them to pour the foundation the next day. Idiot. Tad went through all that trouble to remove Rosa's clothing so they wouldn't be able to identify her if anyone ever found her but forgot to remove her ring. Keith had only begun to berate his grandfather when the old man dropped the nuclear bomb.

"I may be screwed if they ever figure out who Rosa is but you're screwed even if they don't. I know you're chomping at the bit to get Catherine's fortune but her daughter may be alive. She's Catherine's legitimate heir, not you."

"You're full of shit," Keith had protested. "You just told me you found Rosa at Marney's grave."

"Rosa lied. It wasn't Marney. That grave belonged to Amelia Abbott, the little girl Rosa and Marney had been staying with. I found out fourteen years later but by then it was too late. Catherine might have forgiven me when Marney was two but not when she was sixteen."

Keith could only hope his old man was lying. "Nice try. You just want to shut me up."

"Check for yourself," Tad had replied. "*Life Magazine*, circa March, 1959. Search for a girl named Mary Abbott. She'd won some essay contest. It's definitely Marney. She's the spitting image of her father. I thought about going back to Greenview to see if I could find her and bring her back to her mother but decided against it. Catherine would know I blew the yacht and she'd never forgive me. I was a fool. Even after all those years, I still wanted her to love me as much as I loved her. You have no idea how much that woman means to me."

"You are a fool," Keith had replied. "Catherine was never the prize. Whalehead is. Goddamn. Marney, I mean Mary. Is she still in Greenview?"

"I have no idea but if we can find her, we can make this right." Tad patted his chest. "I know you don't give a damn but this ticker isn't going to last much longer. If you can find Marney and reunite her with Catherine, I can go to my grave in peace."

"Peace? You can rot in hell. You may enjoy living like a peon in a caretaker's cottage, but I don't. I've been waiting my entire life for Whalehead and I'm not going to let this Mary Abbott ruin it for me now. I agree. We need find to the bitch. Find her and get rid of her."

It all happened so fast. One minute they were arguing and the next his old man was holding his chest and gasping for air. Idiot. Did he really expect Keith to call 9-1-1? The old man had brought his fate on himself. Years of abuse had forced Keith to walk over to the phone and unplug it. Smiling, he still remembered the last thing he said: "I'll be back. Make it quick. I don't have all day."

Somehow Keith managed to fool Catherine. She interpreted the strained look on his face as exhaustion from his long trip and insisted he have a snack and a cool drink. They chatted for a good half hour before Keith got up to leave. "Should probably be getting back. Pop was out when I got home. Hope he's as happy to see me as you were."

Keith smiled. What a brilliant plan. Everyone believed he walked in and found his grandfather gasping for air. No one questioned his feigned heartbreak that the paramedics failed to get there in time. Sympathy poured in, with one caveat. Here it was, two months later and people were still praising his grandfather unaware of the abject misery he had caused. Two months later and Catherine had yet to name him heir. Always hinting that she wanted to leave Whalehead to him but not doing squat about it. No wonder he was on edge.

Wiping his brow, Keith walked over to the window. It was just as hot outside as it was inside. His inheritance issues would have to wait. His friggin' air conditioner needed a new compressor. Hard to make any rational decisions in this heat.

The landline rang. Keith jumped. It had to be Catherine. No one else had that number. The woman was a witch. She seemed to call every time he thought about her. He walked over to the ugly green phone hanging on the wall. Forcing himself to be pleasant, he said hello.

"Keith, meet me for an early dinner on the veranda. We need to talk. I know these past few months have been difficult for us both and it's time to make things right. Five o'clock."

"Is something wrong?" Keith dared to ask.

"Depends. Like I said, it's time to make things right."

Keith hung up the phone. He smiled at no one in particular. "Make things right"—he liked the sound of that. In his mind there was only one way to do that: officially name him heir to Whalehead. Could his patience finally be paying off? Patting himself on the back, he checked the thermostat. Oddly enough just by opening the window, the temperature had dropped several degrees. It was the last day of June. The days were already getting shorter but maybe, just maybe, this summer could be saved after all.

Chapter Thirteen

June 30th

To Keith, dinner on the veranda was code for not having to wear a jacket and tie. Good thing too. The cottage was stifling. Bad enough he had to slip into a pair of kakis, and a button down shirt. Even worse, he had to give up his flip flops for his docksiders which meant having to coax socks onto his sweaty feet. One of Catherine's pet peeves: no socks, no food. She was too damn prissy for her own good. What was wrong with cut offs and a tee shirt?

Checking the time, Keith headed for the big house. The walk from the cottage could take several minutes. The most direct route was across the large expanse of grass but it was also the sunniest. Given the day's heat, Keith detoured to the path along the Sound. Enjoying the shade and the occasional breezes, he felt energized. 'Make things right,' he kept repeating to himself. Finally.

It had been a long two months and although Keith wanted to credit his successes to his incredible genius, he had to admit that luck seemed to be playing a key role. So far, at every crucial juncture, the ball had bounced in his direction.

Keith was still amazed that no one ever questioned the circumstances of his grandfather's death. Sympathy poured in, giving him no choice but to play along. Like he really cared that his old man was dead. Had it been up to him, he would have would have tossed him into an unmarked grave, just like he had done to Rosa Berman. Instead, he allowed Catherine to make the funeral arrangements. For his kindness he had to endure a two day viewing, dinner each night with a grieving Catherine, an endless funeral and then an elaborate luncheon. Worst of all, he had to listen to all those idiots sing his grandfather's praises.

Then again, all was not lost. Thanks to the old man he now knew what no one else did: that Marney Preston had not died when her father's yacht exploded and that she had grown up as Mary Abbott in the dinky town of Greenview. But where was she now? Did she have any idea who she really was? Would she threaten his inheritance?

Keith was proud of his restraint. As much as he wanted to rush off to Greenview, he forced himself to wait several days after the funeral before making the trip. Finding the Abbott farmhouse had been easy. Dealing with John Abbott, not so much. Two seconds after stepping into the farmhouse, Keith knew he was wasting his time. The man reeked of alcohol. He couldn't remember what he had for lunch much less give credible information on Mary's whereabouts.

How could Keith have known that the moron would follow him up the steps, nipping at his heels? How could he have known he would grab his shirt? Of course he shoved him away. What else was he supposed to do? The shove might have been harder than it had to be but maybe if that banister wasn't so loose, he wouldn't have fallen so far. At least his death had been quick, not like his grandfather who took forever to gasp his last. No matter. The result was the same: two major threats to his inheritance were now gone.

The two weeks that it took for someone to find John's remains turned out to be worth the wait. The newspaper described his body as badly decomposed and called his death an unfortunate accident. Keith liked that. He was officially off the hook. Still he wondered about that neighbor. Was he close to John? Did he know anything about Mary? He had been tempted to go back and ask around but felt it might be too risky. Better to keep a low profile.

In the distance Keith could see Catherine standing on the veranda, staring at the water. He felt uneasy. For someone about to make things right, she looked stiff, uncomfortable. Finally she glanced in his direction. He waved and then hurried to greet her. She welcomed him warmly. "Oh, my. Look at you, all perspired. We can go inside if you'd like."

Inside seemed like a no brainer until Keith noticed how glassy Catherine's normally bright blue eyes were. Damn. She'd been crying. What the hell. He'd been expecting a good news announcement. Now he didn't know what to think. "No, no, no," he replied. "I know how much you love to be out here. I'll be fine."

Keith took Catherine's arm and walked her over to her favorite chair, the one with the best view of the water. He waited until she sat down and then gently pushed it in for her. Of the three other chairs arranged around the table, Keith took the one directly across from Catherine. His back was to the water and his only view was of Catherine's sad face.

A gentle breeze was blowing. The cook stepped onto the veranda. She placed two bowls of freshly cut fruit on the table, advised Catherine that the quiche would be ready shortly and then asked if they needed anything else. Catherine waved her away. Smiling at Keith, she speared a ball of cantaloupe. "You know, I still remember the day your father left you on your grandfather's doorstep. Tad was so lost; had no idea what to do but I just knew it would all work out. I know he could be a little gruff but he was really proud of you. I'm so grateful that you got home when you did. If you hadn't, he might have died alone and that would have haunted me. I can't thank you enough."

Keith forced a smile. *If only you knew*, he mused.

Catherine hesitated. "I hate to bring up that terrible day, but while you were holding your grandfather in your arms, did he say anything, tell you something he wanted to get off his chest?"

Keith could feel his face flush. He hated the way Catherine was watching him, studying his every move. Where the hell was she going with this? "I have no idea. We had so little time."

"I know but something's come to my attention, something rather disturbing. So I must ask. Did your grandfather say anything to you about a letter?"

"A letter?" Keith repeated, hoping his expression didn't give him away. "What kind of letter? If it was something Pop wrote, I could search his computer."

"No, no, no. It was handwritten and I believe it was the last letter Rosa wrote to her sister. Rosa and Helga died within weeks of each other sixty-five years ago, but all of a sudden that letter has become an issue. I want to make things right. Your great grandmother was married to Edward Preston so it makes perfect sense for me to want to leave my estate to you. Unfortunately, if Henry Weinstein has his way that will never happen."

Henry Weinstein, Keith mused. He never met the man but he knew Henry and his grandfather didn't get along, probably with good reason. Henry was Charles Preston's best friend. Tad was Charles' despised stepbrother. "Please," Keith replied. "I don't want to cause any trouble."

"You're not the one causing trouble." Catherine reached for Keith's hand. "If you're going to be my heir, you need to know the truth. You see, your grandfather and I were once in love. We made some mistakes, mistakes that had terrible consequences and I'm afraid it was all my fault. I was very unhappy the summer your grandfather came to Whalehead. I realized my marriage to Charles was a mistake. I felt trapped. When I met your grandfather...I didn't set out to cheat on my husband but it happened and it was wrong. I suspected Charles knew what was going on but he never said anything, to me that is. There I was selfishly enjoying the best summer of my life until I realized I was pregnant with your grandfather's child."

"My grandfather's child? I…I had no idea."

Catherine waved her hand in dismissal. "There was no reason to announce our sin to the world. September came very quickly that year. I dreaded going back to the winter estate. On departure day I was nauseated and exhausted. Still, I knew I had to keep up appearances. When Marney kicked up a fuss about going on the yacht, I didn't have the energy to argue. The biggest mistake of my life. Had I known there were issues with one of the engines and that your grandfather had warned Charles to wait until he could replace a part, I never would have let her go. When I found out that the yacht exploded, I knew that was my punishment from God—cruel but deserved."

"I'm so sorry," Keith replied. "So very sorry."

"Thank you. I hate to bother you with this." Catherine hesitated. "After Marney died, things were never the same between me and your grandfather. I loved him and trusted him till the day he died but now Henry has me wondering if I made a mistake all because of this letter. Please. Let me explain."

Keith listened in stunned silence as Catherine recounted her conversation with Henry. Too bad the bastard was right. Not only was there a letter, Tad had used it to find Rosa and then to kill her. Now what? Could a stupid letter written sixty-five years ago derail his inheritance? Just when it looked as though Whalehead would be his, this comes up. Silently he cursed his grandfather, cursed Henry Weinstein. "I don't understand," Keith finally replied. "I can see how upset you are. Why is Henry doing this?"

Catherine sighed. "A long time ago, Henry made a promise to Charles that he would never allow your grandfather to get his hand on any of the Preston money, especially Whalehead. This letter is his latest weapon and I need your help. Are you sure your grandfather never mentioned it?"

Keith wiped his brow. Like it wasn't already hot enough. He had no choice but to go for the jugular. "I don't want to upset you but just before pop died, even though he could barely speak, he managed to call your name."

Tears welled in Catherine's sad blue eyes. "You have no idea how much I want to remember your grandfather with warm feelings, but Henry has beaten me down. He just wouldn't stop. He kept going back to this crazy notion that Rosa might not have been on the yacht when it exploded or even more ridiculous—that she somehow survived. It was so unsettling."

"I'm sure it was," Keith replied. "Do you think he might be right?"

"Of course not. If Rosa wasn't on the yacht or if she somehow survived, I would have been the first person she contacted."

Keith felt oddly relieved.

"Unfortunately Henry has struck a nerve, a very raw one. It's always bothered me that nothing of Marney's or Rosa's ever washed ashore even though several things that we believe belonged to Charles did. For years, I've clung to the hope that somehow Marney was alive and that one day she would find her way home."

Goddamn, Keith mused. *Henry.* He never met the bastard but now he wanted to pop him. "I'm so sorry. I feel responsible. If you hadn't tried to make me your heir, none of this would have happened."

"It is what it is. I just wish your grandfather had told me about his argument with Henry, about that letter. I had no answer for Henry. I tried to close my ears but the whole time Henry was spewing his hatred, all I could think of was why, why your grandfather never said anything to me about it. I honestly believed we had no secrets, but this letter is making me think otherwise. Henry claims he can keep me from changing my will and has no qualms about using my past against me. Unfortunately, I have no real defense."

A seagull squawked overhead. Catherine waited until it had flown away. "The thing is: you're family whether Henry likes it or not. This is why I need your help. I want you to search for that letter. You know your grandfather. He never threw anything out that had even the slightest importance. I know in my heart that if this letter ever existed, he would still have it. Please. Scour the cottage, the workshop, the New York estate. Take as much time as you need."

"Of course," Keith replied, impressed by the brilliant idea already mushrooming in his head. "You know you can count on me."

"Yes," Catherine whispered, patting Keith's hand. For several seconds, she stared at the water, recalling that terrible day that she gave into her little girl's demands to go on the yacht. "Honestly, I don't know what will make me happier. That you find that letter or that you don't. If you find it and it proves Henry's accusations, I will be crushed but if you don't find it, it will leave us in limbo. Please understand that I want Whalehead to go to you, but I don't want to second guess anything. I love this place. It was here that I said goodbye to the three people I loved most in this world. We must get this right."

"Of course, but whatever happens, I hope you know that Pop would never want to cause you more pain."

"I know that. He was a wonderful man and I'm so grateful that I have you. In so many ways you remind me of your grandfather. I know how much you idolized him. We both did. But we must be realistic. Henry may be an old man but with or without that letter, he'll be a formidable opponent. If we don't disarm him, we won't have a moment's peace. I trust you with all my heart and will be praying that you find a reasonable explanation."

Chapter Fourteen

June 30th

Despite his dismal mood, Dave Schubert couldn't help but smile as he turned onto the driveway that led to his grandmother's house. Even though the Fourth of July was still days away, the entire wraparound porch of the two-story farmhouse was draped in patriotic bunting. No doubt the woman he affectionately called Gam loved holidays, and Independence Day was one of her favorites.

A lifelong resident of Greenview, Emelda Schubert not only took great pride in her community, she had not missed a town hall meeting in forty years. She read the daily newspaper from front to back, voted in every election and like many of her friends, was keenly disappointed when construction on the long debated highway interchange began.

Although her house was miles away from the site, Emelda swore construction dust not only soiled the clean laundry that she liked to hang outside, it seeped in through the windows and covered every flat surface in her meticulously kept home. She had been at the market the day she learned that construction had come to a screeching halt. At first she welcomed the reprieve. Then she learned the reason why.

Like everyone else in Greenview, Emelda was shocked to hear that human remains had been discovered under the foundation of the Old Heidelberg Hotel. In a matter of hours, the peaceful little town, where crime was low and murder unheard of, was overrun with reporters and TV crews. Emelda felt violated. Naturally she called her grandson who was studying to be a journalist and made a perfectly logical case for why he should jump into this story. She was over the moon when he agreed to check it out.

From the beginning, Dave knew his grandmother's enthusiasm was about more than a story. It was about the unpleasant changes that Father Time had wrought upon her, her family, her friends and her town. It was about the encroaching loneliness that seemed to spread every time she lost another acquaintance due to death or dementia.

When Dave took on the story, he figured he had a win-win. As an aspiring journalist, he would get the chance to cover what could be a real blockbuster and he could do so without having to incur the expense of room and board. In exchange, his lonely grandmother would have a reason to change the sheets in the guest bedroom and to cook meals that she could never justify making for only one person.

It didn't matter to Dave that as an untested investigative reporter the odds of identifying a sixty-five year old skeleton were bleak. He embraced the challenge but the hours were long and progress was slow until Laura Hunter agreed to help. What a coup. He could barely get Neeka to say hello and yet she told Laura everything she knew. He felt so good about the progress he was making, until today.

Taking a deep breath, Dave killed his engine. Not quite ready to go inside, he stared at the delicately curtained windows, each opened exactly 11 inches. He stared at the colorful wreath that adorned the front door. Quietly he counted the planters, brimming with soft pink flowers that hung evenly spaced between the porch posts. Order, order everywhere…everywhere but in his own head.

The long shadows of the summer evening were just beginning to creep across the lawn. Dave sighed. The day was losing its light and so was his investigation. He was bummed. Maybe it was a little cocky of him never to doubt that his cemetery drawings were right on. That police report gave him every reason to believe that Jane Doe was visiting the Abbott gravesite when she was accosted. It all made sense.

Dave sighed. Where would he be right now if Laura hadn't insisted that he speak to the officers who responded to that 9-1-1 call? Having read their report, Dave hadn't expected his interview with Jeff Robinson and Mark Lungrin to be easy but he also hadn't expected it to land such a crushing blow to both his confidence and his ego.

It came as no surprise that neither of the officers wanted to speak with him; it kind of went with the territory. He was young and he was an outsider. Who was he to question their work? After some serious arm twisting, Dave got them to agree to meet: McDonald's, twelve noon sharp. Fifteen minutes and not one second more.

Dave was sitting in the parking lot when Robinson and Lungrin arrived a good half hour early. "Yes!" he whispered. He may be new at this but he wasn't born yesterday. The old bait and switch. They would eat and run. If Dave complained, they would claim he was the no show and not them. Having carefully researched both men, it was exactly what he expected.

Jeff Lungrin was ten years from retirement while Mark Robinson was ten years out of high school. Dave knew the type. In exchange for showing up for work whenever scheduled, they performed their jobs with a pervasive boredom and had absolutely no interest in thinking outside the box.

Dave waited until they had gone into the restaurant before getting out of his car. He stepped into the line two registers away from where they were waiting and managed to get served at exactly the same time. Dave introduced himself just as they were sitting down in a booth at the far end of the restaurant; Jeff on one side, Mark on the other. "I won't keep you," he promised, setting his tray at the end of the booth and pulling up a chair.

The older officer was annoyed but the younger one seemed amused, perhaps because he had won some kind of bet. "Good," Lungrin replied. "We don't got all day."

Dave waited for the officers to unwrap their sandwiches. He watched as they poured several packets of ketchup onto their wrappers and, paying no attention to him, dipped several fries into the mixture and then stuffed them into their mouths. He waited as they took ravenous bites of their burgers, followed by loud gulps of soda. Although the delay ate into his fifteen minutes, Dave correctly figured they would be less hostile with a little food in their stomachs. "If you don't mind," he finally chanced, "I've got a couple of questions about the fatal fall at the Abbott Farmhouse."

Lungrin who was about to take another bite of his sandwich froze. "Read the report."

Dave shook a packet of salt over his french fries. "Already did. Several times. Still got a few questions. Did either of you know John Abbott, ever meet him before that 9-1-1 call?"

Lungrin took the question. "Why?"

Dave shrugged. "I'm curious. Gotta wonder why someone whose land is worth a fortune would live in such a dump. Any ideas?"

Lungrin tapped his index finger against his temple several times. "Whadda you think? The guy was crazy. Didn't actually know him but my oldest brother and George went to school together. Sometimes he'd drag me over to the farmhouse. I couldn't of been more than eight years old. Abbott scared me to death but I felt sorry for George. Guy was a loner. Hardly said boo. Had a nice sister though."

"Mary? Did you know her?"

"Nah. She was pretty. Would say hello but never stuck around."

"Were George and Mr. Abbott close?"

"You kidding? Abbott was a prick. Treated George like dirt, especially after the mom died. My brother wondered why George never moved away. Then again, where would he go?"

"Yeah," Dave nodded. "I understand George died about four years ago."

"Yep. Abbott just plopped him in the ground. No viewing, no funeral. Guy was a bastard. Rottin' on the floor for two weeks. Guess what goes round comes round."

"So they say," Dave replied. "What about the neighbors who found Mr. Abbott. Know anything about them?"

"Not really. Almost as weird as Abbott. Must be somethin' in the water at that end of town. The husband said his wife cooked for the old man, washed his clothes. She even went over to clean ever so often. Can't image what the place woulda looked like if she hadn't. What a pit. You shoulda seen it."

"Yeah, I heard. I understand looters had a field day and that by the time the house burned down, there wasn't much left."

Lungrin shrugged. "Looters. I guess we shoulda seen that coming. Damn kids. Don't know what they was thinking. I gotta tell you, the place reeked. A lotta rotting goes on in two weeks and that's a smell you never get rid of. The way it stunk. Figured no one in his right mind would step foot in there."

Dave was surprised that Lungrin was actually being cordial. "So, you found the old man at the bottom of his stairs. Your report said it appeared to be a fall. Did you notice anything that might make you think otherwise?"

"Such as?"

"The position of the body."

"Two weeks in that heat? Hard to tell anythin'."

"Is that why you called in the coroner?"

"Routine."

"Did it bother you that there was no autopsy?"

"Who cares? Abbott ain't the first old man to fall down his steps."

"You sure it was a fall?"

"Don't see no other way to wind up dead at the bottom of your steps."

"What about a push, a shove?"

"Guy lived alone. Two neighbors, that's all."

"Any idea why it took so long for them to find him?"

"They was away. Two weeks or so. The husband was the last one to see Abbott alive."

"Yeah, I got that. Based on the condition of the body you figured Mr. Abbott was dead for about two weeks. That means he must have died shortly after the neighbors left. You said the husband was the last person to see Mr. Abbott alive. Did he say anything about his demeanor?"

"His what?"

"The way he was acting. Was he upset about anything?"

"Was who upset?"

"Mr. Abbott. Did the neighbor think he seemed upset?"

"What the hell kind of question is that? The guy finds his neighbor rotting at the bottom of his steps. What you expect him to do? Shake the stiff and ask what was bothering him?"

"Okay, okay," Dave replied, not wanting to piss Lungrin off. "What about the house? Did you notice anything unusual?"

"You kiddin'? The place was a dump. It stunk to high heaven. That count as unusual?"

"Right," Dave replied. "Any chance Mr. Abbott's fall was not an accident?"

Lungrin took another bite of his sandwich. "If it was, we wouldda said so. Let me ask you this. You ever poke a rottin' corpse, in the heat, with flies buzzin' everywhere, not to mention the stench so bad you could hardly breathe? I hope you ain't sayin' we didn't do our job."

"Not at all. Just wanted to be sure. Got some new information the other day. The remains found under that hotel. Turns out Mr. Abbott may have known the woman. They discover those remains and a short time later Mr. Abbott is dead. Makes you wonder if there's some kind of connection."

Lungrin propped his elbows on the table and leaned in Dave's direction. "Listen kid. Only thing you gotta wonder about is why Abbott didn't fall sooner. Them steps. Ask Robinson. Went up nice and careful and still almost killed himself. The place was a fallin' down dump. Warped steps, loose banister. No big mystery. Your fifteen minutes is up. We gotta get goin'."

"Sure," Dave replied. "I appreciate your time. Just to be clear, you didn't notice anything out of place, didn't find anything unusual?"

Lungrin plopped back into his seat. "Just to be clear," he repeated, his tone oozing sarcasm, "what might be unusual to you don't mean shit to us. We see things for what they are. You ever deal with old folks? You got any idea the kind a calls we get? 'My watch is missin', my radio's gone.' These people take things out, don't remember where they put 'em and then they call us complainin' someone stole their shit. You oughtta read those reports, see some of the weird places we find their things. Now this Abbott guy. Might a been a little more touched than most but findin' him like that and seein' the crap we see, it's about right."

"Gotcha," Dave replied, figuring he had one last shot. "Just one more question. If we could prove there's a link between the Abbotts and the remains that were discovered several weeks ago, would you look at his fall differently? Would you consider the possibility that the old man's death wasn't the accident it appeared to be?"

"That's two questions, kid. Two questions, one answer. I don't give a shit. We heard about them remains. They're sixty-five years old. You wanna make some kind a link between them and old man Abbott, go right ahead. That's the problem with you reporters. Always tryin' to make mountains outta mole hills."

"Just connecting the dots. There's an interesting police report dated the day before the hotel foundation was poured. That's the same day they think Jane Doe was murdered. October 14, 1945."

"So what?'

"So according to the report, the cemetery caretaker witnessed an argument between a young couple at a newly dug gravesite. He'd just come out of his office when he heard the yelling. The man tried to grab the woman, but she broke free and ran across the field. He got into his car which was parked just a few feet away and went after her. Here's why that report's significant. The next day they poured the foundation for the Old Heidelberg Hotel, the very place where they discovered those remains."

"Whoopdeedoo. What's that got to do with old man Abbott?"

"The car the caretaker mentioned. It was parked just a few feet away from the Abbott gravesite. Here," Dave said, pulling his smart phone from his pocket. He tapped the screen several times and then handed the phone to Lungrin. "I spent hours in the cemetery trying to recreate what the place looked like in 1945 and I'm sure I have it right. At that time, the Abbott gravesite was the only newly dug grave where a car could park that close. Take a look."

Reluctantly Lungrin grabbed the phone and glanced at the picture. Sneering, he handed the phone back. "That's the east entrance."

"That's right," Dave replied. "The only way in and the only way out. Only place you could park that close to a gravesite."

"Wrong." Lungrin squeezed his sandwich wrapper into a tight ball. "You spent all them hours dickin' around and you didn't notice the area where the tombstones ain't evenly spaced?'

Dave felt defensive. "Actually I did, but it didn't seem like such a big deal."

"That's 'cause you don't know shit. Long time ago there was two entrances, one on either side of the caretaker's office. East entrance was fine, on a straight away. Easy to pull out, make sure no cars were coming. The west entrance was a death trap. That bend in the road. Couldn't see shit. Tons a accidents—people slammed from behind pullin' into the cemetery, hit broadside pullin' out. They closed the damn entrance about twenty years ago."

Dave was rattled. "Twenty years?"

"Give or take. You college kids is all alike. Think you know everythin'. You got no idea that you ain't even close and you're too dumb to figure it out. Do us all a favor. Go home and take your fancy ideas with you. Let old man Abbott rest in peace."

All of a sudden, Dave realized that his grandmother was waiting for him at her front door. *Damn*, he mused, knowing she would want to hear all about his investigation. She had been so proud of him, so certain he would be the one to identify Jane Doe.

Trying to put on a happy face, Dave got out of his car. He felt defeated. Laura Hunter had been right. First impressions were often wrong. He had been so sure of his cemetery drawings, so sure of a link between Jane Doe and the Abbott family. Now, after checking the gravesites where that second entrance once was, he realized that there were several other families that might be linked to Jane Doe. That could easily set his investigation back several more days, possibly several weeks and maybe forever.

As he approached the porch, Dave swore he could smell his grandmother's awesome apple pie. In the grand scheme of things, maybe this evening wouldn't be as difficult as he expected. If nothing else, he would be well fed. Buoyed by the loving expression on his grandmother's face Dave suddenly realized that he still had one ace left, one card yet to be revealed: the DNA. If that result was positive, it wouldn't matter that there was a second entrance. A positive result would prove that he was on the right track. Cheered by the prospect of getting good news, Dave kissed his grandmother on the cheek. He was keenly aware that she smelled the same way she did when he was a little boy coming for a visit. As pleasant childhood recollections began flooding his memory bank, Dave made a decision. He would not let Jane Doe, Jeff Lungrin or Mark Robinson ruin his evening. Tomorrow was another day. He would deal with it then.

Chapter Fifteen

July 1st

Keith Quigley put his pen down and rubbed his eyes. Through the open windows of the caretaker's cottage, he could hear the telltale sounds of the breaking dawn. He had been up all night and yet he felt energized. Smiling, he looked over his brilliant creation. He had done it. In less than twenty-four hours he had found a way to answer Catherine's doubts about that stupid letter.

Who said he couldn't match wits with Henry Weinstein? The old man had been right about that letter, right to suspect that Rosa Berman had not been on the yacht when it exploded, right to think that Tad Quigley had possession of that letter and that he had used it to find Rosa. But he had been wrong to think it could get Catherine to change her mind, so very wrong.

Keith's goal was simple: produce a letter that would put all Catherine's doubts to rest and be sure to make Tad Quigley look like a hero and Henry Weinstein look like an idiot. It had to be written in German on stationery that would appear to be sixty-five years old. Most important of all, it had to look like Rosa's handwriting. With all that was at stake, Keith never doubted he could meet the many challenges.

A shower or some shut eye? Keith was trying to decide when his landline rang. He knew right away that it had to be Catherine and he knew he wasn't quite ready to talk to her. No doubt she'd want to know if he found anything. The letter was good but it needed a careful proofreading. Keith seriously considered ignoring the call but he knew damn well that Catherine would just keep trying. He reached for the phone, not entirely sure what he would say.

"Keith, my dear. I owe you an apology. I've put you in a very awkward position. This isn't really an excuse but I was so angry with Henry yesterday and truth to tell, even with your grandfather. Henry made me question your grandfather's loyalty and as much as I hated that, I did the same to you. This letter situation is my problem. I don't want you to worry about it."

You gotta be kidding, Keith mused. He just spent the entire night slaving over his brilliant masterpiece. The thoughtful side of his brain told him to keep his mouth shut, to hang back, to make sure he had all the i's dotted and all the t's crossed. "But I found it!" he blurted before he could stop himself. "In an old book. Late last night. It's written in German and I didn't want to bother you until I could translate it. Took me all night."

Catherine gasped and for several seconds the line was quiet. "You...you found it? Oh, my. Henry was right? There really was a letter?"

"He was right about the letter but so wrong about why Pop never told you. Henry owes him and you an apology. It's a very moving letter, moving but difficult."

"What are you saying?"

"I'm afraid Pop had good reason to keep this letter from you. He was trying to protect you. You see, Rosa survived the explosion and I should warn you, she wrote some very disturbing things, things she didn't want you to know. She specifically asked that they remain secret. Pop was only honoring her request and at the same time, protecting you."

"Survived the explosion? How?"

"I guess it just wasn't her time. This letter. Pop did the right thing. It will only cause you more pain."

"What could be more painful than losing a child?"

Keith chose his words carefully. "Being reminded of it. I don't understand why Henry would cause you all this pain for a letter that essentially proves him wrong about Pop. Worked really hard on that translation and I think I got it right."

"That's good. If you didn't Henry will rake you over the coals. He speaks fluent German and French. Please. Come for breakfast and bring the letter. We'll discuss it then. In an hour, on the veranda."

"German!" Keith exploded as he hung up the phone. "The bastard speaks German?" That possibility never occurred to him. Damn! Would his masterpiece wilt under Henry's scrutiny? Henry knew Rosa. Would he expect her German to be perfect or would he expect it to be flawed with slang and improper phrasing? Keith had used a computer program to translate the letter that he'd composed. Would Henry figure it out? Would he cause even more trouble?

After dressing to please Catherine, Keith slipped the letter into an old leatherbound book and began his trek to the big house. The grass had just been cut so rather than muck up his shoes, he took the path parallel to the bay. Catherine was sitting on the veranda waiting for him. Keith kissed her on the cheek and then took his usual seat. He wasn't exactly thrilled to see the bowl of fresh fruit that had been centered on his place mat. Hard to eat anything with his stomach in knots.

"You look tired," Catherine said. She pushed the pewter carafe across the table. "Have some coffee."

"Thanks. It was a long night. Had I known Henry spoke German I wouldn't have wasted all that time trying to translate that letter."

"Is it a long one?"

"Not terribly. I'm guessing Rosa was in a great deal of pain when she wrote it. She was badly burned. It's amazing she lived as long as she did."

Catherine cringed. To distract herself, she cut a strawberry into several pieces. "Poor Rosa. I can't believe she survived the explosion. Her letter. Did she say anything about Marney? I'm afraid to ask. Did…did she survive the explosion?"

Keith took a deep breath. Catherine's pain was palpable and all of a sudden he realized that parts of the letter might be a bit too graphic. "I'm not sure. If my translation is correct, Charles was in the engine room when it exploded. Obviously he didn't stand a chance. Rosa and Marney were heading toward the opposite end of the boat."

"Were they wearing their life vests? That was my rule, you know. Marney could not be on the boat without one."

"They were and Rosa tried desperately to save Marney. She was devastated that she was the only one to survive. Apparently someone pulled her out of the water. She must have been in pretty bad shape. I believe she wrote the letter several days after the explosion. She didn't want you to know she had survived when Charles and Marney hadn't. She felt guilty."

"At least her guilt only lasted a few days. Mine has lasted all these years. If I hadn't been so wrapped up in myself that day, I never would have let Marney and Rosa go on the boat. To this day, I've been angry with myself, angry with your grandfather, angry with Charles. He knew there were issues with the engine and yet he put his own daughter in harm's way. I don't really care that he blew himself up, but my little girl."

"You couldn't have known."

Catherine sighed. She picked up the book. "You found the letter in here? That's so odd. I don't know what your grandfather could have been thinking. *Moby Dick*. I gave that book to him after our first, after the first time we were together. It was Charles' favorite. I don't know why I did that. I guess I wanted to give anything and everything that meant something to Charles to Tad. Your grandfather hated to read and that book is so tedious. I'm surprised he kept it. How I wish I could undo all the stupid things I've done."

Keith was grateful when the cook appeared carrying individual plates of pancakes, bacon and fried eggs. He was even happier when he saw two glasses filled with Bloody Marys.

Catherine placed the book on the table without opening it. "All these years, I wish I had known. It's odd, you know—that your grandfather would have honored Rosa's wishes. I don't think they ever agreed on anything. I'm impressed that in keeping that letter secret, he stood up to Henry's demands for Rosa's sake. He was braver than I thought."

"I'm sure it wasn't easy for him. This letter. I never knew Rosa or Marney but it was hard for me to read. I can paraphrase it for you. That might be easier."

"No, no, no. You don't understand. There's nothing in that letter that can do any more damage. You see, that letter proves something I've never wanted to accept: that I will never see my daughter again. In my heart I guess I was waiting, waiting until something of Marney's washed ashore, waiting until something…something like this. Do you know there were times, in my darkest moments, that I imagined hearing her voice, running into the kitchen out of breath, demanding a glass of cold milk? How silly. If Marney had survived, she would have been sixty-seven this September. Can you imagine a sixty-seven year old demanding a glass of cold milk?"

Keith was at a loss for words.

Catherine toyed with the celery stick in her Bloody Mary. "I feel so bad for doubting your grandfather." She reached for the book, pulled the letter out and then handed it to Keith. "Please, read this before I lose my nerve."

Keith hesitated. Henry's proficiency with German loomed large and he wanted a little more time to go over it. He tried to convince Catherine that it would be better to wait but she wouldn't hear of it. Seeing no other option, Keith unfolded the letter and held it at just the right angle so that he could monitor Catherine's reaction.

My dearest Helga,

By now you've probably heard about that awful explosion and you probably think I am gone. Honestly, I wish I was. I am suffering with terrible burns on my arms, legs and face but the worst thing of all is Marney. That poor little girl. She is gone and it's all my fault. Those last moments on the yacht will forever haunt me. Charles got very agitated when he noticed smoke coming from the engine room. He yelled for us to go to the opposite end of the boat but Marney wouldn't listen. She was fascinated by the smoke. I was carrying her, kicking and screaming away from the engine when it exploded. I'm sure Charles died immediately. It was so loud, so hot. Next thing I knew, we were in the water. There was wreckage everywhere. I remember screaming for Marney but I couldn't find her. I kept telling myself to stay calm. Luckily we were wearing our life vests and I can't tell you how happy I was when I saw Marney's vest bobbing up and down. I hate to tell you this but Marney wasn't in it. Poor Catherine. She was so strict about Marney wearing that vest. I was too but it was so hot on the boat and Marney kept unzipping it. I scolded her several times and re-zipped it for her but I should have checked that zipper the moment Charles realized there was a problem. If I had, Marney might be here today.

"Zipper?" Catherine interrupted. "We'll have to ask Henry about that. Marney's life vest had buckles, not zippers. They were tight little buggers. She could be very stubborn at times but I can't imagine she was strong enough to unsnap them herself."

Damn, Keith mused. Buckles, zippers. How was he supposed to know? He shrugged. "Guess I was more tired than I thought. No need to bother Henry. I'll just check my program."

Catherine took a deep breath. "My poor little girl. Poor Rosa. She loved Marney almost as much as I did. She shouldn't have blamed herself. I know she would have done everything to save her. I just know it. Please. Go on."

Keith hesitated. What other mistakes had he made? If only he could destroy the letter. Pretend it never existed. "Are you sure?"

Closing her eyes, Catherine nodded.

Please destroy this letter as soon as you read it. It's my final goodbye to you. I am sorry that I can't tell you in person. It doesn't matter how I made it to shore or who is helping me but he has promised to mail this letter for me and to lay me to rest. My wounds are infected so it's only a matter of time. I pray the end comes sooner rather than later.

As much as I admired Charles, I blame him for what happened. Tad warned him that there was a problem with the engine but he didn't listen. Please do whatever you can to comfort Catherine but you must never let her know. We must take this secret to our graves, the both of us. God speed. See you on the other side.

Your loving sister.

Tears were streaming down Catherine's face. "If only I had known. We could have brought Rosa back. Buried her here. At least I would have a gravesite to visit."

Keith opened the book and then placed the letter along with the translation between the pages. "I'm very sorry. I wish things had been different."

Catherine patted Keith's hand. "It's not your fault. You were only doing what I asked. I want you to be with me when we show this to Henry. Your grandfather was only trying to protect me. We must show Henry how wrong he was. What's today?"

"July first."

"Oh dear. That means Henry's daughter's in town. We'll never get him here, not till she leaves."

Keith felt enormously relieved. "When will that be?"

"Sometime after the Fourth. Henry's daughter started a charity event some time ago, always the first week of July. It was sad. Her only grandchild had died of leukemia. Problem is I don't remember if they do it on the second, third, or fourth. Doesn't really matter. I know Henry. He'd turn down an invitation from the President if it interfered with his daughter's visit. We'll just have to put this on hold, at least for a few days. You don't mind, do you?"

"Not at all," Keith replied. He put the letter back in the book, thinking he would have plenty of time to work on it. He froze when Catherine reached for it.

"Then it's settled," Catherine replied. "I'll keep this in the safe until we can get Henry over here. In the meantime, I'll have a little peace. Just knowing your grandfather stuck his neck out for me. It means so much."

Keith knew better than to argue. Once Catherine decides to do something no one could get her to change her mind. For appearance's sake, Keith finished his breakfast, hoping it would stay down. He walked slowly back to his cottage. What had begun as such a brilliant idea could now ruin him. Henry Weinstein was a suspicious son of a bitch who not only hated his grandfather; he was obsessively determined that no Quigley would ever own a morsel of the Preston estate. Zipper, buckles. Even if Keith managed to come up with an improved letter and to somehow switch it without getting caught, Henry would probably see through the ruse. He'd figure it out. Bastard.

Abundant sunshine made the cottage feel like an oven. Keith slammed the door and then walked over to the refrigerator for a cold beer. He kicked off his shoes, tore off his shirt and then threw it on the floor. Plopping onto his grandfather's lounge chair, he popped off the tab and then gulped down half the can. His thoughts were racing. Goddamned Henry Weinstein. He could only hope Catherine was right; that Henry wouldn't do squat while his daughter was in town. That gave him three to four more days to figure out what to do.

Just as Keith downed the last of his beer, his landline rang. "Christ Almighty," he muttered. His head was still spinning and Catherine Preston was the last person he wanted to talk to. Then again, it made no sense to prolong the agony. His mind blank, he walked across the room and picked up the phone. Several seconds later he found himself trying to calm a sobbing Catherine. "Please, please. Slow down. I can't understand what you're saying."

"It's Henry. His daughter just called. He's had another stroke, early this morning. This time they couldn't help him. I feel awful, just awful."

Chapter Sixteen

July 2nd

To Laura Hunter, it didn't seem possible that the fourth day of their vacation was already in the books. They were at the half way mark. Tonight would be her fourth night away from home with four more to go. So far, she couldn't believe how well things were going. Even the weather was cooperating.

Sunrise, several hours earlier, had brought a welcomed break in the oppressive humidity. The minute Laura stepped out onto her patio she noticed that there were no dewdrops on the furniture and that there was no haze dimming her view of the ocean. Although it would be a comfortable morning for tennis and biking, Laura had something else in mind. Today would be the perfect day to take her kids to Roanoke Island and tour both the Lost Colony and the Elizabethan Gardens. It had been on her to do list for years but whenever the weather had cooperated, the kids hadn't.

It turned out to be a beautiful day for outside activities. Having recently seen *The Pirates of the Caribbean,* the kids were fascinated by the ships docked at Roanoke Island. They walked wide eyed through the log cabins and the mock-up of the hamlet built to represent the living conditions of the Lost Colony. They toured the Elizabethan Gardens and listened to theories as to what might have happened to the lost settlers. After lunching on the patio of a colonial era café, they visited the museum where they bought several authentic looking souvenirs. On the way home, they stopped at Kill Devil Hills to tour the Wright Brothers National Memorial. They arrived at

Gatekeeper with just enough time to visit the swim club and to do a few laps.

With no interest in cooking, Laura suggested to unanimous approval that they dine at Smokey's, a pleasant family restaurant whose specialty was the onion burst, a sweet onion, carefully sliced and delicately seasoned, quick fried and then served with a choice of dips. No one seemed to mind their relatively brief wait and everyone enjoyed their dinner. Wanting to keep the perfect day going, Laura offered to take the kids to the beach to throw a line or two into the surf as soon as they got home. They all agreed that there would be no curfews and no rigid bedtimes. It was vacation.

Moonlight Surf Fish went into operation the minute they returned to Gatekeeper. Meg went up to the kitchen to prepare coffee and hot chocolate to bring to the beach while Laura helped the younger children find their flip flops and their windbreakers. Scott singlehandedly prepared the bait and tackle. Their walk to the beach was filled with joyful anticipation and the fish did not disappoint. Laura was still marveling at what a perfect day it had been and by the time she kissed her children goodnight, she was blissfully exhausted.

Laura and Meg were sitting on the patio enjoying a nightcap when they realized their glasses were empty. Seconds after Meg went inside for refills, Laura's phone rang. Hoping it was Mike, she was disappointed to see Dave's name on her caller ID. She answered the call.

"Mrs. H," Dave stammered. "I...I'm sorry for bothering you at this hour, but I just read the DNA report. Have you seen it?"

Laura took a deep breath. She hadn't checked her email all day, not just because she'd been busy but because she really didn't want anything to ruin the mood. "I'm afraid not. What's it say?"

"Well, the size of the ring. You might have been onto something. Jane Doe is not your grandmother. Confidence ninety-nine percent, no match."

"Wow!" Laura replied. "That thing was tiny but I didn't really think it would matter that much. I mean, until now, everything else suggested Jane was my grandmother. I'm a little disappointed. Jane was really growing on me. If what she told the Abbotts was true, she not only walked away from an allegedly rich and powerful husband, she somehow managed to save my mother."

Dave sighed. "Guess this takes us back to square one. I'm bummed. I was really counting us having a match. I screwed up, big time."

"Don't be silly. Just because we don't have a DNA match doesn't mean Jane Doe isn't the woman who brought my mother to Greenview. Think about it. Your cemetery drawings, the location of the Abbott gravesite, Linda, whatever her real name is, going up to the cemetery and not coming back, the date she disappeared. It fits, not as neatly as I would like, but it still fits."

"Not exactly, Mrs. H. My cemetery drawings: I based those diagrams on there being just one entrance. I was wrong. Sixty-five years ago there was a second entrance that was also visible from the caretaker's office."

"A second entrance?" Laura replied, watching as Meg returned with two full glasses. Dry mouthed, she took a long sip.

"Yeah, apparently at one time there were two entrances to the cemetery, east and west. They closed the west entrance years ago for safety reasons. The curve in the road created a terrible blind spot. Too many accidents, some of them fatal. When I did those drawings I obviously used the wrong plot plan. Lungrin set me straight."

"Lungrin. Who's he?"

"They," Dave corrected. "Lungrin and Robinson, the cops who responded to the 9-1-1 call at the Abbott farmhouse. I gotta admit. I wasn't all that keen on interviewing these guys, but the more I thought about the timing of John's death and the fact that he was the only living soul in Greenview who might have known Jane Doe, the more convinced I was that these guys might change their story. Instead, they turned the tables on me, big time."

Laura shrugged. She realized she was grinding her teeth and that she was more annoyed with herself than she was with Dave. She had been so infected by his enthusiasm and his reputation that it never occurred to her to doublecheck the accuracy of his plot plan. "So tell me," she finally replied. "That second entrance. Does it make any difference?"

"It could. I found several other families who buried loved ones around the same time as the Abbotts did; all close enough to where that entrance was to be significant. I wouldn't care about that entrance if the DNA matched but it doesn't. Sure wish I knew all this before I got you involved. Could have saved you a lot of grief."

"Don't worry about it," Laura replied half-heartedly. "That's the way these things go and besides, if it wasn't for you, I never would have known the real reason my mother left Greenview. Not all that thrilling but I'd rather have it this way."

"That's generous of you Mrs. H, but you were right, you and the rest of the reporters who showed up when those remains were first uncovered. I should have taken the hint and left when they did. It's going to take an army to identify Jane Doe. I've been barking up the wrong tree all this time. Probably should have quit weeks ago. I've caused you all this angst for nothing."

"Listen Dave. My angst didn't come from you. It came from my mother not telling me the truth and that's not your problem. I hear your frustration and I get it, but you've still got a viable story."

"Mrs. H, this story was on life support before the DNA. I think it's time to pull the plug."

"Come on, Dave. You've still got that ring and there's no telling where that may lead. Besides, tormented as you may feel, you really haven't been at this for all that long. Something could still turn up. One of the things I've learned over the years is never to quit on the heels of bad news. Take a breather, kick back for a bit, let this all sink in. You're lucky. The Fourth is right around the corner and a few days off will do you good, give you a new perspective."

"I don't know, Mrs. H."

"Trust me, Dave. Snap decisions rarely pan out. Believe it or not, some of my best investigations were ones I had all but given up on. Look, you've got good instincts. Give it more time. What do you have to lose? I'll call you as soon as we get back. We can go over everything one more time just to be sure we haven't missed anything."

Yeah right, Dave mused. He imagined that if they came up with anything it would be more ways that he'd screwed up. Then again, the idea of taking some time off sounded really good. "Okay, Mrs. H. I'll give it a few more days. Enjoy the rest of your vacation. Happy Fourth."

It took several seconds after she hung up for Laura to realize that she was holding her breath. She looked at Meg. "The DNA is back. Jane Doe is not my grandmother."

"Wow," Meg replied. "Just when you were getting used to the idea that she was."

"Yeah, it sucks for a number of reasons, the worst being that Dave wants to quit. You know, it's odd. The only reason I agreed to mentor Dave was because Sandy made such a big deal about how bright he was and how Greenview was a total waste of time. She really wanted me to steer him toward a more doable project. To be perfectly honest, I had every intention of doing just that until Dave linked my mother's family to those remains. For selfish reasons, I encouraged him. Made suggestions. I knew identifying Jane Doe was a long shot, especially after all this time. I was being selfish. If Dave gives up now, it'll take forever to get his confidence back. He'll be a mess and it'll be my fault."

Meg hesitated. "You don't know that. Didn't you just tell Dave that something could still turn up?"

"What was I supposed to do? I was just stalling. Dave's right. It is time to hang it up but he has to do it the right way. Dave needs to understand that he did an incredible job for a novice and that's a pep talk best done face to face."

Meg shrugged. "Makes sense, I guess. On the bright side, if your mother's family has nothing to do with Jane Doe than it's highly unlikely John's death was anything more than an unfortunate accident. You're off the hook. You can turn your alarm off. Stop looking over your shoulder."

Laura considered Meg's suggestion. "I could but I probably won't, at least not for a while, not until I'm absolutely sure no one is looking for my mother."

"And how will you know that?"

Laura sighed. "I'll have to go back to Greenview. See if anyone's been asking about the Abbott Farmstead. Maybe even claim it for myself. Dave was right. It might be the only way to pull Jane's killer out of hiding."

"Wow! This is getting better by the minute," Meg replied, her voice oozing sarcasm. "What happened to you wanting no part of the farmstead until you knew who Jane Doe was and how she wound up under that hotel?"

"I still feel that way, but I owe it to Dave."

"Owe it to Dave? What about your kids? Boy, would I like to be a fly on the wall when you tell Mike."

"Speaking of Mike," Laura replied, grateful for the chance to change the subject. "He keeps asking me when we plan to go crabbing. How 'bout tomorrow? That chicken's getting pretty ripe. It'll be fun. I promise."

They sat outside chatting until they finished their drinks. After rinsing their glasses and officially ending their day, Laura went downstairs determined to get a restful night sleep. She checked on her kids and then walked into her bedroom. She washed her face, brushed her teeth and then put her nightgown on. She was plumping her pillow when her cell phone rang. Seeing that it was Mike, she lay back and took the call.

They talked for almost an hour and by the time Laura closed her eyes, she felt enormously peaceful. Maybe it was the wine or maybe it was Mike's comforting tone but for some reason, the DNA no longer mattered. In the recesses of her mind, Laura figured at some point she'd uncover a plausible explanation but for now, she felt no sense of urgency. Dave was taking a much needed break so there was no reason she couldn't do the same. If the next few days were even half as perfect as today, her children would have wonderful stories to share with the one man who might someday become their father. With that thought in mind and a big smile on her face, Laura drifted off to sleep.

Chapter Seventeen

July 3rd

Catherine Preston knew what time it was even before she opened her eyes. Since Tad Quigley's death she hadn't slept past 5AM. Her thoughts, constantly racing, always seemed more vivid just before dawn—vivid and disturbing. To think she had known Tad for sixty-five years and that they had been lovers for only a matter of weeks. While those weeks were the happiest she had ever known; they had extracted a heavy price. With each passing day, she became more and more convinced that had it not been for their brief affair, her little girl would be alive today. The letter that Keith found was only adding to her misery.

The house was quiet. It would be at least another half hour before the cook would venture into the kitchen to make the coffee and begin the day's food preparations. Catherine got out of bed. She thought about going down and making a pot of coffee but for some reason it never tasted as good as when Theresa made it. Best, she decided, to pass the time primping. She'd take a nice long shower, style her hair, dab on a little makeup and put on her favorite dress. With any luck, by the time she opened her bedroom door, the smell of coffee would fill her senses.

The sun was just beginning to brighten the windows when Catherine started down the steps. The coffee was perking and the cook was singing like she so often did. Catherine chuckled. Theresa was a pleasant woman who had no idea how off key her songs were. She greeted Catherine with a warm smile and an excited description of the day's breakfast. "It sounds wonderful," Catherine lied. After a restless night, the very thought of food made her queasy. "If you don't mind, I think I'll head out to the gazebo, enjoy my coffee there and try to figure out if the tide is coming in or going out. I promise to be back in time for breakfast. I shouldn't be more than a half hour."

"Alone? Do you think that's a good idea?" Theresa asked.

"I'll be fine," Catherine replied, gratefully taking the thermal coffee mug that Theresa had prepared. "Believe me. The walk will do me good."

"Well, just be careful. If you're not back in a half hour, I'll call the Calvary to come get you."

Catherine was still smiling as she stepped onto the pebbled path that led to the ocean. The gazebo had been Tad's idea and in her mind, a brilliant one. The Prestons had been boat people and were more interested in sailing the gentle waters of the bay than the unpredictable ocean. No one cared that Catherine loved the beach or that she had been forced to navigate the prickly, overgrown path to the ocean, at least until Tad came along.

Tad, Catherine sighed. Once built, the gazebo and the beach surrounding it topped his opening week to do list. After the electricity and the water at the big house were running efficiently, he would bring the necessary crews down to the gazebo. Rotten wood was replaced, the beach was combed, and each year, Tad added a new upgrade. With running water, heaters and a mini kitchen, it had all the comforts of home.

Wrapping her shawl a little tighter around her shoulders, Catherine climbed the five steps leading into the gazebo. It was both windier and cooler than she expected but at least the sun was strong. She sat in her favorite seat and took a long sip of her coffee. All was quiet except for the crashing waves. Best as she could tell, the tide was coming in.

Mesmerized by the light dancing off the water, Catherine's thoughts drifted to the three men who tried to control her life. Charles, Tad and Henry were all gone but each had made an indelible mark on her psyche. Oddly enough, Catherine hated Charles and Henry equally: Charles for wanting to take Marney from her and Henry for always taking Charles' side. But what about Tad and even his grandson. That letter. Was it for real or was Keith just manipulating her? Zippers. Marney's vest did not have zippers. It had buckles. Was that truly a mistranslation or was it something more?

Catherine was so deep in thought that it took several minutes for her to hone in on a strange flapping noise. Looking up, she saw that it belonged to the impressively long tail of a high flying kite. Awed, she walked over to the top of the gazebo steps and looked to her right, hoping to see who the kite belonged to. All of a sudden the kite began to zigzag, dipping low and then going high. It was just a few feet from where Catherine was standing when she realized the string had snapped. Just as it flew overhead, Catherine reached for the string, certain she could haul it in. Instead, she fell down the steps and landed face first in the sand. Disappointed, she lay in the sand, needing a few seconds to spit the grit from her mouth. Feeling like a klutz and grateful no one had seen her, she began to laugh. Her reaction seemed to startle the children running toward her.

"Are you all right?" the young boy asked.

"Yes, yes, I'm fine," she replied, forcing herself to sit up. "Was that your kite? That was the neatest thing I've seen in a long time. I'm so sorry your string broke."

"Are you sure you're all right?" the girl asked. "We can go get our mother if you need help." She pointed to the roof of a house just beyond the tree line. "We're staying at Gatekeeper. It's right over there."

Catherine smiled. "That won't be necessary but it's very nice of you to offer." Trying not to grunt, she managed to get on her feet and began brushing herself off. She looked to her left, to the last place she had seen the kite. "Well, look at that," she said, pointing to a tall evergreen. "Your kite landed. Let's go see if we can get it down."

As they made their way over to the tree line, Catherine introduced herself and did whatever she could to make the children feel comfortable. She was delighted by the pleasant conversation that followed. By the time they reached the kite, a strong wind had lifted it into the air and was hurling it away. Catherine wasn't sure who was more disappointed, she or the kids. All of sudden, she heard Keith call her name. She turned to see him rushing toward them. The look on his face told her what she already knew. She had lost all track of time.

"Do you know how late it is?" Keith demanded. "Theresa's ready to call 9-1-1."

"Sorry," Catherine replied. "We were chasing a kite. What a beauty. The string broke so it's probably in Virginia by now. These two wonderful children saw me fall down the gazebo steps and ran over to help me."

Keith glared at Scott and Sara Hunter. "And what were these two wonderful children doing on private property?"

"We're sorry," Scott replied. "We didn't mean to ignore the 'No Trespassing' sign but we wanted to get our kite back. It won't happen again."

"You bet it won't. Once is enough. Your parents shoulda been keeping a better eye on you. Go, before they accuse us of kidnapping."

Catherine was painfully quiet on the walk back to the house. "Are you sure you're all right?" Keith asked.

"I would be if I wasn't embarrassed by the way you treated those children. They were only trying to help."

"Help? If they wanted to help they should have stayed off the property. You're lucky you didn't break anything. Do you have any idea how concerned everyone was?"

"Oh, please. I'm not that late. There was absolutely no excuse for you to treat those children like terrorists, especially that little girl. Did you see her? Maybe I'm just blue because Marney's birthday is coming up but she reminded me so much of my little girl."

Keith tried to be patient. He wanted Catherine to focus on the future, to focus on naming him heir. He hated when she wallowed in the past. "Truthfully I hadn't noticed. We'd better get going. Theresa's very worried about you."

Catherine sighed. "I didn't mean to worry Theresa but there's no need to treat me like an invalid. I may be old but I'm fitter than Theresa is. Besides, I've just had my best morning in ages. Those children were so sweet. Just watching that kite." She chuckled. "I can't believe I tried to catch it. That little adventure was a wonderful distraction. I wasn't thinking of your grandfather. I wasn't thinking of Henry and I wasn't thinking of that stupid letter. Such freedom."

"Freedom? You'd be singing a different tune if you got hurt."

"Don't be so dour," Catherine scolded. She grabbed Keith's arm. "I have an idea. I'd like you to replace that kite. Buy one with the longest tail and then bring it over to Gatekeeper. Just be sure to let their mother know how much I appreciate the way her kids tried to help. If I wasn't so tired, I'd come with you, but I want to take a nice warm bath and maybe a short nap. You don't mind, do you?"

"Of course not," Keith lied. Kite shopping wasn't his thing but if it would get Catherine back on track, he could deal with it. They reached the mansion. Keith held the door open. The house staff came rushing toward them. "Mrs. Preston is fine," Keith announced. "She took a little fall at the gazebo but she's fine."

"Please, please," Catherine cried, annoyed by the attention. "No need to fuss. Do what you were doing. I'm sure I'll feel better once I get out of these sandy clothes."

No one said a word as Catherine started toward the staircase. All of a sudden, she stopped and turned around. "Where's Keith?" she asked, making a visor with her hand. "These steps—I just realized I could use a strong arm to lean on."

Keith felt good that Catherine had singled him out. He hurried over and immediately held out his left arm. He was pleasantly surprised by how tightly she clung to him. Did this mean she was no longer annoyed by the way he treated those brats? Even better, did it mean she truly trusted him? Clearly he was making progress.

They took each step slowly, silently and finally reached the top. Thinking this was as far Catherine expected him to go, Keith waited for her to release his arm. Instead she squeezed it tighter. She pulled him across the shiny wooden floor and then stopped at the richly stained door to her bedroom. "Thank you," she whispered. She patted Keith's left arm with her free hand and then slowly untwined her right arm. She opened her bedroom door, took several steps and then stopped. "I just remembered," she said, turning around. "Would you mind starting the bath water? It takes so long for the hot water to make it up here and I just don't have the patience to stand there and wait."

Not sure what to make of Catherine's request, Keith followed her into the bedroom. It felt so strange. He hadn't been in this room since he was a little boy. Looking all around, Keith walked slowly toward the bathroom. Oddly enough, everything looked the same as he remembered. The walls were covered with exquisitely framed pictures, the largest hanging above the bed. It was a portrait of Catherine holding her little girl. Keith couldn't help but stare. In her younger days, Catherine was an exceptionally beautiful woman. No wonder his grandfather fell in love with her. A slightly smaller portrait of two-year old Marney hung on the opposite wall. The room was like a shrine. Beautifully framed pictures but none taken after the explosion. The pictures said it all. Catherine was caught in a time warp.

As expected, the water took forever to get hot. Once it did, Keith plugged the drain and then added just enough cold water to temper the heat. When he returned to the bedroom, Catherine was sitting at her vanity, staring down at a small shiny object. "Your bath is almost ready," he said.

Startled, Catherine dropped the object she had been holding. It hit the vanity where she was sitting and then bounced on the floor. "Oh, my," she whispered, tears clouding her bright blue eyes. "Did you see where that went?"

Keith looked down. He wasn't sure what to look for when a shiny object caught his eye. He bent down to pick it up and was surprised to see what appeared to be a little girl's barrette. "Is this it?" he asked, trying not to stare. Less than two months ago he remembered taking an identical barrette out of the envelope that his grandfather had squirreled away in his desk drawer. It was a reminder he could do without.

"Thank you, thank you," Catherine whispered, returning the barrette to the shadow box that she kept on her vanity. "I should be more careful. These barrettes are all I have left of my little girl—these, a few pictures and some cherished memories. Your grandfather used to tell me I was foolish to keep them on my vanity where anyone could walk off with them but I love looking at them. Charles had five of them made for Marney's second birthday. She was wearing three of them the day…the day the yacht exploded. These two are all I have left."

Keith squirmed uncomfortably, not sure what to say.

Catherine smiled, oblivious to Keith's discomfort. "The stones are real, you know. You have no idea how many times I've held these barrettes, closed my eyes and imagined putting them in Marney's hair. I always hoped it would make me feel better but it never did. The letter you found. I probably should thank you. It's made me realize that I've been holding onto something that will never happen."

That was the idea, Keith mused. "I know how sad that must be for you."

Catherine sighed. "Did you know that every year on the first day down here, I'd spend hours searching the shoreline? I had this silly notion that as long as I never found anything that belonged to Marney that she might be alive. If only your grandfather had showed me that letter. Horrible as it is, it's absolute proof that my little girl is never coming back. I guess he didn't trust me to deal with it."

"I'm sure he was only trying to do what he thought would be best."

"Perhaps," Catherine replied. She sighed. "Nothing we can do about it now." She returned the shadow box to the left corner of her vanity and then rose slowly. "Thank you for your help. You have no idea how much I'm looking forward to this bath and a nice nap. Let me know how you make out at the kite store."

"Will do," Keith replied. He stepped out into the hall, taking a moment to check out the last door on the right. That would be his room, once he owned Whalehead. It was a corner suite, facing the water.

It was relatively early and the kite store didn't open until ten. Keith returned to his cottage and made himself a hearty breakfast. He was amazed that a woman as bright as Catherine was still expecting something of her daughter's to wash ashore and that his grandfather had been dumb enough to sit on the very item that could have ended her misery. Knowing Catherine's habit of combing the shoreline, he could have placed the barrette where she might have found it or perhaps claimed to have found it himself. Catherine could have moved on years ago.

Keith put his dish in the sink, walked into the bathroom and then turned on the shower. Several minutes later, he got out. He was feeling good. After drying his hair, Keith stood in front of the mirror. He was pleased with the way the sun had bleached his dirty blond hair. He knew he looked good, handsome, kind and friendly. So much had happened since the day he watched his grandfather die, since the day he shoved John Abbott down the steps, but all things considered, it was the letter that he was most proud of. It wasn't perfect but with Henry Weinstein gone, that no longer mattered. All he had to do now was to find that damn kite and deliver it to Gatekeeper. *Piece of cake*, he mused, grabbing his car keys. *Piece of cake.*

Chapter Eighteen

July 3rd

Laura Hunter had just gotten out of the shower when she heard the doorbell. Thinking it was the boy next door who was always calling on her kids, she quickly slipped into her yellow sundress, grabbed a hair clip and then headed into the foyer. As she rushed to the door, she pulled her wet hair into a pony tail, twisted it and then pinned it to the back of her head. Without checking to see who it was, she opened the door. She was surprised to see a tall handsome man standing there. "Can I help you?" she asked, wishing she had been less impulsive.

"Are you Mrs. Hunter?" Keith asked, trying not to stare. In bare feet, Laura Hunter was about 5' 7" tall but it wasn't her height that threw him; it wasn't her milky white complexion, her bright dark eyes, her shiny brunette hair or her butter soft skin, still glistening from the shower she had just taken. It was the sense that he'd seen her before, perhaps not too long ago. Feeling a bit uncomfortable, he forced a smile. "I'm Keith Quigley. I'm Catherine Preston's grandson."

"Mrs. Preston from Whalehead?"

"That's right," Keith replied. Something about Laura's tone made him feel defensive.

"Really?" Laura asked. As far as she knew, Catherine Preston's only child had been killed years ago and the young widow never remarried. "Please don't be offended Mr. Quigley, but I didn't think Mrs. Preston had a grandson."

"No offense taken," Keith lied. "Blanche Quigley is my paternal grandmother. She was married to Edward Preston, Catherine's late father-in-law. Catherine's husband

and my grandfather were step-brothers. Technically, Mrs. Preston is my step-grandmother. My father dumped me on my grandfather's doorstep when I was little. Pop passed away about two months ago. Mrs. Preston is the only mother I've ever known."

"Oh, I'm so sorry." Laura replied, feeling a bit foolish. "I've heard many wonderful things about Mrs. Preston. You're lucky. Sounds like you have a special relationship."

Keith was mildly placated. "We do, and she asked me to bring this over." He held up the kite. "I'm afraid the tail on this kite isn't quite as long as the one your little boy lost but Mrs. Preston wanted to thank your children for what they did."

Laura looked at the kite and then at Keith. "I'm not sure I understand. How did Mrs. Preston know about their kite?"

Keith was somewhat surprised that the Hunter kids hadn't told their mother about their trespassing adventure, but he was extremely pleased. If they hadn't mentioned Catherine, then they couldn't have complained about him. He had a clean slate. "Mrs. Preston was relaxing in her gazebo this morning when your son's kite caught her eye. For some reason, when the string broke, she thought she could catch it for them. Instead, she fell down the gazebo steps. Your kids came to help. I don't think they understood they were on private property."

"Oh, my. They told me about their string breaking and how they tried to catch it but they never mentioned Mrs. Preston. Guess I should have asked more questions. Is she all right?"

"Yes, yes, she's fine. The fall sounds worse than it was and to hear Mrs. Preston tell it, she actually enjoyed her mishap. Your children were very polite. They didn't hesitate to help. Mrs. Preston figured replacing their kite would be a nice way to thank them. Here. I hope they like it."

Laura took the kite. All of a sudden she was aware of how flushed Keith's face was. He was handsome, well dressed, came from the oldest family on the island and appeared to be a perfect gentleman. "Would you like to come in for a cold drink?"

"Thank you," Keith replied. It had been his original intention to drop off the kite and leave but now he was curious. Laura seemed so familiar to him and he wanted to know why.

Laura placed the kite on the foyer table. "A twenty foot tail? These are pretty hard to come by. Where did you get this?"

"The kite store at Tim Buck II. Last one. My next stop would have been Duck and then Kitty Hawk. Good thing your kids told Mrs. Preston where they were staying. She would have had me begging all the real estate people down here for your address. Once she makes her mind up about something there's no changing it. I hope I haven't inconvenienced you."

"Not at all. I wasn't thrilled when I found out my kids had gone down to the beach by themselves this morning. My friend, Meg. She's staying here with me. She's always telling me I'm overprotective. Thing about kids; if you don't ask the right questions you don't get the right answers. Iced tea okay?"

"Yes, thank you."

Keith followed Laura up the steps. "Hey, what's that delicious smell?"

"Crab sauce. One of our traditions whenever we come down here. We caught a few crabs this morning. My mother was the master of sauce but she passed away several weeks ago. My friend and I are winging it. Hope it turns out."

"It should as long as you don't overcook the crabs. You don't want them to get chewy."

"You sound like a pro."

"Not really. I just have a better idea what not to do than what to do."

Laura chuckled. For some reason she felt an instant connection to Keith. Meg would probably call her a snob and insist that had he not been connected to the richest woman on the island, she wouldn't have given him the time of day. Then again, to make up for the ruckus her kids might have caused, it couldn't hurt to be friendly. She walked over to the stove and took the lid off the pot. "So what do you think?"

Keith was impressed. For some reason this beautiful woman actually wanted his opinion, or maybe... He walked tentatively toward the stove and stood as close to Laura as he dared. Maybe she was as attracted to him as he was to her. "Looks good. One of my grandfather's favorite things. Catch a few crabs, throw them in some tomato sauce, toss in some Old Bay and then simmer."

"You don't clean the crabs first?"

Keith cringed. "Do you?"

"Absolutely." Laura gestured to the kitchen counter, to one of several bar stools. She waited until Keith sat down. "My husband insisted. I hate it. Scares me to death. Throw them in boiling water till they stop moving and then cut their guts out. I think it's gross and I feel like I'm killing those poor things twice. On the plus side, it does make eating them more pleasant."

"Why didn't your husband clean the crabs?"

"He used to. He passed away shortly after my youngest was born."

"I'm so sorry," Keith replied. He watched Laura's every move as she walked over to the refrigerator, took out a pitcher of iced tea and then placed it on the counter. "How old is your youngest?"

"Almost four."

Keith tried not to stare at the V of Laura's halter sundress as she reached into the cabinet and took down two glasses. "Well, if he's half as nice as your other two, you're doing a fabulous job."

"Thanks. My mother was a big help. She moved in with me after my husband died. Was big on manners. She probably wouldn't have been too happy about my kids going on private property."

"Not a big deal," Keith lied. He knew he was leering, but he couldn't help himself. That halter. He needed a distraction. He wasn't his grandfather. He knew better than to think with his dick.

Laura poured two glasses. "Have you lived down here all your life?"

"Just summers. When I was a kid we'd go back to the New York estate. Now I only go there for Thanksgiving and Christmas. I teach during the school year so I have summers off. It's worked out pretty well for me. How 'bout you? Where you from?"

"A small Jersey town not too far from Philadelphia. Born there. Raised there. Left for college and then came back. I was an only child. My father died when I was three. Kind of felt I owed it to my mother."

"That's nice. Loyalty's a lost art these days."

Laura sighed. "I wouldn't have it any other way. I'm painfully aware that tomorrow's guaranteed to no one. My mother's death was a real shock. What I wouldn't give for five more minutes. I have all kinds of questions."

Keith nodded. "I know what you mean. Pop never talked about his life before his mother married Edward Preston. Made me all the more curious about where he grew up."

Laura sighed. "Funny the way that works. When I was little I was always bugging my mother to take me back to see the town where she grew up. She was patient but firm: no way. Over and over she'd tell me how her house burned to the ground when she was seventeen and killed her entire family. She left town shortly after the funerals and refused to go back. I understood her house was gone but I had this fascination with cemeteries. Would have given anything to see where her family was buried. I was especially curious about my mother's twin sister who died when she was two. I admit it was a morbid fascination."

"I agree, but if you're really that curious and you know where they're buried, you can probably look it up on line. Amazing what you can find these days."

"Truthfully, I hadn't thought about it for years but about two weeks ago, I was asked to mentor one of our journalism interns. I'm an investigative reporter. He's trying to identify skeletal remains found under a sixty-five year old hotel. It was so strange. Turns out, my mother's fire story wasn't true and her house was still standing. Kind of blew me away and after all these years, I actually made it to Greenview and got to see what was left of the Abbott Farmstead."

Keith almost choked on his iced tea. "The Abbott farmstead? What's that?"

"My mother grew up on a farm. Her last name was Abbott so they called it the Abbott farmstead. It's pretty cool, about eighty acres a little off the beaten path. John and Ethel owned the farm. They had a son George and a daughter Amelia. My mother's name was MaryAnne but everyone called her Mary. After she married my father she dropped the Mary and went by Anne. Anne Zimmer."

Goddamn, Keith mused. Had he heard correctly? Was Anne Zimmer the Mary Abbott he'd been searching for? No wonder he couldn't find her. His thoughts were racing. He tried not to stare but he couldn't stop himself from mentally comparing Laura's even features to the portrait of a much younger Catherine Preston. The coloring was different but the resemblance was uncanny. No wonder she looked so damn familiar. Keith was struggling for words when Laura's little girl came up the steps. A man wearing a work uniform was right behind her. "Mommy, this man wants to talk to you."

Laura thanked her daughter and then reminded her that she needed to get her bathing suit on. As the little girl headed down the steps, the stranger walked across the room. Laura was about to ream him out for coming into her house without an adult invitation when Keith jumped out of his chair. "Harry!" he cried, relieved for the distraction. They shook hands.

"What are you doing here?" Harry asked. "You need to get off your duff and help us out. That approaching cold front's killing us."

"What cold front? Last time I looked it was hotter than hell outside."

"Right now it is, but just wait. Thursday through Saturday. Even if the Weather Channel is hyping this thing it sounds like a real bummer. Wind, rain and temps low enough to get the bikini crowd cranking up their heaters. Realtors are freaking out, especially after what happened last year."

Keith squinted. "What are you talking about?"

"Had something like this blow in end of summer. Don't you remember?"

"Wasn't here. Remember. I've got a real job mid-August to mid-May."

Harry chuckled. "Oh, yeah. Forgot. Mr. Education. You missed a close one. It got really uncomfortable and people were turning their heaters on left and right. You, of all people, know the issues we have down here with heaters just sitting over the winter and their burners quietly corroding. Almost lost an entire family, carbon monoxide."

"Had no idea."

"They lucked out. No permanent injuries but they're suing the owners and the real estate company. Nothing like a big, fat law suit to shake things up."

"No kidding."

"Realtors are driving Dutch crazy. Don't want a repeat. Got a ton of heaters they want us to inspect, just in case. No excuses."

For a couple of minutes, the two men talked shop. "Better do a good job," Keith warned as the man finally headed toward the steps.

Laura squinted. "You, of all people? What did that man mean?"

"Nothing really. I was still in high school when my grandfather made me get certified as an HVAC technician. I've worked on air conditioners and heaters just about every summer since I was eighteen. Last few years, I got to doing early pre-season checks and uncovered dozens of heaters with dangerously corroded burners. Salted air, heaters not used very much. Bad combination."

"Corroded burners?"

"Yeah. If you don't get a clean burn, carbon monoxide builds. Frankly, I think they're all chasing their tails. A working carbon monoxide sensor is a lot more effective than a hurried inspection. As far as I know most houses, including this one, have sensors on all the sleeping floors and I'm pretty sure the ones in this house are hard wired. Don't worry. If you have a problem, you'll know it."

"Well, I'm glad for that. Do you really think it's going to get that cold?"

Keith shrugged. "Who knows? The Weather Channel hypes everything. I'm guessing it won't get that cold but wind might be an issue. Beautiful houses, not well insulated. It could get uncomfortable."

Laura squinted. "Did that man say Thursday through Saturday?"

"Yeah. Tans might suffer but at least it won't mess with the Fourth. Fireworks down here are spectacular. Have you ever seen them?"

"No. This will be our first. We're really...."

Keith waited. Really what, he wanted to ask. All of a sudden he realized Laura was more interested in what was going on across the room. He turned to see Laura's little girl hurrying in, tugging on her bathing suit.

"Mommy, I'm stuck. These straps are always getting twisted."

"Why don't you wear the pink one?"

"It's still wet."

Keith watched in disbelief as the little girl approached. Having pinned her hair away from her face, she looked very different. She had long legs and a slender torso. Keith had to turn his head as Laura fixed her straps. He was afraid his expression would give him away. It wasn't her body that fixated him. It was the two sparkling barrettes that she had pinned on either side of her head. They appeared to be identical to the ones Catherine had showed him just a short time ago.

Oblivious to Keith's discomfort, Laura fixed the straps and then held her hand out. "The barrettes," she said, waving her fingers.

"But Mom, they look so pretty."

"I know they do but that's not what we agreed to. I told you, you can't wear them until after I get them appraised. Hand them over."

"Will you give them back?"

"Why should I? You broke our agreement. Those things were supposed to stay in your doll's hair, under a bonnet and never to be taken out of the house."

"Grandmom would want me to have them."

"Grandmom would want you to keep your promise. Go get the sunscreen. I'll give you twenty-four hours. If you don't nag, I just might give them back but only under the original agreement."

"Sorry about that," Laura said as her daughter sulked out of the room. "These barrettes have been a thorn in my side. They belonged to my mother when she was little. Didn't know she had them until recently. Sorry. I didn't mean to bother you with my issues."

Keith forced a smile. He didn't dare respond. Mary Abbott, Greenview, Laura's striking resemblance to Catherine. Christ Almighty, he didn't need an elephant to step on his head. "That's okay. I probably should be going. I can see you have your hands full."

As cool as it had been in the house, Keith was sweating profusely by the time he got into his car. He felt tighter than a stretched rubber band. What started out as a pleasant interlude was turning into a disturbing nightmare. Laura Hunter was beautiful and friendly, potentially someone he would enjoy getting to know. Unfortunately, there was little doubt that her mother was the long lost heir to the Preston fortune. No future in that. Even though she seemed to have no idea who she was, getting close to her would be like holding a lit firecracker in your hand and hoping to toss it before it exploded. Christ Almighty. Now what?

Keith was still muttering to himself when he walked into his cottage, the hot, stuffy dump that his grandfather had sentenced him to. He yanked a beer from the refrigerator and plopped down. Goddamn. He had been aware that his inheritance could be affected by Catherine's daughter but he never expected this. He felt an odd sense of relief to know that Mary Abbott was dead but what about Laura and her children? Bad enough they were staying just a stone's throw away but it was downright sickening that they had attracted Catherine's attention.

Keith closed his eyes. Unlike his grandfather and John Abbott, Laura Hunter had no idea of the power she could wield. She had no idea that Catherine Preston was her long lost grandmother and as long as it remained that way, it might be possible for them to peacefully coexist. But for how long? Catherine was so damned unpredictable. She'd already met two of her great grandchildren. What options would he have if she wanted to meet the rest of the family? Today was Tuesday and the day was almost over. That left three more days before Laura and company would make the Saturday exodus and be out of his hair. Given all that was at stake, three days was a lifetime. Once again Keith cursed his situation. Had Catherine already signed on the dotted line, he wouldn't give a damn.

Keith knew he had to keep Catherine and Laura as far apart as possible, but how? He imagined sitting on his hands and hoping that the next three days would pass without incident. *Yeah right*, he told himself. That was a little like dumping ice cubes into boiling water and hoping they wouldn't melt. Somehow he had to come up with a better plan than that.

Three days. For the next three days, he'd be hanging on tenterhooks. He could leave his fate in Catherine's hands or he could come up with a way to eliminate a young mother, her three children and the friend staying with them. He'd have to be ready on a minute's notice and his plan would have to be foolproof. He looked around. This morning, he was certain his days in this dump were numbered. Now a beautiful young woman stood in his way. *Think*, he told himself. *Think.*

Chapter Nineteen

July 4th

Keith Quigley awoke to a string of fireworks exploding somewhere near the lighthouse. He didn't give a damn that it was the Fourth of July. It was too friggin' early for all that noise. Muttering to himself, he rolled over. It happened every year. Tourists, having loaded up with all sorts of pyrotechnics as they passed through Virginia, simply couldn't wait till dark to set off their new toys. He held his breath. Years of experience had taught him that a single round of fireworks was always followed by a second round, kind of like dueling banjos. A short time later, someone on the ocean side of the road answered. Cycle complete. Keith got out of bed.

It was still hot and uncomfortable, but the oppressive humidity seemed to be dissipating. Or maybe Keith was just in an exceptionally good mood and why not? Good things were finally happening. His love life had taken a sharp turn last night; he no longer had to worry about Henry Weinstein screwing things up for him and his long search for Mary Abbott was over. There were still issues, to be sure, but his dream of inheriting the Preston fortune was coming into focus.

Keith was walking past the window when the mansion caught his eye. He loved the way the early morning sunlight illuminated his future home. Smiling, he imagined the day when he would wake up over there, step out onto his balcony and enjoy the view. He would demand that the cook carry his tray up those many steps and serve his breakfast out there. Everyone would cater to his wishes.

Everyone would want to please him, the new master of Whalehead. From peon to prince. Such power.

Relishing the thought, Keith walked into the kitchen to prepare his coffee. For some reason it was never quite as good as the coffee at Whalehead and although he hated to admit it, Keith was a little disturbed that Catherine hadn't invited him to breakfast. For as long as he could remember, she was always in an exceptionally good mood on the Fourth. Then again, maybe she had finally come to respect that he did have a social life, one that could make rising at the crack of dawn somewhat difficult.

Still, there was something about being with Catherine last evening that bothered him. As the coffee brewed, Keith sat down in his grandfather's lounge chair and then clicked on the TV. Catherine had been pleasant enough, but he liked predictable and last night she was anything but. Knowing her the way he did, he fully expected her to regale him with all the boring details of her adventure with the Hunter brats and their damn kite. Instead, she barely mentioned it. She simply asked where he found the replacement and then thanked him for his effort. No questions on whether it was well received or if Laura Hunter gushed over her gesture. As curious as she seemed to be about Laura, she never even asked what she looked like. Was he being paranoid or was Catherine plotting something behind his back?

Trying to decide how to handle Laura Hunter and her children was like walking through a mine field with two very dangerous trip wires: Laura's resemblance to a younger Catherine and those goddamned barrettes. The resemblance might not be such a big issue, given that Catherine believed she had no living relatives, but stepping on those barrettes might cause the explosion from hell. Barrettes. Could something that innocuous really cause major problems or was he just looking for trouble?

Keith rested his head against the back of the recliner. He didn't need this aggravation, not when everything finally seemed to be going his way. He closed his eyes, trying to visualize his future. He was not a greedy man. Of all the Preston holdings, Whalehead was the only one he really cared about. He loved the place so much that once it was his, he might even find a way to stay down here year round. He would have to keep enough of a staff to meet his every need but given the vast Preston fortune, money would be no object. If it got too cold, he would simply jet to a warmer clime.

Whalehead. What might it look like once he took over? What would he do first? Gussy up the grounds or redecorate the house? He opened his eyes. And what about this dump? With him at the mansion, there was no need to keep it. Then again, it was somewhat quaint and it was nicely isolated. Once he fixed it up, it could be the perfect place to bring a guest that he didn't want the house staff or maybe even his wife, to know about.

Whatever he decided to do, Keith knew that his social life would greatly improve once he was the owner of Whalehead. Nothing like a little charm and a copious amount of wealth to turn those pretty heads in his direction. He couldn't wait. Anything would be better than the The Islander, the only nightclub at this end of the island. Keith hated having to compete with all the other guys looking for an easy hook up, and it pissed him off that the women who already knew him often ignored him. Some even had the nerve to advise the newbies to steer clear. For a change, that hadn't happened last night and it felt good to think that his luck was finally turning around.

Smiling, Keith recalled last night's adventure. He had been in an unusually charming mood when he headed over to the Islander. Although he had planned to be fashionably late he was annoyed that the parking lot was jammed. No real surprise. It wasn't a Saturday but it was the night before the Fourth.

As usual, the music was loud and the drinks were flowing. Keith was just about to down his first drink when a pretty young thing approached him. They drank, they dined and they danced. It had cost Keith a fortune but as they closed down the club, Cinderella seemed intrigued by his invitation to join him later tonight to watch the fireworks at the exclusive Whalehead gazebo. She had even keyed her number directly into his contacts so that, given all the noise, there would be no misunderstanding.

The coffee maker beeped. About time, Keith mused, getting up to make himself some scrambled eggs and toast. If tonight came close to meeting his expectations, he would need his strength. He returned to his grandfather's recliner, placed his breakfast tray on his lap and mentally planned his day. Given the growing chatter about an approaching cold front, Keith figured it would be wise to check the heaters at the gazebo. Even on the hottest days it could become uncomfortably cool after dark and the last thing he wanted was to have his cute little chick wrapped tightly in a blanket.

Once again, Keith imagined all that could happen tonight. Cinderella was nothing like the bitch from the bicycle shop. She had approached him and was clearly into him even before he told her that he lived at Whalehead. At this very moment, she was probably bragging to her friends that her date for tonight was not only drop dead gorgeous, but that they would be making their own fireworks at the Whalehead gazebo.

Surprised by how quickly he wolfed down his food, Keith brought his empty tray into the kitchen. He showered, dressed and then headed down to the gazebo to check the heaters. As much as he wanted to call his potential playmate, he figured it best to wait until he was sure he could get the heaters up and running. It also didn't hurt to make her squirm, to make her wait until he contacted her. She was probably carrying her phone around waiting for his call. It felt so good to be in control.

As he neared the gazebo, Keith heard what sounded like a vacuum cleaner. "What the hell," he muttered. The Whalehead gazebo was probably the only one on the entire island with a janitor's closet. Just as he walked up the steps, he saw someone from the grounds crew stocking the refrigerator with boxes of both white and chocolate milk as well as cans of coke and root beer. "What's going on?" he asked.

"For tonight. The fireworks party," the middle-aged man answered. "We'll be out of your way as soon as we put the bunting on the roof."

"The bunting?" Keith asked, suddenly aware of the packages of red, white and blue fabric.

"Fireworks. Mrs. Preston is very excited. Wants to make sure those kids have a wonderful time."

"What kids?"

The man shrugged. "All's I know is she met them yesterday."

"Hey boss," one of the workers called. "This heater. Can't get it to turn on."

No kidding, Keith mused. He'd been watching the man screw up the ignition sequence but decided not to say anything. "Shoulda checked that first, man. Been having problems with these things. Even if you can get them to turn on, they might not be safe to use."

"But we need 'em. You know how Mrs. Preston hates to be cold. Can you do something?"

Keith walked over to the heater. Of course he could do something, but why would he? Catherine hadn't had the decency to let him know that she planned to use the gazebo. She hadn't even considered that he might want to use it. Even worse, she was clearly chumming it up with Laura

Hunter. Keith made a feeble attempt to turn the heater on. "Looks like its busted. Sorry."

The man's walkie talkie went off. It was his supervisor. "You guys about ready to wrap it up? I need you by the fish pond."

"Almost. Still got the bunting and the heaters. Having a hell of a problem getting these damn things to turn on."

"Don't worry about it. Party's off. Sick kid."

"Still want us to hang the bunting?"

"Nah. Tourists might take it as an open invitation. By the way. Seen Quigley around?"

"Yeah, he's right here."

"Good. Tell him Mrs. Preston wants him at the big house asap."

"Roger. Tell her he's on his way."

The man turned to Keith. "Hear that?"

"Yeah, I heard it and just so you know, I can speak for myself."

The worker gestured surrender. "Sorry, man. Didn't mean nothing by it."

Keith stormed away. The walk to the big house from the gazebo was approximately twice as long as the walk from the cottage and it gave Keith time to calm down, to figure it all out. Catherine had gone behind his back and he wanted to know why. Was it because of his behavior toward those brats? Could she still be holding it against him? He apologized, for God's sake. What the hell else did she want?

As the mansion came into view, Keith took out his phone. He needed something to temper his mood and since he was confident that he could get the heaters going, he decided to confirm tonight's festivities. He flipped to contacts, tapped his latest addition and then listened. Barely a full ring and the call went through. A good sign. His new friend was as eager as he was.

Keith was about to say something when he realized he was listening to a recording. The number his little princess had keyed into his phone was not a working line. He stopped dead in his tracks. He was pissed, really pissed. It had happened again.

Taking a deep breath, Keith looked around. *Focus,* he told himself. *Focus.* A few steps later a sense of relief washed over him. As much as he hated to admit it, Laura Hunter was weighing heavily on his mind. What if his growing obsession with her became a drag on his performance? Better to put his love life on hold than to make an ass of himself. Better to wait until Hunter was out of the picture, until Catherine officially named him heir. From that day on, all the bitches who ever rejected him would rue their stupidity. He would be king and they would all be lapping at his feet. Sweet.

As he neared the house, Keith could see that Catherine was sitting on the veranda. She was wearing her reading glasses and seemed very intent as she flipped through what seemed to be a short packet of papers. Could it be, he wondered. Was she finally ready to make the appropriate changes to her will? Was this why it was so urgent that she see him?

Catherine welcomed him warmly. "Just the man I wanted to see. Sit. I've sent Theresa in to get you an iced tea. Is that okay? Would you like anything else?"

"No, iced tea would be fine." He pointed to her papers. "You look busy."

Catherine looked down. She closed the folder she'd been sorting through. "Menus. Just trying to get ideas." She leaned closer as if what she was about to tell him was a classified secret. "I'm so glad you came over. I've got good news and bad news. Mrs. Hunter called right after you left last evening, to thank me for the kite. We were having such a nice conversation and I realized how nice it would be to actually meet her so I invited her to bring her children and her friend to the gazebo tonight to watch the fireworks."

"That was nice," Keith lied.

"I thought so too but unfortunately that's not going to happen. Mrs. Hunter called a short time ago to let me know her little one isn't feeling well and that they won't be able to come. Poor Edwardo. He's been working like a dog to get the gazebo ready."

Keith feigned concerned. "What a shame. The kid. Nothing serious I hope."

"Sore throat, fever. Mrs. Hunter didn't sound terribly concerned. Matter of fact she seemed to be more worried about this storm. These weather people. Honestly I don't understand them. This constant drumbeat of doom and gloom. They keep this up and half the tourists will be checking out first thing in the morning."

"Probably not a bad idea. If we get as much rain as they say, the main road outta here will be impassable Thursday night into Friday night."

Catherine brought her index finger up to her lips. "Shhh. That's exactly what I'm hoping for. If Mrs. Hunter's little boy is feeling better in the morning, she plans to head for home, to get ahead of this storm. If he's not, and this storm comes in as they say, she figures she'll be stuck here until Saturday. Fingers crossed. If that happens, she's agreed to come for brunch on Friday."

The very idea made Keith ill. "Friday? Why not Saturday?" he asked hoping to buy more time.

"Because Saturday's departure day and you know how bad traffic gets. Mrs. Hunter was firm. If she's still here on that day, she plans to leave at the crack of dawn. Today's Wednesday so we have two more days. I'm trying not to panic but there are so many things I want to get done."

Keith couldn't believe his ears. In his mind, Catherine meeting Laura Hunter was a recipe for disaster.

If Mother Nature didn't keep it from happening, he'd have to find a way. "I'm not sure I understand. Are you asking me to help you prepare for a brunch that might or might not happen?"

"Don't be such a curmudgeon. Theresa and I will take care of the food, but I need you to make sure the house is comfortable. Start with the furnace. Even if it doesn't get as cold as they say, the wind alone will make this place unbearable. I don't mind throwing on a shawl or an extra blanket but I won't do that to my guests. We don't have a moment to lose. You know how long it takes for this house to heat up."

"Actually I don't. I haven't been down here past the middle of August since I finished high school. Pop was a master at opening and closing this place. Sometimes I think it annoyed him that I arrived after everything was up and running and left before it had to be shut down."

"Well, I'm afraid we had some issues with the heater this year when we first got down here, but then it got so warm that we didn't bother with it. Your grandfather had a plan but I don't know what it was. You'll have to figure that out and you'll have to be quick about it. These weather people. Maybe it's just the power of suggestion but I'm already feeling a bit chilly. I can count on you, can't I?"

Keith hesitated. Helping Catherine meet her long lost granddaughter was a little like digging his own grave. Then again, somehow he'd think of something; he always did. "Of course, but it's an old heater and we might have a problem if we need parts."

"Do whatever you have to do. Just get it going. Like I said. Theresa and I will take care of the food but when you're done with the furnace, I need you to call Happy Hippo and have them send over a few age appropriate toys for the children. Whatever you think they'll like. You did such a great job on the kite."

Keith stifled a groan. He was grateful when the cook stepped onto the veranda. She seemed rather somber. She placed a glass of iced tea in front of Keith and then turned to Catherine. "I'm afraid the light's out in my oven. Would you mind if Keith took a look?"

What the hell, Keith muttered to himself as he followed the rotund woman into the kitchen. Since when did he get his marching orders from the cook? He walked over to the oven and was about to ream her out when she opened the oven door. The light went on.

"Shh," she said, raising her finger to her lips. "There's nothing wrong with the light. We need to talk. I...I hate to say this but I think Mrs. Preston has flipped. I've known her for a very long time and I just don't understand her fascination with this Mrs. Hunter. It's all she's been talking about. Something weird is going on in her head and I'm really worried. You've got to do something before she makes a complete fool of herself."

Keith was spooked. "A complete fool? That's a little harsh. Does she know how concerned you are?"

"I've tried to talk to her but she just looks at me like I have three heads and then she starts rambling about that little girl and about how much she reminds her of Marney. You ready for this? I heard her ask Hazel to shine up Marney's barrettes. You've probably never seen them. Scottie dogs. Mr. Preston had them specially made for her second birthday. They're platinum with real gemstones, worth a small fortune. She's kept them in a box on her vanity table for years, like a shrine. This is what's really making me crazy. She told Hazel that she's thinking of giving those barrettes to that little girl. Can you imagine? Giving her most prized possession to a perfect stranger."

The alarm bells clanging in Keith's head were getting louder. Even if Catherine didn't give those stupid barrettes away, just showing them to Laura would be disastrous. His thoughts were racing. "That's insane. We can't let her do that."

"Well, this is all your fault. You started it and now you're going to have to stop it."

"Started it? What the hell you talking about?"

Theresa shrugged. "Some letter you found with your grandfather's things. Somehow it finally convinced Mrs. Preston that Marney is never coming back. You have to stop her. You can't let her give those barrettes away. She'll regret it for the rest of her life."

"No kidding," Keith replied. He promised to talk to Catherine although he had no idea what he would say.

"Well, talk fast," Theresa replied. "And while you're at it, see if you can derail this silly brunch. Last thing I want to do is to cook up a storm for perfect strangers."

"I'd rather do that than crawl around in that damn basement just to get the heater going."

Theresa gestured surrender. "Okay, okay, you win. You're definitely getting the raw end of the stick. Hang tough. Let's see what tomorrow brings."

Keith sighed. He could only hope that by tomorrow, the Hunter brat would be feeling better. With just a little luck, Laura would be on her way home and the crisis would be averted. Yet despite the reprieve, the reality wouldn't change. A beautiful woman had become a fly buzzing around his soup, a meal he'd waited his whole life for. How many times could he swat her away? Would she keep coming back? Would she eventually land in his soup and ruin everything? Goddamn. Just when things were going so well.

Keith returned to the veranda and sat down. Catherine smiled warmly. Keith forced himself to reciprocate. He knew damn well that once the old biddy met her long lost granddaughter she'd cast him aside like a spoiled fish head. His thoughts racing, Keith downed the last of his tea and then got up from his chair. "That furnace. You'll have to excuse me. No telling how long it'll take me to get that relic to work."

"Right, right," Catherine replied. "I knew I could count on you."

Keith nodded politely and then turned to leave. He didn't trust himself to say anything. Catherine had once counted on his grandfather and now she was counting on him. He feared the outcome would be the same as much as he feared it wouldn't.

By the time Keith reached the cottage, the ugly truth had become painfully clear. Laura Hunter could ruin everything for him in the same way that his grandfather, John Abbott and Henry Weinstein could have, with one difference. Laura wasn't looking to destroy him. She didn't even know that she could. Dare he wait till she figured that out, or should he preemptively eliminate her?

Racked by indecision, Keith changed his clothes and grabbed his tool box. Needing time to think, he walked back to the big house. The tool box was heavy and it weighed him down. Sixty-five years ago, his grandfather had committed an unthinkable crime and for sixty-five years Catherine acted as if he walked on water. It wasn't fair. It simply wasn't fair. Now he had to deal with the repercussions. Why hadn't he ratted on his old man when he had the chance?

Keith unlocked the basement door and stepped inside. "Jesus Christ," he muttered. It was cold, dark and dank. He walked over to the massive furnace and slammed his tool box onto a nearby bench. "Sonofabitch," he whispered, to no one in particular. What the hell was he doing? He was the future heir to Whalehead and yet somehow he was supposed to bring this piece of crap to life so that the one person who could ruin his future would be comfortable. There had to be a better way. There just had to be.

Chapter Twenty

July 4th

Dave Schubert loved the Fourth of July. He loved the history, the parades, the barbecues, the fireworks and in recent times, he loved the idea of taking some time off. Too bad that won't be happening today, he mused. Instead he was on his way back to Greenview to help his grandmother pour through undelivered letters recently discovered at her soon to be demolished post office. Why, he wondered, had he agreed help with this boring project when he could be spending the day at his girlfriend's seaside home?

Dave glanced over at his girlfriend, now sound asleep in the passenger seat. He and Julie had gotten up at the crack of dawn so that they could be in Greenview by noon. It had been a relatively pleasant ride but now it had gotten a little too quiet. "Jules," Dave whispered, hoping she would wake up. She looked so peaceful, so perfect and on top of that, she had actually been looking forward to their little adventure. Clearly she was a keeper. Who else would give up a day at the shore for a hot, stuffy post office? "Jules," he whispered again. She didn't move.

"Damn," Dave muttered. The first leg of their journey had been fun. It began with a stop at the local convenience store where, not surprisingly, Julie immediately began ranking on the items Dave selected for his breakfast. While she picked out fresh fruit and spring water, Dave bought two breakfast burritos, a large coffee and a box of donuts to sustain himself on their long ride. Julie feigned horror at Dave's choices and after a halfhearted lecture on nutrition, she asked for a bite of his burrito. A mini food fight ensued, ending with a knocked over cup of coffee and a spontaneous kiss.

Dave chuckled as he downed the last of his coffee. Luckily, during their food fight, the cup had landed in his lap and the lid had remained intact. He did have a tiny dark stain on his shorts but they had both agreed he had gotten a lucky break.

In a way Dave was grateful that Julie was asleep. The coffee was now a good three hours old and she always made such a fuss whenever he insisted on finishing it. "Good to the last drop, my eye," she would say, sticking her finger in her mouth and pretending to gag. "I don't understand how you could do that. You use creamer. It spoils. One of these days you're going to get violently ill."

Breakfast had put them both in an expansive mood. They laughed and joked about the silly things they had done as kids to celebrate the fourth. They talked about family, about friends and about their future. As some point, Julie took her sandals off, propped her pedicured feet on the dashboard, coaxed her seat to a more comfortable position and then closed her eyes. "Wake me up when we get there," she had joked.

Dave sighed. Julie was either incredibly naïve or incredibly gracious. She had actually been looking forward to helping his grandmother with her post office project. "It's so romantic," she had told him. "All those letters that have never been delivered. I don't understand why you're not the least bit curious. If we get even one single letter into the hands of its rightful recipient, it'll be worth it."

Worth it, Dave mused. That was the same thing he thought two months ago when he started his investigation. So much promise: his senior year and the perfect story had been dumped in his lap, one that would write his ticket to either a fabulous internship or to a well paying job. The remote town of Greenview, skeletal remains. At first it felt good to be one of the many reporters who had flocked to the scene, all hoping to learn more about the female body that had been dumped at a construction site sometime before October 15, 1945. First buzzkill: the victim was from out of town. Second buzzkill: the mass exodus of reporters. Maybe it was naïve of him to hone in on that ring and to convince himself that the design had to be a family crest. Weeks later he finally realized what everyone else already had. Jane Doe would probably remain Jane Doe.

Dave sighed as he recalled the past few days. New York, the jeweler who specialized in family crests. So much hope. Dashed. Barrettes—unique, expensive as all get out but with no useful markings. Dashed again. Brilliant cemetery drawings—not so brilliant after all. Hard not to feel like a punching bag that was losing air, easy to knock down but hard to get up. Still, he hadn't been ready to call it quits, at least not until the DNA came back. Surely a positive result would bolster his case. Didn't happen. Jane Doe and Laura Hunter were not related. Hard to rebound from that one.

Thanks to E-Z pass, Dave breezed through the interchange. He was turning onto the two lane road that would take them to the town of Greenview, when Julie punched him in the arm. "I didn't hear it," she said. "Thank you for insisting I get E-Z Pass."

"Ah, Sleeping Beauty awakens."

"I didn't hear it. You can say it. It's easy. T-h-a-n-k…"

"Are you kidding? We were the only car at the toll. Essentially I just wasted twelve dollars, a dollar for each month I have that stupid pass."

"You just wasted three cents and that's dividing 1 by thirty and not thirty-one. Three cents won't break the budget. You should do the math before you complain."

"Yeah, yeah, yeah," he replied. "You still want to see the Abbott Farmstead?"

Julie repositioned her seat so she could get a better look out the window. "Of course. The farmstead, the cemetery and the construction site. Whatever order works best."

"Well, look to your right. We're coming up to the construction site. I'm afraid there's not much left to see. One of the first things they did when work resumed was to fill in the pit where they found Jane's remains. They did such a great job of leveling the ground that you can't even guess where the hotel once stood."

Julie craned her neck to see. "God, that is so weird. This whole thing. A body being there all this time. Who would have thought? It's so peaceful up here."

"The cemetery's on your left. We can stop there now or on the way back. What do you think?"

"On the way back. I'm dying to see the farmstead."

"You got it," Dave replied, pulling onto the deeply rutted driveway that led to the Abbott farmhouse. He turned to Julie. "The house was a little further down but this is as far as I dare go. We'll have to walk the rest of the way. Just be careful. These pot holes are deeper than they look."

They reached the pile of charred timber. The acrid smell that hung in the air just a short time ago was barely noticeable. Julie was bummed. "Good thing you took those pictures when you had the chance. The setting here is beautiful. I didn't know John Abbott but I feel sorry for him. Sitting on a gold mine but living in squalor. Two weeks decomposing on his living room floor. That's so sad. What do you think will happen here? Will Mrs. Hunter claim the estate?"

Dave shrugged. "Not sure what she plans to do. She mentioned several legal issues that need to be addressed. At this point, it's not my problem."

Julie refused to leave until she saw the stream behind the house and the wooded path that led to Neeka's. "Good enough," she said as they got into the car. "You look so glum. Don't tell me you're still planning to bail.

I'm telling you, that's a mistake. The DNA could be wrong. It happens, you know."

"Yeah and so does winning the mega millions. Look, Jules. I screwed up. Laura had some doubts about Jane Doe being her grandmother and she was right. I honed in on the wrong family."

"You don't know that. So there was a second entrance to the cemetery. That doesn't mean the Abbotts aren't your family. I don't get you. Why are you throwing out the entire puzzle just because you don't have all the pieces?"

"I'm throwing the puzzle out because it sucks."

They headed for the car. Julie grabbed Dave's arm and pulled him along. "Let's move it. It's almost noon. I don't want to keep your grandmother waiting but I don't want to skimp on the cemetery either. Tombstones. Did I ever tell you how much they fascinate me? The older the better."

"Great. I'm in love with a cemetery crawler. I knew it. I knew there was something weird about you the moment we met."

The ride to the cemetery was a short one. They got out of the car to copious sunshine and oppressive humidity. Dave led Julie over to the Abbott tombstone. "Take as much time as you want. My grandmother won't mind having to wait and if you get this out of your system now, you won't insist we come back. On the plus side, for every minute that we're late, we get a little more time to breathe normally. Trust me. It's going to be suffocating inside that post office."

"Oh, stop complaining," Julie replied, studying the tombstones. "This is so cool. I don't care what you say. I really think you're onto something." She made a visor with her right hand and peered across the road. "Look. The construction site is almost a direct line from here. That second entrance would have been way too far down. I doubt a woman running from there would have run to the construction site. I'm telling you, this is your gravesite. I don't care what those cops say. They're just jealous because you saw something they didn't. I would love to see the look on their faces when you identify Jane Doe."

Smiling, Dave reached for a strand of hair that had fallen out of Julie's clip. He gently lifted it off her face and then slipped it behind her ear. "You amaze me. You never give up. Everything's sunshine and roses. I just hope you feel that way after spending several hours in that damn post office. Did I mention it isn't airconditioned?"

"Several times." Julie stepped closer to Dave. Standing tip toed, she brought her lips to his ear. "Why do you think I'm wearing this halter top?" She started to unbutton his collared shirt. "You know I think it's really nice that you agreed not to wear one of those wife beaters. You know how much I hate those things but I have to admit. I'm going to be much cooler than you. What do you think we should do?"

Dave was wildly distracted. "Well, if you help me out of my shirt, I'll help you out of yours. That would be one way to make this afternoon a little more interesting."

"I'm game," Julie said as she nibbled on Dave's ear. "But don't forget, your grandmother is the only one with clearance and she's required to be with us at all times."

"Killjoy," Dave replied, opening Julie's door. He muttered to himself as he walked around the car and then got in. He started the car and turned the air conditioner on full blast. "I still can't believe we're going to be spending the best part of the day inside that stupid post office. How my grandmother gets herself involved in these things, I'll never know."

"You ought to be happy she stays involved, especially at her age. Besides, I don't care what you say. The Fourth of July is the perfect day to try to bring people together. It's so romantic."

"You say that because you haven't seen this post office. Trust me. This is a race against time. They're tearing it down before it falls on itself."

Several hours later, Dave and Julie were speeding back to Philadelphia, not only because they wanted to catch the fireworks but because of something Dave was sure could be far more explosive—a letter, written in German, dated October 10, 1945. "Your roommate," Dave said. "Do you really think she could translate that letter?"

"I've already left two messages. She's not answering her phone."

"Try again."

"Stop! I'm as excited as you are but there's a limit. I can't keep bugging Audrey and I guarantee she's not going to drop everything and come home to translate this letter."

"We can scan it and email it."

"Oh please. Put yourself in her position. How would you like to be an exchange student who hasn't seen her boyfriend for months? Would you waste your time translating a letter that could wait a few more hours? Besides, if she's not answering her phone, she's not going to answer her email."

"Yeah, yeah, yeah, I know you're right but if this letter was written by the woman we've been trying to identify, it would be a coup, an incredible coup."

"True but if it's a coup tonight, it'll be coup in a few more days. Besides. A woman named Rosa Berman wrote this letter. I still don't understand how you can connect Rosa Berman to Linda Ferina?"

"Are you kidding? That's what has me so convinced I'm on the right track. I dated a girl in high school and for almost two years I thought her name was Linda. Picture this: graduation. We're all seated in alphabetical order and frankly, there were only two names that I was listening for: hers and mine. Her last name was Bennett so I didn't have to wait too long but when they announced her name, I didn't know who they were talking about. Do you know what her real name was? Rosalinda. She wanted to make sure no one ever call her Rose or Rosa so she told everyone her name was Linda. Linda Ferina could have done the same thing."

Julie chuckled. "You dated someone named Rosalinda? For two years? What happened to her?"

"Linda. She called herself Linda. She went to California after high school. Wanted to become an actress. Met some dude who had the same ambitions she did. Haven't heard from her since."

"An actress?" Julie shrugged. "Well, she has the right last name. I'll have to watch for her."

"Stop! I only brought her up to prove that Linda Ferina and Rosa Berman could be the same person."

"I doubt that," Julie replied. "So far the only thing Linda and Rosa have in common is their internet presence: zilch. Nothing on either one of them, at least nothing that fits your timeline. It's time to chill."

"Okay, okay. Just try Audrey one more time. I'm dying to know what that letter says."

"I know you are but she'll call back when she's ready. Look, if you're so desperate, maybe you should try the language lab. Someone there has to be proficient in German."

"Already thought about that. The lab is closed for the holiday and won't be open till Monday. Maybe I could download a translation program."

"Really? In case you forgot, today's the Fourth of July. Independence Day, freedom. We just spent the entire day in a hot, stuffy post office. I'm not complaining but I think we should reward ourselves. This will be a great night for fireworks, first at Penn's landing and then who knows? Ask yourself, how often do we get the apartment to ourselves?"

Dave smiled. "Well, if you put it that way. Just one thing. Let's go to Forest Hills tomorrow, to the address on the envelope. I'll check Google Earth to make sure the place still exists."

Julie sighed. "I'll think about it but under two conditions: you don't mention Audrey's name tonight and you don't make me get up at the crack of dawn."

"Deal," Dave replied. As he reached over to grab her hand, he noticed how loose her halter top had become. *Goddamn*, he mused, staring at her cleavage. All of a sudden he realized how nice it would be to get home, to an empty apartment, no roommate, no distractions. Fireworks before Penn's Landing and fireworks after. Julie was right. A little time off was exactly what they needed.

Chapter Twenty-One

July 4th

Keith Quigley stepped into his shower. His skin was crawling. He had just finished servicing the heater at the big house. Dirt, grease, thousand leggers, spider webs. It was disgusting. Had he known the job would have been such a pain in the ass, he would have farmed it out. He might be the best HVAC technician on the island but the heater at Whalehead didn't need brilliance. It needed replacing. Of course, he had gotten it to work but he couldn't guarantee for how long.

He washed his hair. He scrubbed his nails. A new heater. One more thing to add to the list of changes he would have to make. How could his grandfather have let it get that bad? True, Catherine was a naturalist. If it was too hot, she would open the windows. If it got too cold she would close them. She hated air conditioning and only used it for the comfort of her staff. No matter how humid it got, she always slept with her bedroom windows open.

Shaking his head, Keith wrapped himself in a towel. His grandfather was an idiot. If he'd had any brains, he would have told him that there were issues with the heater, but then again, the old bastard rarely spoke to him about anything constructive. If he wasn't criticizing him, he had nothing to say. At least that chapter of his life was over.

Keith grabbed a beer and then plopped onto his grandfather's recliner. He often wondered what Whalehead was like in September. For years he heard the locals brag about how spectacular it was to be on the Outer Banks at that time and finally he'd have the chance to see for himself. From a financial perspective, quitting his teaching job might not have been such a brilliant idea. He had no money, no income, and at the rate he was spending money, by September his credit cards would be maxed out. If Catherine didn't come through soon, he'd be in big trouble.

Catherine. He hated that she was so damn unpredictable. He wanted to believe that even if she met Laura Hunter and even if she actually noticed how much Laura looked like her in her younger days that nothing would come of it. Given that etiquette programmed her every move, she would probably convince herself that it was just her imagination.

Too bad he wasn't as confident about those damn barrettes. Would Catherine really give them to that little brat or was Theresa just playing with his head? He wouldn't put it past her. When his grandfather was alive, she barely noticed him. Now, all of a sudden, she was sharing secrets. Why should he trust her?

Keith downed his beer. He couldn't believe he wasted half the day trying to get the heater going and for what. So that Catherine would have a comfortable place to invite her long lost granddaughter? Why hadn't he told her that getting the heater to run was impossible and that it might even be dangerous? It would have been a seamless way to get her to abort her plans. Stupid, stupid, stupid. He had overlooked a perfect opportunity, not because he didn't want to disappoint Catherine but because if he didn't fix that stupid thing, he'd disappoint himself.

It was getting late and Keith was starving. After spending the day in a dark and dank basement, he realized that he was craving pulled pork and hush puppies. Finishing his beer, he got up to check his wallet. Although Carol's Café had the best pulled pork on the island, it was an antiquated hole in the wall that only accepted cash. Keith smiled. Tax included, he had just enough.

Not wanting to draw attention to himself, Keith took his own car, a brown Toyota with twice as many dings as rust spots. He ordered his food to go, paid for it and then headed over to the brew thru. He was in line debating whether he should buy one case of beer or two when someone in the car next to him called his name. He looked over to see a man wearing a familiar HVAC uniform. "Harry! What the hell you doing here?"

"Same thing you are, only difference is I work for a living."

"So do I. Spent the whole day trying to get the heater at Whalehead going. Only real difference is I didn't get paid."

"Too bad. Dutch is driving me crazy. Can't really complain. Double time. By the way, everything all right between you two?"

Keith shrugged. "Saw him at Pop's funeral. He seemed okay. Why?"

"Just wonderin'. After I saw you at Gatekeeper, I suggested he give you a call. We're swamped. Could use an extra hand. Told me to mind my own business."

"Crusty bastard. He'd cut his nose off to spite his face."

"Yeah, too bad. Could really use your help. You didn't hear this from me but we're wasting our time. Tomorrow's gonna turn to shit and anyone's who listening to those weather idiots will hightail it outta here first thing in the morning. You know how these things go. Everyone loves us when the sun is shining. A few raindrops and we're like the plague. All these houses we're bustin' our humps for, they'll be empty."

Keith's line was moving faster than Harry's. "Yeah, but your wallet will be thicker."

"Tell that to my wife. She's bitchin' cause I'm not around."

"Catch you later," Keith called as he pulled forward. There were two cars ahead of him. "Goddamn," he muttered. Dutch. Why hadn't the old prick given him a call? He was smarter and faster than all his techs combined. What the hell was his problem? The line moved again.

One case or two? Keith couldn't decide. He couldn't decide and he couldn't concentrate. Dutch had gotten under his skin. Corroded burners. Last year the man was kissing his ass because of all the new sales his "discovery" had generated. Now he was dissing him. Two faced bastard.

Keenly aware of his financial squeeze, Keith decided to play it safe and order one case of beer. Taking a deep breath, he waited impatiently for his credit card to clear. What the hell was taking so long? Maybe he was just on edge. Was it possible that his old man had opened his big mouth? That vial. He never should have left it where the self righteous prick could find it. Instead of congratulating him for his brilliance, he made like he was outraged. Keith had been so careful about everything else. He only "discovered" the corrosion in houses that were winterized and whose heaters were infrequently used—conditions that could very well create a hostile environment.

All the way home, Keith tried to convince himself that his grandfather wouldn't have said anything. Yeah, they didn't get along. Yeah, he and Dutch were friends but to snitch on his own flesh and blood? In any event, he was pissed with his grandfather and he was pissed with his former boss. Somehow he would get even.

The beer wasn't as cold as he wanted it to be and his dinner was only lukewarm. The cottage stunk like an abandoned fun house and it only added to Keith's discontent. Dutch, his grandfather, Laura Hunter. Their faces were all swirling before his eyes like a nonstop eddy and it was making him sick. Was Hunter staying or going? Had his grandfather badmouthed him? Had Dutch grown suspicious of the work he had done? He wanted answers and he wanted them now. He'd begun this goddamned day feeling upbeat. Now he felt like shit.

Somewhere between finishing his pork and realizing his hush puppies were all gone, the idea came to him. It was so simple that Keith was annoyed with himself for not thinking of it sooner. He knew exactly how he could stick it to his old boss. All he needed was for Laura Hunter to stay put and for the weather to actually get miserable enough for people to turn their heaters on.

The idea began to mushroom. His old boss had been hired to inspect heaters but what if his poor, overworked HVAC tech screwed up? What if he failed to detect a corroded burner? What if someone actually got sick from carbon monoxide poisoning? What if someone died? What if it happened in a house that Dutch had serviced? Even better, what if it happened at Gatekeeper?

Keith got up to get himself another beer. Too energized to sit, he paced the floor. His palms were sweating, his heart racing. Could it be that the perfect storm had just been dropped in his lap? Would it really get miserable enough for the idiots down here to turn their heaters on? Would the weather forecasters actually get this one right? Time for an update.

Grabbing the remote, Keith clicked the TV on and then waited impatiently for the latest forecast. Several minutes later, Keith was still staring at the TV. He really didn't give a damn that they might see record breaking cold for this time of year. Big deal. It was July, not December. The important thing was that this front would more than likely make it windy and miserable, cold enough for even the diehards to run to their thermostats and turn up their heat. This was almost too good to be true.

Gatekeeper. How hard would it be to rig that heater, a heater that his old boss was on record for having serviced? Stupid prick. Maybe he shouldn't have forced his overworked technician to take on so many jobs. Who could blame the poor guy for not noticing a corroded burner? He was just a cog in a wheel. The responsibility would fall directly on Dutch's shoulders. He would bear the blame if Laura and everyone in her house got deathly sick or even better, if they all croaked.

His thoughts racing, Keith took a deep breath. A chill ran through his body from head to toe. He could ruin his old boss and eliminate the last and final threat to his inheritance in the process. What a rush. Properly executed, Laura and her family would die peacefully in their sleep. No one would suffer and, best of all, no one would know that he was the one responsible.

But could he do it? Could he really do it? A young mother, her three children and a friend who happened to be in the wrong place at the wrong time; did they deserve to die? They were not like his old man, like John Abbott or Henry Weinstein. They really hadn't done anything to him, yet.

Cool your jets, Keith told himself. Whether Laura Hunter stayed or whether she'd be like the rest of the short ballers and head for home, there was no time for indecision. His plan to flood Gatekeeper with lethal levels of carbon monoxide had to be flawless and his margin for error was non-existent. Properly executed this would be the perfect way to secure his future.

No doubt rigging the furnace would be the easy part. With the help of his corrosive mixture, he could make the furnace burn inefficiently and cause it to emit deadly amounts of carbon monoxide. But what about the sensors? In the past, he'd actually serviced the system at Gatekeeper and he remembered that there were three sensors, one on each floor. He'd have to find a way to render them useless. The fix would have to be temporary and easily reversible, but how?

Cutting the wires was out. It would be too hard to splice them back together so that no one would notice. That left the gas inlet. He had to find a way to keep the noxious gas from getting through the inlet. *Think*, he told himself. There had to be something he could put over the inlet, something that would go unnoticed, something easy to remove. The seal didn't have to be air tight, just good enough to buy precious time. Once everyone was unconscious, it wouldn't matter how loudly the sensors beeped.

It caught his eye just as he tossed his empty beer can into the trash. Amid the clutter on the counter sat a roll of white duct tape. Of course. Easy on, easy off and easy to go unnoticed. It was simple yet brilliant. Now all he needed was a plan for getting into the house.

Keith jumped as a string of firecrackers went off. Christ Almighty. It was hard enough to concentrate. He needed to get out; catch a whiff of fresh air; brace himself for the barrage of fireworks that would soon follow. The Islander? Nah. He was in no mood to socialize. The beach? Yeah, right. Just what he wanted to see; all those people milling around, glad to be spending time together. The gazebo? Bingo. Dark, isolated. He could bring a few beers and sit there all by himself.

He changed his clothes and combed his hair. He splashed on some cologne and then walked over to the table where his kept his wallet and his cell phone. "Holy shit," he muttered as he picked it up. He had a text. It was from the cook. "You need to do something. This is getting out of hand."

"Dammit," he muttered. What the hell was Catherine up to now?

He stepped outside. It was a beautiful night for fireworks. Cool and comfortable. The sky was growing darker by the minute and Keith knew from experience that those waiting for the show to begin would not be disappointed. In his mind, this was the best show around, especially the finale: a solid two minutes where the entire sky for as far as the eye could see would be alight with brilliant colors and dazzling configurations, to say nothing of the constant ear popping explosions.

Hoping his time with Catherine would be brief, Keith traversed the soft, green grass. Most days he entered the big house from the veranda, but at night, those doors were locked. Taking the service entrance which led directly into the kitchen, Keith cringed at the strange odor. The minute he saw Catherine, he stopped dead in his tracks. There she was, wearing an apron. Her perfectly coiffed hair was disheveled and her lipstick had long since faded. She was standing at the stove, stirring the contents of a rather large pot. Her frazzled look vanished the minute she saw Keith. "Keith, my dear. You timed that perfectly. I need someone to taste this."

Jesus Christ, Keith mused, craning his neck to see what was in the pot. "What is it?"

Catherine feigned insult. "Chicken noodle soup, minus the noodles. I'll put them in later." She filled a medium sized ladle and then brought it to his lips. "Here. Give it a try."

Keith blew on the ladle, giving himself a chance to see what he was about to eat. Surprisingly it wasn't that bad. "I'm not a soup lover but this is pretty good."

"Thank you. It's the celery and onions. Sweetens the chicken and the broth. I plan to add wide noodles. I know most people use the thinner ones but I like my soup to be hearty."

Keith looked around. He could care less about noodles. "Where's Theresa?"

"She's off, thank God. I love her dearly but she thinks she's the only one qualified to work in this kitchen. When I told her what I wanted to do, she offered to stay and help. I think she was a little put out that I refused. Good thing Dr. Winston came by when he did."

"Dr. Winston? What was he doing here?"

Catherine waved her hand in dismissal. "He came to check on me."

"But I thought he was a pediatrician. Doesn't he run that clinic?"

"He does. Such a kind man. I've known him all his life. His grandmother and I were dear friends."

"Check on you for what?"

"Sore throat. The Hunter children. Now all of them are sick. Apparently the older two have gotten what the little one has. Might be strep. Mrs. Hunter told Joe that I spent some time with Scott and Sara and she's worried I may have been exposed. Joe is going to see the children tomorrow. He'll call me if they test positive. Mrs. Hunter is so sweet to worry about an old lady she's never even met. Making this soup is the least I can do. I'll need you tomorrow to help me bring it over to Gatekeeper."

Holy shit, Keith mused. This was really getting out of hand. "Tomorrow?" he asked trying to think of a reason why he couldn't do that.

"I'd love to bring it tonight," Catherine replied, "but I need time to cool the soup and then skim off the fat. Be here around seven. The pot is heavy so I'll need you to pour the soup into my tureen. It'll look so nice in there."

"Is Mrs. Hunter expecting you?"

"Not yet. I didn't want to say anything about the soup until I was sure it came out okay. I'll call her first thing in the morning. I'm sure she'll love it.'

Keith was speechless. Theresa was right. Catherine was losing her mind. "Didn't you say she had a doctor's appointment?"

"Yes, but the clinic doesn't open till nine. That should give us plenty of time. Early. Be here early. We can drop the soup off before they leave. That should work, shouldn't it?"

"Depends. I'll have to check my schedule. I have an important meeting on the mainland in the morning and I'm not sure if it's at eight or at nine. I'll let you know."

Catherine could not hide her disappointment. For the past several hours, she'd been imagining the look on Laura's face when she brought the soup over. It never occurred to her that she would have to check with Keith first. Resigned, she kissed Keith good night and then walked him over to the door. "Early," she called as he stepped outside. "We must find a way to make this work."

The fireworks finale had just begun by the time Keith started back to his cottage. The sky was ablaze and the noise deafening, but Keith barely noticed. His thoughts were jumping over each other. It was unbelievable. A doctor's appointment was sure to keep Laura Hunter away from Gatekeeper for at least an hour and maybe more, giving him unfettered access to the house, the heater and the sensors. All of a sudden, what once seemed impossible was now potentially doable. Somehow he would have to find a way to keep Catherine at Whalehead, to keep her away from Gatekeeper. The least of his worries for now, Keith decided. He had far more important details to consider.

A deafening quiet replaced the noise of the fireworks by the time Keith stepped into his cottage but he was still on edge. Brilliant as his plan was, it had one potentially fatal flaw: it all depended on the weather. Gatekeeper was a big place and it would take hours for the carbon monoxide to reach lethal levels. If Laura turned her heater on too soon, she might be awake enough to recognize her symptoms and take evasive action. Not only would his plan fail, his part in the near tragedy might be uncovered. Was it worth the risk? Timing was everything.

Keith grabbed a beer, plopped into his grandfather's recliner and then clicked on the TV. As much as he dissed the Weather Channel, he knew it would be his best resource. After squirming through several annoying commercials, he was finally rewarded when a beautiful meteorologist appeared on the screen. Momentarily distracted, Keith forced himself to focus.

"Goddamn," Keith muttered as another commercial came on. How he hated being jerked around. Then again, he liked what he was hearing. For a change, no one was hedging. They were one hundred percent confident that the effects of the storm would not be felt until mid to late afternoon. *Perfect.* That meant he'd have no worries that lethal CO levels would be reached too soon, when Laura was awake enough to recognize her symptoms. *One problem solved.*

Keith savored his perceived success before focusing on his next concern: what if the necessary levels of carbon monoxide were not reached until morning, when everyone was waking up? *Damn.* Unless he could find a way to be sure that everyone slept through the night and beyond, his mission would be an abject failure.

It had been a long day and Keith's head was pounding. No wonder he couldn't think straight. He wanted Whalehead and as much as he wanted to screw his boss so why was he worried that the risk might be too great for the reward? Whalehead, the Preston fortune. Without it his life would continue to be shit. *Think,* he told himself. *Think.*

Getting up from his chair, Keith finished his beer and then tossed the can into the trash. Desperate for relief, he walked into the bathroom and opened the medicine cabinet. As he reached for the Motrin, a bottle with a purple cap caught his attention. Melatonin. Sleep. His old man swore by it.

Keith's ears were ringing as he stared at the bottle. He took it out, shook it and then opened it. Capsules, more than half full. Capsules, its contents easy to remove. All natural. *Holy shit.* Could it be? Could this be the solution he had been looking for?

Not wanting to get ahead of himself, Keith reached for the paper cup dispenser next to the mirror and then placed an empty cup on the sink. He opened a capsule and then dumped the contents into the cup. He turned the water on, filled the cup half way and then stirred it with his finger. Bingo! It was completely soluble. He had done it: he had just found a foolproof way to get five people to sleep for as long as necessary.

Buoyed by his discovery, Keith embraced his next hurdle: delivery and dosage. He headed for the kitchen where he would have more room to experiment. Last time he was at Gatekeeper, he noticed that the jug on the water cooler was relatively new. That meant it had taken them four days to go through the old one. Who drank the water, when did they drink it and how much did they drink? The water cooler might be the perfect delivery system if it didn't have so many damned variables. He was brilliant to be sure but how was he supposed to figure out the right dosage and more importantly, restrict ingestion to late afternoon or evening?

Christ Almighty. Was he back to square one? He groaned. In the morning he'd have to deal with Catherine and her ridiculous need to deliver chicken noodle soup to Laura and her children. What a pain in the ass. Here he was on the cusp of something brilliant and he had to deal with Catherine.

It hit him like a ton of bricks. "Of course," he muttered, annoyed that he hadn't thought of it sooner. The soup. It would be the perfect delivery system. Figures began racing through his head like a calculator on speed. If the normal dose was 10 mg. and if Catherine's tureen held six quarts then all he had to do was to guess what size soup bowls Laura would use. Six or twelve ounces. *Twelve,* he decided. He would make a solution for twelve ounces. Better to have a stronger solution than a weak one. Yes. His headache was gone. This could work. Tonight he would make the solution and tomorrow he'd dump it into the tureen.

Forcing himself to concentrate, Keith emptied the pill bottle onto the counter and then counted exactly how many capsules he would need. For good luck, he added an additional three, his lucky number. He found a small, discrete container, one he could easily hide in his pocket. Opening the capsules took longer than he expected but he was ecstatic when he was done. He walked over to the window. It was dark. Whalehead was just a silhouette against the night sky. He smiled. The irony that Catherine's soup would be the deciding nail in her granddaughter's coffin was remarkable.

Keith got into bed and rested his head on his cheap, smelly pillow. He closed his eyes, imagining what it would be like when he finally got into his bed at Whalehead. The sheets would be cool, the room air conditioned. Even so, he would crack his window so that he could hear the water lapping against the dock. Smiling, he rolled over. "So close," he whispered. "So goddamned close."

Chapter Twenty-Two

July 5th

Dawn had yet to break when Laura stumbled into the kitchen, hoping to grab a cup of coffee and some quiet time. She was pleasantly surprised to find that Meg was already up and had the coffee brewing. "That smells awesome but I can't believe you're up this early."

Meg took two mugs down from the cabinet. "Are you kidding? All this talk about that cold front. This might be the best sunrise of our entire vacation. Can't wait. I even set my alarm."

Laura took the half and half out of the refrigerator. "You really are crazy. You're probably the only person down here excited to have their vacation ruined by two days of yucky weather."

Meg filled both mugs. "That's because I don't expect it to ruin my vacation. I won't have to worry about sunburn and with just the right light, pictures of the ocean will be awesome."

"I rest my case."

Meg chuckled. "All things considered, the biggest shame here isn't the weather; it's the kids getting sick. That's the part that really stinks."

"Yeah, I can't believe I missed all the signs. I knew Jon wasn't feeling well but it never occurred to me to check for fever until the others started complaining about sore throats."

"Well, there goes your Mother of the Year award."

"That's too bad. It would look so nice next to my Daughter of the Year award. Truthfully, I don't feel all that bad about missing the kids. I mean I only had a few hours to realize they were getting sick, but Greenview? I had years to see through my mother's godawful story; not hours, years. Hard not to feel like an idiot."

Meg shrugged. "Well, for what it's worth, your mother was very convincing and as we now know, she had every reason not to want to talk about what happened."

"I agree but it makes me wonder what else she didn't tell me. I feel like I'm missing something. I don't know. Maybe I'm just on edge."

"Well, you do have a lot to think about and I'm sure it doesn't help that the kids are sick. Long as I've known you, you always think the worst."

Laura waved her hand in dismissal. "I'm not all that worried about the kids. I know this is strep and once the doctor starts them on antibiotics, they'll be fine. I just wish Mike had called in an order yesterday. If he had, they'd already be on the mend and last night wouldn't have been such a horror show. A good night's sleep would have gone a long way."

"True but I think Mike was right about the kids being seen by a pediatrician. It's really lucky that his old medical school buddy practices down here and was more than happy to see the kids. What did you say his name was?"

"Joe. Joe Winston. To be honest, I've always wanted to meet this guy. Mike talks about him all the time. They were good friends in Medical School but kind of drifted apart after graduation. Mike went on to do his residency and fellowship in New York. Joe went to Florida. Good thing Mike remembered he was down here. Are you hungry?"

"Starved but I don't have much time. Sunrise in about ten minutes. Do we still have those strudels?"

Laura walked over to the freezer. "Ah, here they are. Raspberry. My favorite." She placed two strudels into the toaster oven, turned it on and then sat down. "Wanna hear something weird? I spent a lot of time with Sara last night. She was really agitated. Kept asking about Keith. Don't know if it was the fever talking but if I was following her correctly, she wanted to know why he kept staring at her."

"Staring at her?" Meg replied. "That's weird. Was this when the kids were chasing their kite?"

"No, it was when Keith brought the new one over. He and I were having such a nice conversation until Sara pranced in. She was trying to get her bathing suit on and her straps got twisted. She was a little whiney."

"Her bathing suit? Staring at a little girl in a bathing suit? I don't like the sounds of that."

Laura shrugged. "It was nothing like that; at least I don't think it was. Matter of fact, I'm almost certain Keith never even looked at Sara until I made her give me my mother's barrettes."

"Your mother's barrettes. What are you talking about?"

"Well, between you and me, Sara really looked cute. She had parted her hair down the middle and had pinned the barrettes on either side. She clearly intended to wear them to the beach and she probably would have done just that if she hadn't had an issue with her bathing suit."

Meg chuckled. "Let me guess. World War III?"

"Not exactly but as you can imagine, she didn't give them up easily. Unfortunately, while we were going round and round, I had my back to Keith, so I have no idea what he was doing. I can tell you though, as soon as Sara walked away, Keith was done. Claimed he had to leave. It was like the lovely conversation we were having never happened. I was kind of disappointed."

The toaster popped. Meg got up, grabbed two dishes from the overhead cabinet, removed the pastries and then slipped one onto each of the dishes. "Answer me this," she said, making a small cut in the corner of the icing packet and then decorating the strudels with squiggly lines of white sugar. She took a second to admire her handiwork and then placed the dish in front of Laura. "When Sara walked out of the room, was Keith watching her?"

Laura nibbled on the corner of her strudel. "Not at all. I don't think little girls are his thing. Full disclosure: up close and personal, Keith is drop dead gorgeous and if it hadn't been for the incident at the bike shop, I'd be searching for a way to get you two together."

"Please, don't do me any favors. I told you that guy had issues."

"Yeah, I know but he was so easy to talk to. He talked about Catherine, his relationship with her, his grandfather and I told him all about my mother, Greenview, the Abbott Farmstead."

"Wow!" Meg replied. "He must have been easy. You're so private."

"I know. I hardly recognized myself. There I was blabbing away. Then Sara walked in and everything changed."

"That's not surprising. Men hate to be interrupted, especially by kids. Some guys are convinced liquid gold pours from their lips."

Laura thought for a moment. "Yeah, but I'm not entirely sure Keith was reacting to Sara. I honestly think that if she hadn't been wearing my mother's barrettes, nothing would have changed. Keith looked so uncomfortable when I told him those barrettes belonged to my mother and that they've been a thorn in my side. It was really awkward."

"Well, chalk it up. Today's Thursday and we'll be leaving Saturday. Highly unlikely you'll ever see him again."

"I hope. I meant to tell you that Mrs. Preston is insisting we come for brunch before we leave."

"When?"

"Friday if the kids are better and if we're still here."

"Still here? What are you talking about?"

Laura hesitated. "Don't look at me like that. Just hear me out. Let's say the kids do have strep and that Dr. Winston starts them immediately on antibiotics. We bring them home, let them rest and then whip this place into shape. If we leave today, we won't have to deal with Keith Quigley."

Meg shrugged. "I'm not sure which is worse. Antibiotics or not, no one slept very well last night, you most of all. You have the potential to be a real detriment behind the wheel."

"I'll take a short nap. Sneak in a little shut-eye and then wash the dishes, pack the clothes and return the bikes. Whip the game room into shape, load the car and be on our way. They're saying this front won't get here until late afternoon. Our appointment's early and hopefully Dr. Winston won't keep us waiting. That should give us plenty of time to get out of here noon, one-thirty at the latest. It'll be fun. We'll be just ahead of the storm."

"Do you hear yourself? Why are you so desperate to get out of here?"

Laura shrugged. "I don't know. I feel like the walls are closing in. You know how much I've always loved coming down here. I was ready to bail after Dan died but my mother talked me out of it. Now she's gone. It's just not the same. Truth to tell, I don't think I even want to come back next year. I realized something last night when I was trying to comfort Sara. This place is my past. Home is my future. I know it's stupid to leave two vacation days on the table but it's not like the weather's gonna cooperate."

Meg took a giant bite of her strudel and then washed it down with a long sip of coffee. She understood Laura's angst although she didn't necessarily agree with her solution. "Why don't you eat? You'll feel better. Never good to make important decisions on an empty stomach."

Laura sighed. "Humor me and at least consider it."

Meg grabbed her camera. "After the sunrise. Maybe we'll both see things a little clearer. I won't be long."

"Take your time," Laura replied. She sipped her coffee and nibbled on her strudel. She felt restless. She wanted desperately to be home, to be in Mike's arms. She looked around. She knew damn well that trying to get everything ready in a couple of hours was pushing the limits but she really didn't care. For the first time in months, she knew exactly what she wanted and more than anything, she wanted share the news with Mike. Problem was, he was over three hundred miles away. She could no longer wait to let him know that she was ready; that she was finally ready to build a new life with the man she had loved for such a long time.

One by one the children sauntered into the kitchen. No one wanted to eat or to drink but they all accepted the ice pops that Laura offered. She had everyone dressed and ready to go well ahead of schedule, but somehow they were several minutes behind when they finally walked out of the house. "How does time vanish like that?" Laura asked Meg as they herded the kids into the car. "It's like doing the laundry. You put twelve socks into the washer and by the time you take them out of the dryer, you've only got ten."

Meg chuckled. "Can't say that ever happened to me but then again, I'm only doing laundry for one."

After buckling her little one in, Laura hurried around the car and got behind the wheel. "Brilliant," she muttered, reaching for her keys. "I left my purse in the kitchen. Keep the doors open. I'll be right back."

Convinced that she was losing her mind Laura raced up the steps, grabbed her purse and without breaking stride, bounded back down. The house phone rang just as she reached the front door. For a split second she considered ignoring it but thinking it might be Mike, she changed her mind. She turned around, ran down the hall and grabbed the phone on her night stand. Out of breath, she expected to hear some off color comment about her panting. "I can't talk right now. Call me on my cell phone."

"Mrs. Hunter? This is Catherine Preston. Have I gotten you at a bad time? You sound winded."

Damn, Laura mused, wishing she had followed her instincts and ignored the call. "Just a little. We're on our way to the doctor's."

"Well, I'm glad I caught you. Dr. Winston stopped by to see me on his way home yesterday. That was very sweet of you to let him know I was exposed to your children. He did tell me strep is going around and has asked me to call him if I should feel ill. He's such a wonderful man. The children will be in good hands."

Laura was keenly aware of the ticking clock. "So I've heard. It's very nice to hear from you but I'm afraid we're in a bit of a time crunch. Would you mind if I call you later?"

"This won't take long. When Dr. Winston told me all your children were sick, I wanted to do something. I'm not all that good in the kitchen but somewhere along the way, I did learn how to make an incredible chicken noodle soup. Cures whatever ails you. Would you mind if Keith brought it over? He's here with me now. He's got the tureen and is ready to walk out the door. Truthfully, I was hoping I could come with him but he's in a very tight time crunch. He has an important meeting on the mainland and can't be late."

Laura shook her head. *Murphy's Law*. Keith Quigley was the man of last night's angst. She hated chicken noodle soup and taking this call already wasted what little time she had. "That's very nice of you Mrs. Preston, but I'm afraid we won't be able to wait. Dr. Winston is doing us a favor by squeezing us in and I don't want to be late. Besides…"

"Don't worry about being late," Catherine interrupted. "You can blame me. I've known Joe since he was in diapers. Please. I don't want to hold Keith up. He needs to get to the mainland and has no idea when he'll be back."

Laura took a deep breath. She didn't have the energy to argue. "I'll tell you what," she heard herself say. "I'll leave the front door unlocked. Keith can put the soup in the refrigerator."

Catherine seemed disappointed that Laura wasn't more appreciative of her efforts. "Well, I guess that will have to do."

Laura tried to sound upbeat. "Thank you. My mother was a great believer in chicken noodle soup. She would love this. It's really thoughtful of you. "

Catherine's voice was warmer now. "My pleasure. You said the front door?"

"Yes. I won't lock it for now. All he'll have to do when he leaves is turn the lock and then pull the door closed."

"What took so long?" Meg asked the minute Laura got into the car.

"The phone. I thought it was Mike."

"Everything okay?"

Laura shrugged as she buckled her seatbelt. "It wasn't Mike. It was Mrs. Preston. Caught me off guard. I probably could have handled the call better than I did."

"What did she want?"

"She made some chicken noodle soup for the kids and wanted us to wait for Keith to drop it off. I told her we couldn't." Laura started the engine and was grateful that Meg didn't ask her to elaborate. They arrived at the clinic with seconds to spare but Laura felt tighter than a stretched rubber band. Somehow Catherine Preston had just convinced her to allow Keith Quigley to come into her house all by his lonesome. She was batting a thousand, compounding one mistake after the other. Early dementia or emotional exhaustion? Hard to know.

Despite the Tylenol and the ice pop, Jon was hotter than before. Laura felt defeated. As much as she wanted to get home, she knew that she couldn't possibly subject her little boy to such a long ride. She looked around. The sky was still a peaceful blue. The air felt cool and crisp. Maybe they should hunker down. If it got too cold, they could turn up the heat, spread out on the living room floor and watch some good movies. Tired as she was, the idea was beginning to appeal to her. Putting Keith Quigley and Catherine Preston out of her mind, she walked into the clinic. What harm could there possibly be in waiting one more day?

Chapter Twenty-Three

July 5th

Keith Quigley made the right turn out of Whalehead just in time to see Laura's large blue Suburban make the left turn and then head in the opposite direction. He hung back, not wanting her to see him. When she passed the indoor sports complex, the only place on the two lane road where she could possibly turn around, he breathed a sigh of relief. So far, so good. Everything was going as planned.

Keith pulled onto the Gatekeeper driveway and drove down to the end, as far out of sight as possible. Laura had left the front door open and although he didn't plan to use it, he made a mental note to remember to lock it. In the interest of progress, many of the upscale homes had digital locks on the lower level doors. The codes to the locks were changed frequently and communicated to high level service workers via email. As an HVAC technician, Keith had access to the codes and even though he wasn't on the payroll this summer, he was still getting the emails. Piece of cake.

First things first. Taking his tool box from his trunk, Keith walked over to the door and then keyed in the code. It didn't work. "Dammit," he muttered, staring at the keypad. Had he pressed the wrong numbers? Impossible. He had an eidetic memory. Shaken, he checked his phone again. He had remembered the numbers correctly but had missed the security code. In a hapless attempt to maintain security, a plus or minus number was always planted somewhere in the email. Today it was a plus two, meaning he had to up the first and last numbers by two. He tried again. It worked.

Forcing himself to focus, Keith brought his tool box into the utility room. He knelt down in front of the heater and unscrewed the protective panels. He was annoyed to think that Harry had done the exact thing less than two days ago. Dutch was such a moron. Why fork out all that overtime when all he had to do was to ask the best HVAC tech there ever was to help out?

For several seconds, Keith stared at the burner. He hesitated. In less than twenty-four hours a young mother, her three children and their friend would all be dead. No doubt their untimely deaths would attract plenty of attention. He had to be careful. His inheritance would be secure but his victory would feel hollow if his old boss got off Scot-free.

Taking a deep breath, Keith proceeded. It didn't help that his hands were shaking. The corrosion process was taking longer than he expected, not because the burner was any big deal but because he could feel himself wimping out. Horrible thoughts were creeping into his head. Laura and company didn't really have to die for him to besmirch Dutch's reputation. They only had to get sick. For a split second, he actually fantasized finding them and rescuing them. He would be a hero. *A hero without an inheritance.*

When he was done, Keith studied his handiwork. Satisfied, he wiped the sweat from his brow and then screwed the panel back into place. He picked up his tool box, turned off the light and then walked out of the room.

Returning to his car, Keith placed the tool box in his trunk and then grabbed the roll of duct tape. Slipping the roll onto his arm, he walked over to the passenger's side and then opened the door. "Shit," he muttered, suddenly aware of an unpleasant smell. The tureen had a cover but it also had a tiny opening that allowed for a ladle to be inserted. Minus the ladle, some of the soup had spilled onto the floor. Like the tan rug wasn't already dirty enough.

Keith lifted the tureen. It was heavy and its ornate handles made it awkward to carry. He kicked the car door closed and then went back into the house. He started up the steps, trying to keep the tureen level. Catherine had insisted that he fill the damn thing almost to the brim and like an idiot, he complied. One wrong tilt and the soup would start sloshing back and forth. "Damnit," Keith muttered. The only sure way to avoid another spill was to inch his way up the steps.

Slow and steady, Keith reached the kitchen without incident. He placed the tureen in the sink. Lifting the lid, he doctored the soup, wiped the sides of the tureen and then placed it in the refrigerator. He kicked the refrigerator door closed and then walked into the living room. He adjusted the thermostat and then taped the third level sensor. Pleased with his progress, he headed downstairs.

The sleeping floor. More to do on this level. *Stay focused,* Keith told himself. He locked the front door and then adjusted the thermostat. Locating the CO sensor, he ripped another strip of duct tape from its roll and carefully placed it on the sensor. "Damn," he muttered, taking a step back. A keen eye would see the tape. Not ideal but with any luck, by the time anyone thought to check the sensor, the tape would be long gone.

Keith checked the time. As much as he wanted to get out of the house, he figured he had two choices. He could look for those goddamn barrettes now or search for them tomorrow morning. In the grand scheme of things, his ultimate success depended on him confiscating those gaudy pieces of crap. Surely Catherine would freak if she ever saw them. *Not something to leave to chance,* he told himself. No telling what might happen tomorrow morning. Best to know where to look. Last he knew Laura had taken the barrettes from her little girl with some kind of vague promise to give them back. *Start there*, he thought. Find the room where the little brat was staying.

There were four bedrooms on the middle level. The master bedroom was closest to the steps. *Not that one*, Keith decided. Opposite the master bedroom were two rooms that shared a bathroom. Definitely used by the boys. Keith turned and walked across the hall into the room adjacent to the master bedroom. He stopped dead in his tracks. On the bed was a doll that looked just like the little brat. The damn thing was so lifelike that he felt as if it were staring at him. That expression, that look on her face, sitting there like friggin' princess, wearing both barrettes in her neatly combed hair.

"Screwballs," Keith muttered. Ugly as they were, those barrettes were worth a fortune. What kind of mother allows her little girl to mess around with something that valuable? Clearly Laura Hunter was just as moronic as her grandfather.

Careful not to touch anything in the room, Keith forced himself to leave. Although he had yet to figure out how to arrange it, he would be the one to discover the bodies, here, in the bedrooms. It would be a telling moment. Up until two months ago, he'd never been up close and personal to a fresh corpse. First his grandfather and then John Abbott. What would Laura Hunter look like dead? What about the kids? He'd read up on CO poisoning. He didn't really give a shit if they passed peacefully, he just didn't want to see vomit. That would be the last straw.

He headed down the steps. *Focus*, he told himself. *Focus*. Tomorrow would be just as important as today, maybe more so. First he had to find an excuse to come to Gatekeeper, alone. He would have to make sure there were no survivors, remove the duct tape, clean the tureen, confiscate those damn barrettes and then make a convincingly frantic 9-1-1 call.

Pleased with his plan, Keith adjusted the thermostat and then doctored the sensor. Believing that he'd thought of everything, he walked over to the door, took one last look around, pulled the door closed and then set the keypad. Done.

Keith drove out of the subdivision feeling relatively calm. He couldn't help but wonder if this was how his grandfather felt after he rigged the yacht. Had he walked away with an enormous feeling of satisfaction or was he a bundle of nerves? In any event, the old man had gotten away with a horrendous crime for sixty-five years. Odd that after spending a lifetime trying to distance himself from the old bastard he now wanted to be just like him.

Keith headed to the mainland. He spent hours wandering aimlessly. Time moved at a snail's pace. When the rain finally began, Keith headed home. He stopped at Catherine's favorite gourmet shop and bought her the honey roasted cashews that she loved. It was one way to prove to her that he was where he said he would be and it would also give him an excuse to stop by to see her.

The winds were howling and the temperature was dropping. Traffic was light but slow due to water ponding on the road. Keith got to Whalehead later than he wanted and was greeted by something he never expected.

"Oh, my, look at you," Catherine said. "You're soaked. Put those nuts in the kitchen and go get yourself a towel. Hurry. I need your help in the living room."

Keith was annoyed that Catherine wasn't more appreciative of his offering but at least the house was comfortable. The heat was on. It was a good sign. He walked into the living room. *What the hell*, he mused.

"So what do you think?" Catherine asked. "I'm so excited. I spoke to Mrs. Hunter a little while ago. She called to thank me for the soup and to tell me that Dr. Winston put the kids on antibiotics and that they're already feeling better. Best of all she's agreed to come for brunch tomorrow morning but only if no one else is around so I'm afraid you and Theresa will have to make yourselves scarce. Mrs. Hunter is so thoughtful. Doesn't want to expose anyone else to strep. I didn't know this but even though the kids are medicated, it takes a good twenty-four hours before they're no longer contagious."

Keith just stared at the baskets of toys sitting on both sides of the fireplace. "You've been busy. It looks like Christmas morning."

Catherine waved her hand in dismissal. "Happy Hippo was wonderful. They told me you called but you didn't tell them how old the children were. No big deal. Once I gave them their ages, they knew exactly what they wanted to send over. The only problem now is the fireplace. I had Edwardo stack the wood but he couldn't find the screen. Do you have any idea where it is?"

For a split second, Keith imagined telling Catherine that her stupid brunch would never happen; that Laura, her brats and her friend would all be dead. Instead, he chose a safer answer. "You realize we haven't used that fireplace in years. If it's still windy, it'll get awfully smoky in here. The downdraft is terrible. Trust me. If you want this room to be comfortable, forget the fire."

Catherine was visibly disappointed. "Oh, my. You're right. Now I remember. Your grandfather was always saying that we should either get a glass screen or build a higher chimney. I'm so disappointed. I wanted everything to be perfect."

Keith looked around. "It'll still be perfect," he replied. "You are a wonderful hostess."

The lights flickered. Catherine grabbed Keith's arm. "What if the power goes out?"

That would suck, Keith mused. No power, no heat. No heat, no carbon monoxide. "Let's hope it doesn't," he replied, leaning over to kiss Catherine on the cheek. It was a Judas kiss and he knew it, and yet he wasn't terribly troubled. It takes a strong man to know when betrayal is the only option. In the end, it was all up to Mother Nature. A torrent of rain slammed against the back windows. Thunder rumbled in the distance. "I'd better get going."

"Oh, my," Catherine whispered. "It's getting so nasty out there. Would you like to stay here for the night? I can have Hazel fix up the corner bedroom."

Keith was tempted. The corner bedroom was the very suite that he planned to lay claim to. *Not now*, he told himself. Tonight of all nights he needed to be able to come and go as he pleased. "That's very nice of you but it's getting late and I don't want to put anyone out. I'll see you in the morning."

By the time Keith got into his car, he was cold, wet and agitated. Was it the barometer or was he drowning in second thoughts? "Goddammit," he muttered. He could barely see where he was going. It was dark and one of his headlights was out. The rain was blinding. It was difficult to stay on the road. Approximately five hundred feet from his front door, he got stuck in the soggy grass. Cursing his bad luck, he got out and ran inside. He flicked on the light but the room remained dark. Was it a bulb or a power failure?

Keith threw his keys onto the table and then inched his way to the bathroom. He flicked the switch. The light went on. Feeling an odd sense of relief, he walked over to the mirror and stared at his reflection. If the power stayed on all night, morning would truly be a new day. If it went out, he'd be back to square one. Goddamn. Too bad his inheritance hung in the balance.

Ripping off his wet clothes, Keith wrapped himself in a towel and then got into bed. Thunder rumbled in the distance, driving rain beat against his window. He closed his eyes but there was no turn off switch. The short time that he'd spent with Laura Hunter was etched in his memory. He could see her face, hear her laugh. It was late and she was probably asleep. It might have been nice. Then again, she would probably reject him just like all the rest.

He turned over and covered his face with his pillow. Now was not the time for second thoughts. Morning could not come soon enough.

Chapter Twenty-Four

July 5th

The house where Helga Berman once lived was still standing. It was a large Tudor on a tree lined street surrounded by homes both larger and smaller. Drawn draperies and empty driveways made the neighborhood seem deserted, not terribly unexpected for an extended holiday weekend. The noon hour was approaching and the sun was almost directly overhead. Dave and Julie stepped off the concrete sidewalk onto the curvy slate path that led up to a stained wooden door. "Hope they're home," Dave whispered as he rang the doorbell.

Several seconds passed. "How old do you think this house is?" Julie asked.

"Was built in the 1930's. The original owners lived here for about sixty years and then sold it to their daughter for one dollar. The parents are no longer alive but the daughter should know something."

When no one answered, Dave rang again. Several more seconds passed before they finally heard footsteps. The brass peephole, approximately three inches in diameter opened. "Who is it?" a young girl called.

"My name is Dave Schubert. I have a letter that was supposed to be delivered to a woman living at this address a long time ago. It's very important that we find her and we're hoping someone here may be able to help us."

"Delivered to whom," the young girl asked.

"Helga. Helga Berman."

"Sorry, no one here by that name."

"I'm not surprised," Dave replied. "It was a long time ago." He held the envelope up to the peephole. "It's a very old letter but we believe Helga lived here at some point. Is there someone else who might be able to help us? It's very important."

"Important to whom, and why?"

Dave pulled out his money clip to show his ID. "I'm a senior at the University of Pennsylvania, Annenberg School of Communication and I'm investigating a sixty-five year old murder."

"What's that got to do with Helga?"

"Well, recently remains were discovered under an old hotel in a small town named Greenview. We think those remains belong to Helga's sister."

The peephole slammed shut. One lock snapped and then another. The door swung open, bringing Dave and Julie face to face with a pretty young girl wearing an NYU tee shirt. "A murder mystery? You're investigating a murder mystery? Wow!" She extended her hand. "Hi. I'm Maria and I just finished my freshman year. I have no idea what I want to do but I've always been fascinated by forensics. That letter sounds really interesting. May I see it?"

Dave complied. "Check out the postmarks. For some reason the letter was delivered here in 1945 but sent back to Greenview as undeliverable. It's been in the dead letter file all these years. Is anyone here who might have been around at that time or can you hook us up with someone who was?"

"Wow. I wish I could. Sixty-five years is a long time. This sister. She have a name?"

"Rosa. Rosalinda Berman."

Never heard of her or her sister. Looks like the letter's been opened. What's it say?"

"Don't know. It's written in German and our translator is temporarily unavailable. In the meantime, we thought we'd try to find Helga. We're kind of in a time crunch."

"A time crunch? More like a time warp. I really wish I could help. That's just too long ago."

A very tall man walked into the room. He did not look pleased to find his daughter talking to strangers but before he could say anything, she introduced him to Dave and Julie. "Don't worry, Dad. He has legitimate ID. They're looking for Helga Berman." She handed her father the envelope. "They came because of this letter. It was delivered here a long time ago but returned to the post office as undeliverable. It's from the dead letter file in a tiny town named Greenview. Dave's from Penn, the Annenberg School of Communication. That letter may have something to do with a sixty-five year old murder."

The man gave Dave and Julie a visual pat down. He then looked down at the envelope. "1945's an awfully long time ago. "What is it that you want?"

"We'd like to talk to anyone, anyone who might have known Helga. Anyone who might have been around at that time—friends, neighbors, workers."

The man shook his head. "I'm sorry. My wife's parents built this house. They would be your best bet but they've been gone for several years now. As for neighbors, most of the homes in this neighborhood are on their fourth or fifth owners."

"What about help?" Julie asked. Although she had yet to see the inside of the house, she could tell by the meticulous landscape that the homeowners more than likely had plenty of help.

The man shrugged. "1945? As you can imagine, anyone working here back then retired a long time ago. Frankly I couldn't even tell you where any of them have gone or how many of them are still alive. Sorry."

"Wait a minute," the girl interrupted. "What about Maud? She's still alive."

The man nodded slowly. "True, but I doubt she'd be much help. Maud was our cook. She and my wife had a special relationship. She started working for my in-laws right after they built this house. If anyone would know about this Helga she would, but unfortunately her memory's shot. Her family put her in East Gate Estates. It's a fancy name for a rather unpleasant nursing home. It's way across town. Not the best neighborhood."

"What's her last name?" Dave asked hopefully.

"Good question," the man replied. "She was just Maud to us and with good reason. No one could ever pronounce her last name. I believe it starts with an s." He handed the envelope back to Dave. "Sorry. You're welcome to leave your contact information. When my wife returns, I'll check with her, just to be sure."

"I'd appreciate that. East Gate Estates. If we are lucky enough to find Maud, may we tell her you were asking for her?"

"Of course but don't be surprised if you get a blank stare. Word of caution: be very careful getting to that nursing home. Like I said, it's not in a very good neighborhood."

The trek to the nursing home was a walk in the park compared to what Dave and Julie found once they got there. From the minute they walked in, they were eyed with suspicion and it took several minutes before they could convince the receptionist that they weren't there to do an impromptu inspection of the facility. They jumped that hurdle only to find the next one even more taxing. There were two patients named Maud, both with long last names that started with S and both in their eighties. An hour and change later, Dave and Julie walked out of the nursing home, tired, frustrated and empty handed. They made their way back to Penn Station.

"Looks like we're back to Audrey," Dave complained. "We won't know squat till we get that letter translated. I can't believe we've wasted an entire day. Instead of coming up here it might have been smarter to go to Brauhaus Schmitz in Olde City. We could have had a beer and then asked the bartender if he could read German."

"Yeah, but then you wouldn't have seen where this Helga Berman lived." Julie grabbed Dave's arm. "You know, I love the way you track down every possible lead. You're gonna figure this out. I just know you will and soon. I have a very strong feeling that your luck is about to change."

They arrived at Penn Station just in time to miss their train. "Really?" Dave asked. "What is it you said about luck?"

Julie just shrugged. "Well, we've got about an hour to kill. Let's make the best of this and grab something to eat."

They settled for a sandwich and a beer. The hot sandwich was cold and the cold beer was warm but they were both too hungry to care. Julie predicted that their train would be coming in on track 4 seconds before anyone else. They managed to be first in line, first to board and first to pick their seats. Exhausted, they settled comfortably for the ride home.

"I just thought of something," Dave said as the train began to pull away. "Why didn't we canvass the neighborhood instead of going to that stupid nursing home? We might have found someone who knew the Berman sisters."

Julie sighed. "Why? If the people who lived in the same house as Helga Berman didn't know her what makes you think anyone else would? Look, if it'll make you feel any better, I'll call Audrey as soon as we get off the train."

"Why wait?"

"Two reasons. We're in a tunnel with no reception. That will certainly improve after we get out but we're in the quiet car."

"The quiet car? So, can't you speak softly?"

Julie placed her index finger on Dave's lips. "Chill," she whispered, resting her head on Dave's shoulder. Predictably the train began picking up speed. Julie sighed, comforted by the rhythmic click clack of metal on metal. "Let's be smart about this. As soon as the conductor passes, we close our eyes. If we nap now, we can have fun later."

They were a good fifteen minutes out of New York, their tickets had been scanned and the gentle swaying of the train was putting them to sleep. Just as they were dozing, someone's cell phone rang. Annoyingly, it was the woman sitting directly across the aisle. Although she was smart enough to use a soft voice, Julie found herself eavesdropping. She wanted to know what was so important that she had to keep talking. Several seconds later, she realized why she was so difficult to understand. Only half of what she was saying was in English. The rest was in German.

"Dave, Dave," she whispered, nudging him awake. "The woman across the aisle. She's on her cell phone. Listen to her. She's speaking in German."

"So?"

Julie was incredulous. "So! If the woman speaks German, maybe she also reads it."

Dave's eyes widened. "You think? You think she might be able to translate our letter?"

Julie shrugged. "Let's ask her. We've got nothing to lose."

Dave took the letter out of his pocket. He waited until the woman ended the call. "Excuse me," he said, not wanting the woman to feel defensive. "Your phone call didn't bother us but we were wondering. Were you speaking German?"

The woman smiled apologetically. "I was and I'm sorry if I disturbed you. My sister. Her baby is sick. When she's upset, she prefers to speak German. I'm a physician's assistant."

"Well, I hope you were able to help."

The woman shrugged. "Sounds like a virus. More messy than anything else. Not much you can do other than keep the patient hydrated. I'm getting off at the next stop, so hopefully I won't bother you again."

"No bother at all but I was wondering." He held up the envelope. "This letter. It's written in German. Do you think you might be able to translate it for us?"

The woman checked the digital readout indicating how many minutes she had until the train reached her stop. "I'll try. I speak better than I read and I haven't done this is in quite some time so I'm a little rusty. Would you mind if I looked it over first?"

"Go right ahead," Dave replied, keenly aware of the fleeting time. "Whenever you're comfortable."

After what felt like an eternity, the woman looked up. "This shouldn't be too hard." She patted the seat next to her. "Sit here. I don't want to be too loud."

Dave moved across the aisle and sat down. With eight minutes until the woman's stop, he realized they had no time for repeats. He took out his smart phone. "Would you mind if I recorded it?"

"Not at all." She cleared her throat.

My dearest Helga,

Although it hasn't been terribly long since I last wrote to you, it feels like a lifetime. Amelia, the little girl I told you about passed away in her sleep several nights ago. It's been so sad. For her parents, for me and even for Marney. That poor mother. The pain she is going through. It's made me think of Mrs. P and all the misery she must be feeling. I don't think I should wait any longer. I've got to get to New York as soon as possible. Marney's safety is my main concern so I will come alone. I've already discussed it with Amelia's parents and they've agreed to take care of Marney until I come back.

I don't understand why no one has come for us and I'm worried about Mrs. P. Please don't say anything but she's with child and I do hope she's OK. If you haven't already, you must get to her without Tad knowing. I hate to think what he might do if he finds out that Marney and I are alive. He rigged the yacht and he knows I can prove it. God only knows what he might do if he finds us.

You can imagine how nervous I am. I know it's a blessing that everyone thinks we died in that explosion but I keep reliving it. Poor Mr. P. I can still see his face when Marney made that fuss about going on the yacht. It was a sunny day but the water was pretty rough. We should have known she would get sick. Mr. P felt so bad to see her suffer. Mama always said there's a silver lining in every cloud. She was right. If he hadn't turned around to drop us off, we all would have died in that explosion.

Enough of the past. Here's what I want to do. Next week, Amelia's father is going to take me back to Philadelphia and help me get on the train to Penn Station. I'm sure I can figure out how to get from there to your house. Please, do what you can to smooth my way to Mrs. P. If you must, get your boss to help you but under no circumstance can you tell her why. Maybe you can get her to invite Mrs. P over for tea. Whatever you do, it has to be a complete surprise. I have to be very careful. We both do. Tad is a very dangerous man. I don't want anything to happen to you, to Marney or to the wonderful family that has taken us in.

I pray this will work out. It calms me to know that the town where we're staying is so far from anywhere and I know Amelia's parents will take good care of Marney. They never questioned my story that I'm running from a crazy husband who tried to kill us.

I can't wait to see you again. It's been so long. Whatever you do, don't let anyone other than Mrs. P see that beautiful barrette I sent to you in my last letter. There are only 5 like it in this entire world. I have 2, Mrs. P has two and now you have one. It's unmistakable proof that Marney is alive. Brace yourself. When Mrs. P sees it, she'll be overjoyed. This will work out. I just know it will.

    Your loving sister, Rosa.

The train began to slow down. The woman handed the letter back to Dave. "Well, I hope that helps. I believe I got it right. Let me give you my phone number in case you have any other questions."

Dave helped the woman retrieve her suitcase from the overhead bin. He thanked her warmly and then returned to his seat. Julie grabbed his arm. She was excited and wanted to know what was in the letter but for the moment, Dave was too shocked to answer. He reached into his pocket and took out his ear buds. He plugged the cord into his phone, placed one bud in his left ear and then handed the other one to Julie. "Here. You're not going to believe this. I'm not sure I do. He waited until Julie was ready and then adjusted the volume. "I'm telling you, Jules. If I heard that woman correctly, forget everything I said before. Today really is our lucky day."

Chapter Twenty-Five

July 5th

Laura woke with a start. Although it was only 4PM, her room was dark. She bolted upright and listened. Judging by the gusts of wind slamming against the house, the nasty weather that forecasters were predicting had arrived. Getting out of bed, Laura couldn't help but smile. Although she rarely napped during the day, she felt like a new person. She stepped out into the hallway to check on the kids. Their beds were empty—an excellent sign.

Embarrassed that she had slept so long, Laura went downstairs to the rec room where she found her kids engaged in their favorite activities. It was hard to remember how sick they had been just twenty-four hours ago. Antibiotics. Amazing how quickly strep can be knocked out.

Smiling, Laura bounded up the two flights of steps leading to the third floor. The TV was on, tuned to the Weather Channel but the room was empty. Laura walked over to Meg's bedroom and knocked on the door. No answer. Above a loud gust of wind, the sliding door opened. Spinning around, Laura watched in disbelief as Meg stepped inside. She was drenched.

"Mistimed that one," Meg chuckled. "Thought I could get down to the ocean and back before the skies opened. The ocean. You gotta see it. It's fabulous. Here." She handed Laura the binoculars that they kept on the table next to the door. "There's just enough light. Take a look. I'll be right back."

Laura walked over to the sliding door and looked out. The ocean was a sea of white foam set against a backdrop of a dark angry horizon. A brief flash of lightening lit up the sky. *Not bad*, Laura mused, for anyone who likes that sort of thing.

Meg returned from the bedroom wearing dry clothes and a terrycloth turban. "I don't know about you but I'm starving." She walked over to the refrigerator and took out an unopened package of Brie. "This, crackers and wine. Whadda say?" She put the Brie on the counter. "By the way, where'd that tureen come from? It's gorgeous."

"The tureen," Laura replied. "I forgot all about it." She opened the refrigerator. "Wow! It really is pretty. Thank Catherine Preston. When she found out the kids were sick, she whipped up a crock of chicken noodle soup. Keith dropped it off when we were at the doctor's."

"Keith? Dropped it off when we weren't here? How'd that happen?"

"Long story. Remember Mrs. Preston calling this morning, just as we were leaving? She had made that soup and was annoyingly insistent that Keith drop it off. Wanted us to wait till he got here. Apparently he was in as much of a hurry as we were. Easiest thing to do was for me to leave the front door unlocked with the understanding that Keith put the soup in the refrigerator and then lock the door on his way out."

"Wow! I can't believe you trusted that creep in here by himself."

"Two minutes. What could possibly happen in two minutes? Don't worry. I checked when we got home. Everything was exactly like we left it. You know. I have to say. This storm. So far, so good. It's actually pretty comfortable in here despite all that wind."

"Yeah, the heating company must have come by to turn the heat on while we were out. All the thermostats were set to seventy-two. Seemed a little high for up here so I turned this one down to sixty-eight. I hate to sleep in a hot room but if it gets too cold we can turn it up until you all go to bed."

"Nah. I think we're all right for now."

"Good. You hungry? I'm dying for a nice thick pizza. Listen to that wind. Carbs and nasty weather; the perfect combo."

"Yeah but what about all the food we already have? Pizza tonight, brunch tomorrow. If we ate nonstop from now till we leave, we'd still have enough left over to choke an elephant. You know how I hate waste."

"So, we take it with us. Bag the dry goods and put the cold stuff in the cooler. I can bring whatever survives to the shelter."

Laura considered the proposal. "Okay, you convinced me but let's serve the soup as an appetizer. That way we can clean the tureen and bring it back to Mrs. Preston in the morning." Laura checked the time. "If we want delivery we'd better call for the pizza now. It's a tad early but if half the people who are still here have the same idea, we won't get our pizza until midnight."

Laura's cell phone rang. "I hope this is Mike. The kids are doing great and I'm dying to do the I told you so speech. Mind if I take it?"

"No, but try to be charming. You don't want Mike to know he can never be right until after the wedding. Take your time. I'll call for the pizza."

"Thanks. There's a magnet on the refrigerator that has the number. You have to use the landline. They won't take delivery orders from phones outside the local area code."

After countless busy signals, Meg finally got through to the pizza shop. She placed their order and was about to complain about the lengthy wait time when she realized Laura was still on the phone, pacing back and forth. She opened a bottle of wine and prepared a tray of Brie and crackers. It was several seconds before she realized Laura had ended her call and had plopped onto the living room sofa. "What happened?" Meg asked, not sure what to make of the look on Laura's face. "You don't look very happy."

"That wasn't Mike. It was Sally Harrington, Robert Feldman's daughter, the man who supposedly designed my mother's barrettes, you know, Steve Jankowitz' former partner. She apologized for not calling sooner. Sally didn't remember very much about the barrettes and wanted to wait until after she spoke with her mother. Took longer than she expected."

"So what did she say?"

Laura rubbed her temples. "I'm not sure where to begin. Sally just put her mother in an assisted living facility. Memory issues. Apparently Mrs. Feldman can't remember what she had for lunch but for some reason she remembered every little thing about those barrettes. Robert Feldman sounds like a real character. Every piece of jewelry he ever created had to have a trademark. His Scottie dog pins were a real hit. The barrettes came about thanks to Chuck and Kay Ferarra."

Meg handed Laura a glass of wine. "How so?"

"Well, Kay and Mrs. Feldman were good friends. Kay had a little girl who loved Scottie dogs. She was just a toddler but apparently had a gorgeous head of hair. She had a ton of little girl barrettes, but none of them could hold her hair back. Kay complained to Mrs. Feldman about the hair and about finding something special for her kid's second birthday. Mrs. Feldman came up with the perfect solution. She loved the Scottie dog pins that her husband had been making so she twisted his arm and got him to make the Scottie dog barrettes. It was kind of last minute and Robert worked like crazy to get five barrettes ready in time. Kay was thrilled when she saw the final product but her husband flipped when he turned one over and saw Robert's trademark. Chuck thought the trademark was crass and over Kay's objections, sent Robert back to his workshop to make five new ones with no visible markings."

"Wow. This Ferarra guy sounds like the client from hell."

"No kidding. Robert balked big time. He considered the Ferarra's to be his wife's friends, not his and wasn't at all thrilled to be pushed around. For him, no trademark meant no barrettes. That's when Mrs. Feldman suggested that he secretly inscribe his trademark under the stones. Robert loved the idea and to further amuse himself, he even inscribed the kid's birth date. Turns out Sally and the Ferarra kid had the same birthday. Same day, different year. Robert finished the barrettes with time to spare. Everyone was happy. The parents got their barrettes and Feldman got his secret inscription."

Meg chuckled. "Clever."

"Here's the really weird part. Mrs. Feldman thinks it's wonderful that there are only five barrettes in the whole world that have her husband's trademark and her daughter's birthday."

Meg agreed. "Well, that is kind of cool. Why do you look like you just sucked on a lemon?"

Laura took a deep breath. "The date. You'll never guess: September sixth."

"Same day as your mother's? That's really weird. What did Sally say when you told her?"

"Didn't see any reason to mention it. All five of those barrettes are gone. According to Mrs. Feldman, the little girl and her father were killed in a boating accident a short time later. Those barrettes, the ones her husband worked so hard on have been sitting in salt water for the past sixty-five years."

"That stinks. Guess that means your mother's barrettes are forgeries."

"Not necessarily. Sally thinks it might be possible that her father had other clients who didn't want any visible trademarks and she strongly suggests that I get a jeweler to take a look."

"That's so strange," Meg replied. "Buying jewelry with an invisible trademark is like buying designer clothing with all the labels cut out. Just doesn't make sense."

"No kidding. But here's the best part. Sally's pretty sure the Ferarra's are figments of her mother's imagination. Sally claims to have a good memory for names but she swears her parents never mentioned the Ferarras before. She was six at the time and thought maybe she was just too young to remember. It bothered her so much that she went home and rifled through her mother's old address books. No one."

Meg shrugged. "Interesting. Now what?"

"Well, fortunately Robert Feldman kept receipts from every sale he ever made. Unfortunately Sally's selling her mother's house and has been cleaning things out. Right now all her father's files are sitting in a dumpster on their driveway and will be picked up sometime next week. Sally's gonna get someone to crawl through the dumpster to try and find those files. She's really motivated. Wants to know whether or not her father actually had a client named Ferarra. In the meantime, she thinks I should find a jeweler to check out my mother's barrettes, see if there might be some kind of inscription."

"Why do you need a jeweler?" Meg asked. "How hard could it be for you to look under a few stones? Piece of cake."

"What if I break the prongs?"

Meg shrugged. "Then you find a jeweler to fix them. Look, there's a tool box in the utility room. Gotta have something we can use, preferably needle nose pliers. Whadda you think?"

A gust of wind shook the house. Laura sighed. "Sounds like the perfect distraction. As soon as the kids go down."

Meg prepared a cracker for Laura. "And you wanted to go home. You know, this could turn out to be a really fun evening. Aren't you glad you stayed?"

The lights flickered. "I'd be a lot happier if I was sure we wouldn't lose power."

"Don't worry about that. We have a ton of candles and if they burn out, we can always use the flashlight app on our phone."

A car door slammed. Meg walked over to the kitchen window. "Hey, the pizza's here. That was quick. I'll nuke the soup."

"Great." Laura grabbed her wallet and was halfway down the steps when there was a loud bang. "What was that?" she called to Meg.

"The patio furniture. We probably should have brought it closer to the house."

"Too late now," Laura replied. She paid the delivery person and because of the weather, she tipped him generously. By the time she closed the door, a cold chill had invaded the area. Wanting everyone to be comfortable when they went to bed, she walked down the hall and turned the thermostat up a few degrees. To her delight, the heater responded almost immediately. Taking that as a good sign, she called her kids up for dinner.

Just as they were charging past her, another gust of wind rattled the windows. Although it made her heart pound, she was the only one who noticed. Climbing the steps, she felt foolish. She was supposed to be the grown-up in the room.

The kids were thrilled to see the soup. Laura had to laugh. She felt like a black sheep. She was the only one worried about the storm, and she was the only one who wouldn't be having soup. Holding the pizza box over her head, she pranced into the room. The soft yellow light glowing from the dining room chandelier provided a sharp contrast to the blackened windows and doors. Although it was still relatively early, all remnants of daylight had vanished. Thunder rumbled overhead but no one else seemed to care. *Don't be such a wimp*, Laura told herself. It was just a storm. By morning it would all be over. No doubt she was a bit out of her comfort zone but wasn't that what pizza and vacations were for?

Chapter Twenty-Six

July 5th

The pizza was even better than Laura expected and judging by Catherine Preston's empty tureen, so was the chicken noodle soup. While everyone else had enjoyed the soup, Laura opted for an extra slice of pizza. Now she was stuffed. She patted her stomach. Maybe if she got moving, she wouldn't feel so bloated.

Laura looked around. Except for the battering wind, the rain, and the soft drone of the TV, all was quiet. *Strange,* she mused somewhat perplexed by the sudden exodus from the table. No one brought their dishes over to the sink and no one offered to help. Instead, the kids had crashed on the living room floor in front of the TV and Meg, who just wanted to close her eyes for a few minutes, was also sound asleep. Laura tried not to begrudge them. No one slept very well last night, nor did anyone take as long a nap as she had.

Picking a mushroom off one of the leftover slices, Laura placed the remaining pizza in a plastic bag and then put it in the refrigerator. She crushed the pizza box and stuffed it in the trash. Next, she took the soup bowls over to the sink. She rinsed the bowls and put them in the dishwasher. Carefully, very carefully, she washed and dried Catherine Preston's tureen.

Lonely and a bit rattled by the storm, Laura again tried to get in touch with Mike. She knew she would feel better once she heard his voice but all she got was his voicemail. She pined to be home. A shiver coursed through her body. She rubbed her hands up and down her arms.

Even though the heat was on, the third level was uncomfortably chilly but it was just the way Meg liked it. Rather than up the thermostat, Laura went downstairs, grabbed pillows and blankets for the kids and gently covered them. She kissed their angelic faces. They seemed so peaceful, a sharp contrast to how sick they were last night.

Laura returned to the kitchen. She was tired and enormously distracted by her conversation with Sally Harrington. Still, wanting to get a jump on preparations for their eventual departure, she gathered the dish towels and the place mats, brought them downstairs and then tossed them into the washing machine. Knowing that they had to leave the house as neat as they found it, she went into the rec room. She was disappointed but not terribly surprised by the mess.

Structurally insulated from the wind and rain, the room was blissfully quiet. Laura looked around. She shrugged. There were worse ways to kill time. She began sorting the games and puzzle pieces. At first she was unwilling to just throw anything anywhere and labored to make sure everything wound up where it belonged. Several puzzles later, bored and queasy, she began to compromise. Close enough mattered more than one hundred percent accuracy.

The washer beeped the end of its cycle. Laura hurried into the laundry room, tossed the wet items into the dryer and turned it on. She started up the steps. Although she was sweating, she felt chilled. She upped the thermostat a few degrees and then walked into her bedroom. She figured she had two choices. She could close her eyes for a few minutes or she could continue her departure preparations. Her ring tone made the decision for her. She plopped onto her bed, hoping that Mike was finally returning her many calls.

"Hey, Mrs. H! It's Dave. I understand it's storming down there. Can you hear me okay"

"Yeah, I can hear you fine," Laura replied, annoyed that she felt so queasy. She stacked a couple of pillows against the headboard and leaned back. "What's up?"

Dave hesitated. He checked the time. It was relatively early but Laura sounded groggy. "I didn't wake you up, did I?"

"No, no, you didn't. Actually, I'm glad you called. Everyone corked off right after dinner so it's nice to have someone to talk to. This storm—the lights have flickered a few times. I just hope the power stays on, not so much for the light but for the heat."

"It's July, Mrs. H. How cold could it get?"

"It's not the cold as much as the winds. Think March. You know. When it's not really that cold but the wind blows right through the window panes and no matter how high the thermostat is set, it's hard to feel warm. That's what it's like right now."

"Sorry to hear that," Dave replied, "but I've got great news. I'm pretty sure I've identified Jane Doe. Her name is Rosa Berman. I don't have a lot on her right now but there's a definite link between her and Linda Ferina."

Laura was stunned. "How do you know?"

"Well, late yesterday, we found a letter that Rosa wrote to her sister in October 1945. It's been sitting in the dead letter file of the Greenview Post Office all these years. It's her, Mrs. H. The woman who brought your mother to Greenview. She mentions the Abbotts and the man she was running from: the man who tried to kill her and your mother. We think Rosa might be short for Rosalinda and that could be why she called herself Linda. Not sure where Ferina came from. Shelving that for now."

"Wow! That's really interesting. This letter. Can you email it to me? I'd love to read it."

"Wouldn't do you much good. It's written in German and all I have right now is a recorded translation. Because of the holiday we couldn't find anyone to translate it for us so Julie and I went to NY to see the house where this letter was sent. The house was a bust but on the train home we realized the lady sitting across from us was speaking German. Didn't have time to do a written translation, so she read the letter out loud and I recorded it. As soon as things settle down, I'll do a written transcription. In the meantime, the recording is all I have. It's a bit choppy and it might be hard to understand in places but do you want to hear it?"

"Of course. I'm really impressed."

"Okay, Okay. Here goes."

Although it hasn't been terribly long since I last wrote to you, it feels like a lifetime. The little girl I told you about passed away in her sleep several nights ago. It's been so sad. For her parents, for me and even for Marney.

"Marney? Who's Marney?"

"We believe it's your mother. Marney, Mary. If you take the n and the e out of Marney, you get Mary, which is the name everyone called your mother when she lived in Greenview."

"Marney," Laura whispered. "What a pretty name." She closed her eyes and gently placed her hand on her stomach. She wasn't sure what she regretted more, that last piece of pizza or the wine and cheese. "Go on. I wanna hear more."

That poor mother. The pain she is going through. It's made me think of Mrs. P and all the misery...

"Mrs. P? Who's Mrs. P?"

"Well if Marney's your mother, Mrs. P has to be your grandmother. Unfortunately, we still don't know what the P stands for. Do you remember how Linda told the Abbotts that everyone thought she and your mother had died in a fire? Well, based on this letter, we don't think it was a fire. It was an explosion. Rosa mentions it a little later on. It appears that Rosa, your mother and your grandfather were sailing on your grandfather's yacht when your mother got seasick. Your grandfather brought Rosa and your mother back to shore and then apparently continued on his way. When Rosa realized the boat exploded, she ran, believing that someone named Tad was responsible. In her mind, he was a monster bent on killing her and your mother. Don't know if that was fact or fantasy but he was the man Linda was running from, not some abusive husband.

"It's the explosion that's key, here, Mrs. H. We figured yachts don't explode without some kind of media coverage. I know it was a long time ago, but the Penn Library is incredible and Julie is a genius when it comes to discovery. We've been researching boating accidents circa Labor Day, 1945 since we got off the train. Julie's gotten a few serious hits so she's reached out to some of her friends. You know how it is. This one knows that one, who knows that one. Everyone's scrambling. With any luck should have a better idea who this Mr. and Mrs. P are fairly soon."

"Wow. You two are incredible. Do me a favor and start that letter from the beginning. I promise not to interrupt."

Dave complied and by the time he was done, Laura's heart was pounding. "This is amazing. Amelia's parents. Rosa must be talking about the couple who raised my mother. The timeline fits. My mother grew up thinking she had a twin sister named Amelia who died September, 1945 at the age of two. Honestly, Dave. This is making my head spin."

"I know. This letter's amazing in what it says and what it doesn't say. For example, this letter doesn't exactly explain Marney's relationship to Rosa but given that Mr. P was sailing a yacht, well, yacht to me says wealth. DNA has told us Rosa is not your mother's mother so I'm thinking she might have been some kind of nanny or governess. She and your mother must have been pretty close, close enough for Rosa to convince everyone they were mother and daughter."

"Good point. A governess, very expensive barrettes. The pieces are really starting to fit."

"There's more, Mrs. H. Remember the ring? Aaron pointed out six initials: FCP and GRB. R could be for Rosa, B for Berman and P could be for whoever Mrs. P is. The letter also mentions a barrette. No description but I'll betcha anything it's a Scottie dog."

"Wow! If this Marney really is my mother, then Mr. and Mrs. P must be my grandparents. I can't believe this. I never thought we'd get this far."

"Well, don't get too excited. If our information is correct, Mr. P was killed in that explosion and we have no idea if Mrs. P is still alive. We need her for DNA and until we get that, all we have is theory. Wait. Julie's got something. Hold the line. I'll be right back."

"Come on, come on, come on," Laura whispered as she waited and waited. Finally after what felt like an eternity, Dave came back.

"Mrs. H. Have you ever heard of an estate called Whalehead? Based on our timeline, we think the yacht that exploded belonged to the family that lived there. Julie's friend says it quite a place and at one time it took up the entire northern end of the Outer Banks."

Laura was speechless. "Dear God," she muttered. She tried to sit up but the room was spinning. "Don't tell me. The P stands for Preston."

"How'd you know?"

"My kids were flying a kite the other day and wound up on Whalehead property. I haven't met Mrs. Preston but I've spoken to her a couple of times. Oh, my God. This can't be, Dave. There's gotta be some kind of mistake."

"There's more. That Tad fellow, the one in the letter. We've got a last name. Quigley. Tad Quigley was the one Rosa was running from, the one she thought rigged the yacht."

"That can't be right. I happen to know that Tad and Mrs. Preston were close friends. He died just a couple of weeks ago but until then he was the caretaker for both her winter and summer estates. It just doesn't compute."

"Maybe, maybe not but according to Julie's friend, Quigley was Charles Preston's step-brother and Rosa wasn't the only one suspicious of him. There are others who think he blew the yacht because he hated his step brother and because he wanted Whalehead."

"Well, I can tell you that never happened. Tad Quigley died where he lived: in the caretaker's cottage. I know that because I met his grandson, Keith. He came here to drop off a kite for the kids, from his grandmother. Keith seemed like a really nice guy. We were having a very nice conversation until Sara walked in wearing my mother's barrettes."

"Your mother's barrettes?" Dave repeated. "What was she doing with your mother's barrettes?"

Laura sighed. "Long story."

Dave felt uneasy. Perhaps he was being unfair. Just because Keith was Tad's grandson didn't make him guilty by association. Then again, was Keith aware that his grandfather blew the Preston yacht? Did he have any idea how significant those barrettes might be? "So your daughter pranced in wearing your mother's barrettes. What happened after that?"

"Nothing really. I took them from her. Told her if she didn't nag me, I might give them back."

"Not with Sara, Mrs. H. With Keith. What did he do? How did he react? Think. This could be important."

Laura cringed. She was disturbed by the urgency in Dave's voice. "Why? Do you know something I don't?"

"Depends. My sources claim Catherine Preston has no living relatives. Keith's just a step grandson but he is the only game in town. For all we know, he feels entitled to the Preston fortune. If that's the case, how happy could he have been when your daughter walked in wearing barrettes that once belonged to Marney Preston?"

Laura didn't respond.

"I hate to say this, Mrs. H. but if Keith's anything like his grandfather, there's no telling what he's capable of. Look, I know it might be hard to wrap your head around this but if your mother really was Mrs. Preston's daughter, you're the legitimate heir to her fortune, not Keith. If he realizes the significance of those barrettes, who knows what he might do. Try to remember. How did he react?"

Laura closed her eyes. "This is so strange. Meg and I were talking about this earlier today. Keith did act a little odd when Sara pranced in wearing those barrettes but at first I thought it was because she interrupted. Last night Sara had a pretty high temp. She was kind of loopy but she kept talking about Keith and even asked me why he was staring at her."

"Was he?"

Trying desperately to keep her thoughts straight, Laura felt like crying. "Meg asked me the same thing but I can't say for sure. Keith was standing behind me when I made Sara give me the barrettes. I can tell you Keith made a quick exit right after that. Oh, my God. What could that mean?"

Dave hesitated. "Is there any chance that instead of staring at Sara, Keith might have been staring at those barrettes?"

Laura's heart was pounding. "I don't know," she whined. "Possibly, probably. I can't believe I told Keith as much about myself as I did. Looking back, he kind of stiffened when I mentioned the Abbott Farmstead. God only knows what he can glean from that."

"Nothing you can do about that now, Mrs. H. Look, I don't want to upset you but it's a good idea to put those barrettes under lock and key. They're your ace in the hole. I'll betcha anything Mrs. Preston balks when you tell her what we've discovered. Show her those barrettes and you're golden."

"When I tell her what we've discovered? I thought this was your story."

"It is but Mrs. Preston needs to know as soon as possible and you've already spoken to her. You can wait for me if you want. I'll head down at first light but I probably won't get there till early afternoon."

"I'm afraid that won't work," Laura replied. "Mrs. Preston is expecting us for brunch tomorrow, nine-ish."

"Perfect," Dave replied. "The sooner, the better."

Laura sighed. She felt sicker than ever. "Easy for you to say. Really wish I had that letter. English, German, who cares. Can you email it to me?"

"I can, but there's nothing like the real thing. I can't wait for you to see it. It's awesome. It's all yellowed. It even smells like a dusty old post office."

Despite her angst, Laura chuckled. "Okay, okay, I'll wait till you get here. Just be careful on your way down. Start texting me when you get to the Chesapeake Bay Bridge. That'll give me an idea when to expect you."

"Will do, Mrs. H. In the meantime, make sure all your doors are locked. Keep your phone charged and if you see or hear anything out of the ordinary, call 9-1-1."

"You're so reassuring," Laura complained. "If I have nightmares tonight, I'm gonna blame you."

"You'll be fine, Mrs. H. Just think. In a few more hours we might have this whole thing wrapped up. See you tomorrow. Can't wait."

Laura just nodded. "You know there was something I wanted to tell you but I can't remember. In my head one minute, gone the next. So annoying. One lousy glass of wine and I can barely string two thoughts together."

"It's been a long couple of days, Mrs. H. I'm sure you'll feel better in the morning."

"Right," Laura sighed. Just as she ended the call, an angry gust of wind shook the house. She tried to sit up but the room kept spinning. She leaned back. Closing her eyes, she took several deep breaths, hoping she would feel better. Instead, she was startled by a shrill beep.

"Dammit," she muttered, patting her chest for her phone. Between her stomach and her head, noise was the last thing she needed. All of a sudden, she could feel her ears pop, followed by the sound of rushing air. It was coming from the lower level. She groaned. The rushing air could only mean one thing: the door had somehow blown open. Laura listened. All of a sudden the noise stopped. *Thank God*, Laura mused. Last thing she wanted to do was to drag herself downstairs to close the door. As it was, she could barely move.

The room was dark and Laura could feel herself drifting off. Sleep. If only she could sleep. Maybe the nausea would go away. That beep. That shrill beep. How was she supposed to sleep with her phone going off? Damn. "Please stop," she whispered, patting the mattress for her phone. All of a sudden, it crashed to the floor. That beep. That shrill beep. It was louder than ever.

Willing herself to get up and turn the damn phone off, Laura was startled by a different sound. Wide-eyed, she fell back onto her pillow. What was going on? Footsteps? They were getting closer. It wasn't her imagination. "Meg?" No answer.

A large silhouette suddenly appeared in the doorway. Groggy as she was, Laura knew right away that it was Keith. He was walking toward her. Terrified, Laura tried to get up but he nudged her back onto the bed. Her children. She had to protect her children. Her head was spinning but she forced her eyes open just in time to see hands coming toward her face. She recoiled. "Please," she begged, gasping for air. "My children. Don't hurt my children."

It was the last thing she said.

Chapter Twenty-Seven

July 6th

For Keith Quigley the night seemed endless. On the plus side, Laura Hunter and her children were gone. They could no longer hurt him but it still wasn't over. Dawn may have broken but in many ways, the hardest part was yet to come.

Taking a deep breath, Keith walked over to the window. The storm had left its mark. Amid a clutter of broken tree branches the green field that he often took to get to the big house was dotted by puddles of water. He squinted. Against the brightening sky, the outline of the mansion was coming into view. He couldn't wait to wake up over there and look back on the dump where he had spent far too many years.

Keith turned from the window. He checked the time. After all he'd been through he was not about to do anything foolish. He would trust his instincts to do and to say all the right things. If his grandfather, a man with half his intellect, could live a lie for sixty-five years, he could certainly get through the next few days.

After days of ungodly heat, Keith longed for a nice hot cup of coffee. He went into the kitchen, prepared the pot and then grabbed two pieces of bread. Ignoring the tiny flecks of mold just beginning to grow, he popped them into the toaster. Several seconds later, he sat down at the kitchen table. He ran his hand over the scratched, uneven surface. It was a sharp contrast to the polished tables at the mansion. Today for some reason, it seemed especially annoying.

As he sipped his coffee, Keith wondered what his old man would say about his brilliant scheme. No doubt the old coot was threatened by his genius and would want him to fail. Keith got it. It was the only way his old man could feel superior. "Ain't gonna happen," he muttered.

The coffee sucked, as did the toast. Unable to sit still, Keith got up from the table. He checked the time. Catherine wanted him at the big house early to help her prepare for a brunch that wasn't going to happen. Keith knew that having to put up with Catherine's stupid questions and unfettered excitement could make for a long, tedious morning. He could only hope the moment when Catherine realized the Hunters were not coming would happen sooner rather than later. That was the moment when the greatest act of his life would begin.

Not wanting to get too far ahead of himself, Keith stuck his nose out of his cottage door. Although the rain had stopped, a persistent breeze was blowing. He looked around. On a morning like this, he knew exactly what his grandfather would be doing. He'd be down at the beach with all the other fishermen. For years Keith had listened to his old man go on and on about a storm's aftermath. 'If you can't catch a fish after a halfway decent storm, you might as well hang it up. Only an idiot would sit around.'

Keith shook his head, his thoughts drifting back to that storm twenty-eight years ago. At age eight, Keith still believed he could do something to please his old man. A Category Three hurricane had passed through the area and had left a delightfully rough surf in its wake. Like an idiot, Keith thought it would be the perfect opportunity to accompany his grandfather to the ocean.

Step by step, he still remembered the walk. Anticipation ran high. Dawn was just beginning to break. The old man was as expansive as Keith had ever seen him. Keith had been so sure this would be a turning point; that this time together would catapult their relationship into more positive territory.

As expected, the surf was rough. Keith followed his grandfather across the sand as he staked out the best available spot. Instinctively he glanced into the buckets of the people down there before them. Everyone seemed to be catching fish. Keith couldn't wait. Finally he would do something to win his grandfather's approval.

The tide was coming in. Supposedly a good sign. Squeamishly Keith baited his own hook. Cast, reel, cast, reel. Nothing. All around him everyone was catching something, everyone but him. What had he been doing wrong? Not wanting to disappoint his grandfather, he persisted. His head ached. His hands hurt but he kept at it. They started for home once his grandfather's bucket was full. The entire way back, and for years and years after that, all Keith ever got for his efforts were mocking reminders of how miserably he had failed.

Keith never went fishing again. He hated anything that reminded him of that day. When his grandfather died, he wanted to toss out all the old man's possessions, especially his fishing garb, his fishing poles, his bait and tackle. He knew that the sooner he got rid of all those painful reminders, the better he would feel. But he wasn't stupid. He had to show some sentimentality. He was the grieving grandson. Good sense dictated that he wait until they closed Whalehead for the season. Now he was glad for that he had.

His grandfather had been right. After storms like yesterday's everyone suddenly becomes a fisherman. People were already out and about, making it harder for him to sneak into Gatekeeper unnoticed.

Stay calm, Keith told himself. The to-do list was long and needed to be done as quickly and carefully as possible. *Challenging, but not impossible.* Keith knew the best way to get to and from Gatekeeper without attracting any undue attention was to blend in with all the other morons heading to the beach. All he had to do was to look like a fisherman.

Walking into his grandfather's bedroom, Keith once again patted himself on the back for holding onto his grandfather's crap. Standing in the closet, he donned his old man's fishing vest and hat. Reluctantly he slipped his stocking feet into his old man's smelly beach shoes and then took a large plastic bait and tackle bucket from the corner of the closet. Grabbing a fishing rod, he walked over to the mirror. *Good deal,* he told himself. Feeling confident, he set out for the path that ran from the cottage to the beach.

It still amazed Keith that his grandfather knew so little about him. He'd always called him a lazy dreamer who wouldn't amount to anything and yet in less than two months time, he'd quietly changed the lives of eight people. Nothing explosive. No destruction of property.

Since learning of his grandfather's crime, Keith's feelings for the old man had rotated through a carousel of emotions. Some days he was angry, some days he was jealous and some days he was actually proud. The man had been a bastard and yet he had gotten away with an unspeakable crime. That had to take a considerable amount of genius. Then again, forensic science was still in its infancy and as curious as people were at to what caused Charles Preston's yacht to explode, no one could prove anything.

Fast forward sixty-five years. Keith accepted that he had many more challenges. He knew damn well that the deaths of a young mother, her three children and her best friend would be intensively investigated. He also knew that once he sterilized the crime scene and confiscated those stupid barrettes, no one would know. The rightful heir to the Preston fortune would be interred with her children and life would go on.

As he made his way to Gatekeeper, Keith reminded himself that he had done the right thing and unlike his grandfather, he had been kind. Rather than blowing his victims to bits, he had found a way to allow them to pass away peacefully in their sleep. Carbon monoxide poisoning was a much better solution. It was quiet, neat, and clean. It sucked that his grandfather had forced him to become an executioner but at least he had figured out a way to be a gentle one.

Since Whalehead was private property, Keith decided to make his way to the gazebo and from there slip through the tree line over to Gatekeeper. Unfortunately the path to the gazebo was soggier than Keith expected and he regretted not having worn his grandfather's boots instead of his beach shoes. Now, when he got to the house, he'd not only have to remove his sopping wet shoes, he'd have to remove his socks. So much for getting in and getting out in record time.

By the time he reached Gatekeeper, Keith's nerves were on edge. He stood outside under the car port and listened. No blaring carbon monoxide sensors. A good sign and a not-so-good sign. How did he know if it was safe to go inside? He was confident that no one had seen him but it was still chilly. Was the heater running? If not, how long ago had it turned off? *Fifteen minutes*, he decided. Surely he would be safe for that amount of time. Get in and get out.

As he removed his shoes and socks, Keith fully understood that the final phase of his scheme would be the hardest. Once his crime scene was secured he would wend his way back to the cottage. He would shower, dress and maybe spend a few minutes in front of the mirror rehearsing his lines. No doubt Catherine would react badly to the news of Laura's demise. Keith would not only have to comfort her, but his own shock and grief would have to be convincing. He knew he'd be taking a page from his grandfather's playbook, but he was glad for one major difference. Like his grandfather, he would console Catherine all the while knowing he was the one responsible for her grief but at least he wouldn't have to spend sixty-five years doing it. With any luck, age and depression would hasten Catherine's demise and he would be free. The Quigley quest that had begun sixty-five years ago would finally be complete.

Taking a long look around, Keith went over his game plan one more time. First he would remove the duct tape from the lower level sensor on the wall next to the staircase. Then he would head up to the middle level and take care of that sensor. He would go into the little girl's room, grab those barrettes and then make his way up to the third floor. He would remove the tape from that sensor, wash the tureen, exit through the sliding door and then come down the outside steps. Once at the carport, he would put his shoes on and be on his way.

Taking a deep breath, Keith stepped inside. Given the early hour, the lower level was dark, but not dark enough to have to turn on the light. The house was deadly quiet, quiet but a bit chilly. Keith scrunched his nose. That smell. What the hell was it?

Walking slowly, Keith headed for the steps. He was about to walk around the staircase to get to the sensor when something caught his eye. He stopped dead in his tracks. A strange looking object was lying on the steps.

"What the hell," he whispered. His heart was pounding. He moved closer. "Goddamn," he muttered. The little girl's doll was lying face up on the fourth step from the bottom. As he reached for the doll, he looked up. For several seconds, he stared mouth agape at the tiny figure lying at the head of the steps, her hand draped over the first step. He hadn't counted on this. That rotten brat must have gotten up at some point during the night.

Rattled, Keith yanked the doll off the step. Annoyed that his hand was shaking, he removed one barrette and then the other. He slipped them both into his pocket, tossed the doll onto the steps and then made his way around the staircase. *One step at a time*, he told himself, reaching for the sensor. Dammit. His hands were still shaking and he was having trouble breathing. Although the house was somewhat chilly, he worried that the CO levels were still lethal.

Knowing that he had to hurry, Keith knelt down. Not wanting to leave any residue, he slowly removed the duct tape. Perfect. Two more to go.

Trying to ignore the pulsing in his ears, Keith started up the steps. The light was dim, but it was enough for him to see that the kid was lying sideways, deliberately blocking his path. He climbed slowly, very slowly. *Why*, he wondered. Why did the miserable brat look bigger than he remembered? Her hair seemed a bit stringier but he was grateful that it was covering her face. He couldn't help but wonder if she had died with her eyes open or closed.

All of a sudden Keith noticed a shadow. He froze. Someone was in the house. What the hell. This was not part of his plan. Dammit. *Be calm*, he told himself. Of course the duct tape on the remaining sensors would be incriminating but if he got out unseen, no one could prove that he was the one responsible. He turned around. Fighting the urge to run, he tiptoed down; one step, two steps. *Almost there. Don't panic. Don't panic.*

He reached the bottom step and was just a short distance from safety when he heard someone call to him. He bolted. As yet, no one had seen his face. Grabbing the doorknob, he flung the door open. A man in uniform was blocking his path. He stepped forward and was about to push his way to freedom when someone grabbed him from behind. "Keith Quigley, you're under arrest for the attempted murder of Laura Hunter, Scott Hunter, Sara Hunter, Jon Hunter and Meg Richards. You have the right to remain silent…."

Chapter Twenty-Eight

July 6th

Laura knew she was in trouble, big trouble. She was almost three hundred miles from home and yet she thought she heard Mike Romano's voice. *It had to be wishful thinking,* she decided, trying to recall her last waking moments. She had a vague recollection of feeling ill and of being afraid.

She opened her eyes. Blinking against the harsh white light, she began to panic. Nothing looked familiar. She became aware of a strange noise, soft but persistent. Curious, she looked down. Clear plastic tubes were positioned across her cheeks, just under her eyes. Something was in her nose. She took it out. The strange noise changed. Oxygen. Why was she breathing oxygen? Her left arm hurt and she felt something strange on her finger. She checked it out. An oxygen sensor was pinched to the tip of her finger. The needle stuck in her vein was attached to an IV pump. Clearly she wasn't at the Ritz.

Laura looked around. She remembered the darkness, the wind and rain, wanting to go home, of being all alone. But she wasn't alone. Someone had been in the house. All of a sudden, she bolted upright. Her children! Where were her children? Having kinked the line to her IV, it started beeping. Footsteps began running toward her. "Laura! Wait!"

The kids. Where were her kids? Cursing the spinning room, she tried to get up but she could feel herself falling. Someone grabbed her. Sat her on the bed and then sat down beside her. "It's all right, Laura. Everything's all right."

As much as she wanted to see, Laura closed her eyes, hoping to stop the spinning sensation. That voice. It sounded so comforting, so soothing. She opened her eyes. "Mike!" She reached for his face just to make sure it was really him. "Where am I? Where are the kids?"

"You're in the hospital. I brought you in last night. The kids and Meg are fine."

Laura studied Mike's somber expression. She'd known him since they were in high school. If he wasn't being one hundred percent truthful, she'd know right away. "Where are they?"

"They're with Joe and Judy Winston."

"Joe and Judy? Why?"

"It wasn't safe to stay at Gatekeeper."

"Why not?"

"Carbon monoxide."

"Carbon monoxide? That's impossible. I know our heater was safe to use. The HVAC Company sent a tech to check the heater. Said it was fine."

Mike just nodded. Laura had been through a lot and he wasn't sure she was ready to hear all the disturbing details. "They're looking into that."

"Who's they?"

Mike hesitated. The look on Laura's face said it all. She wanted to know and she wanted to know now. "The police, the F.B.I."

"The F.B.I? You gotta be kidding. Why?"

Mike shrugged. "I don't know the whole story but they've been looking into the activities of a local HVAC tech. He came to light because of the number of heaters he's recommended replacing over the years due to high levels of carbon monoxide. Most of the old heaters are gone but one in particular caught their attention. The Corolla Post Office. They suspect the burners had been deliberately corroded. Federal building, federal crime."

"What's that got to do with Gatekeeper?"

Mike turned the oxygen off and then lifted the tubes over Laura's head. He gestured to the IV bottle. "Let's get that out of your arm."

Laura watched as Mike turned off the IV, removed the needle, placed a sterile pad on her arm and then gently pressed a strip of tape over it. She waited for him to answer her question. Instead he asked her how she was feeling.

"I'd feel a lot better if I knew what was going on."

"Headache?"

Laura shook her head.

"Nausea?"

"No. Mike. What's going on?"

"You want to get out of here?"

"Of course I do, but I want you to tell me what's going on."

"First show me how well you can walk. I'll help you get started."

"I don't need any help."

"Suit yourself. I'm here. Grab my arm if you need to."

Wanting to prove that she was fine, Laura stood up. Feeling surprisingly woozy, she reached for Mike's arm. "I can walk. I know I can."

"I know you can too. I'll walk you over to the door. You walk back by yourself."

With each step, Laura felt stronger. Then it occurred to her. If she needed oxygen and an IV, how could the kids and Meg be okay? She stopped dead in her tracks. "Why won't you tell me what happened? Are you sure the kids are okay?"

"Absolutely." Mike guided her into the bathroom. "They're not only okay, they're all waiting for you. I'll tell you everything on the way to Joe's." Mike handed Laura her clothes and an overnight pack. "I'll be at the front desk."

"Oh, my God," Laura whispered, catching her reflection in the bathroom mirror. Her skin was pasty white. She couldn't let her kids see her like this. She washed her face and pinched her cheeks. She brushed her teeth and then combed her hair. Mike had just finished speaking to the doctor in charge when she walked out. He looked over and smiled. There was no need for either of them to say anything, not just yet.

"I've figured it out," Laura said several minutes later as Mike pulled out of the parking lot. "It's all coming back. That HVAC tech was Keith Quigley, wasn't it"

Mike nodded. "I'm afraid so. They arrested him at Gatekeeper a little while ago for attempted murder. How'd you know it was Keith?"

"Wild guess. Keith mentioned that he spent every adult summer working as an HVAC tech. I got the impression he really knew what he was doing. If anyone would know how to fill a house with carbon monoxide, he would."

Mike smiled. "You're pretty sharp. No memory issues. Glad to see that."

"Don't get too excited. I remember talking to Dave about Keith and I remember him warning me to be careful but I don't remember why. I remember being scared."

Mike hesitated. He didn't want to dump everything on Laura all at once. "What else did you and Dave talk about?"

Laura took a moment to compose her thoughts. "Well, Dave called because found a letter in the dead letter file of the Greenview Post Office. It was written by a woman named Rosa Berman, aka, Jane Doe, the woman we've been trying to identify."

Mike smiled. "So far, so good. What else do you remember?"

Laura ran her hand through her hair. She hesitated. "Dave thinks my mother's real name was Marney. Marney Preston."

Mike was pleased. "I'm impressed. Dave mentioned that you've spoken to Mrs. Preston several times and that Scott and Sara have already met her. That should make things a little easier."

Laura squinted. "What things?"

"Letting Catherine Preston know she's your long lost grandmother; getting her to agree to DNA."

Laura closed her eyes. She rested her head against the head rest. "I knew that. I sort of remember Dave and I talking about that last night."

"Good," Mike replied, pleased that Laura's memory seemed to be all right. "Last night. Thank God we got there when we did."

"When did you realize it was carbon monoxide?"

"Almost immediately. When we got to Gatekeeper, the CO sensor on the middle level was just starting to beep. Joe thought that was odd, given how sick you were. Those sensors should have been blaring. Once we got everyone situated, Joe called the police chief and took him back to the house. No big surprise. The sensors had been tampered with. Dave figured out the rest."

"Dave? When'd you speak to Dave?"

"Last night. He called your cell about an hour after we got you here."

Intuitively Laura began patting her pockets. "Darn. I must have left my phone at the house."

"No, you didn't," Mike replied, reaching into his pocket and then handing the phone to Laura. "Sorry about the screen. It was on the floor when I got there and I accidently stepped on it. Truthfully, I didn't realize I'd slipped it into my pocket until I heard your ring tone. It works, but you've gotta let me get you a new one."

Laura ran her finger over the cracked screen. "Why would I want a new phone? Every time I use this one, I'll think of you."

"Yeah, and you'll remind me what a klutz I was."

"No, I won't. I'll remind you that you saved my life."

Mike shrugged. "All I did was beat Dave to it. He was pretty upset after he talked to you. He planned to call you back just to make sure you were okay. I assure you, he would have called 9-1-1 if you didn't answer. Only difference, they wouldn't have such a solid case against Keith right now."

"A solid case? What do you mean?'"

"Well, Joe says that if Dave ever changes his mind about being an investigative reporter, he should be a lawyer. He had Keith figured out from the get go. Claimed if Keith was smart enough to tamper with the CO sensors, he'd be smart enough to come back and remove the evidence. Made the case for the authorities to be at Gatekeeper so they could catch him in the act."

Laura squinted, studying Mike's facial expression. "What's so funny?"

Mike shook his head. "Nothing. Well, Joe. In a lot of ways, he hasn't changed. He was always a prankster. This time it really paid off. They figured when Keith came back, he'd probably go in through the door on the bottom floor, where no one would see him. You might not like this but Joe got them to use one of his child size dummies, you know the ones they use to teach CPR. Long dark hair. They laid the dummy face down at the top of the stairs on the second floor and Sara's doll several steps below so it would look as though she dropped it when she fell. Joe claimed at first glance that it looked pretty convincing."

Laura imagined the scenario. She cringed. "That's really disturbing."

"Well what was more disturbing is that Keith ignored the dummy and picked up Sara's doll. Here's the part I still don't understand. He took the time to remove the barrettes that were in the doll's hair. According to Dave, short of DNA, those barrettes might be the only solid evidence linking your mother to Catherine Preston."

Laura sighed. "Yeah. Dave was pretty set on that. Wait till you see these things: platinum shaped Scottie dogs covered with real gemstones, diamonds, rubies and onyx. Did Meg tell you how they wound up down here?"

Mike chuckled. "She did and somehow I'm not surprised."

"Speaking of surprises; whatever possessed you to come down?"

"I was missing you and the kids so I managed to wrangle a few days off. I reserved an SUV at the airport but my flight was delayed and by the time I got there, all they could give me was a sedan. Between the rain and the flooding, I kept stalling. The car finally died right in front of that big grocery store. I coasted into the parking lot. Didn't want to call you and ruin the surprise so I called Joe. He came to get me and brought me to Gatekeeper. He planned to just drop me off but at the last minute decided to come in. Good thing too."

Laura sighed. "You know, this kind of reminds me of that day in the emergency room. I was terrified. Scott's arm looked like a pretzel and you walked by. Once again, I really needed someone and there you were. You know, I think I'm ready to make this a permanent thing. Is the offer still on the table?"

Mike pulled onto a long winding driveway. "I don't know. If I'm following Dave and Joe correctly, you might be an heiress and I'm not sure I want to deal with all that drama. Heiress, high maintenance: who needs it?"

Laura punched Mike in the arm. After a long kiss, they walked arm in arm up to the house. Even before they reached the front porch, they could hear the kids running out to greet them. After hugs that were tighter and longer than usual, Joe and Judy Winston led them into the kitchen for what turned out to be a loud and boisterous breakfast.

"We need to get going," Joe said to Laura as the children finished eating and then bounded outside. "I'm not sure how much longer we should keep this thing hanging. Word travels fast around here and I don't want Catherine to hear about what happened from anyone else."

Laura took a deep breath. "I'm not sure I'm ready for this."

"For what?" Joe asked. "For telling a sweet old lady who thinks she's all alone in the world that she may very well have a granddaughter and three wonderful great grandchildren?"

"You're not looking at the whole picture, Joe. What about my mother? Catherine Preston has lived her whole life thinking her only child died sixty-five years ago. Her whole life. All that emptiness, all that sorrow. For what? How am I supposed to tell her what we think happened without her feeling that she's lost her only daughter twice? Shouldn't we wait till we're absolutely sure?"

"I'm already sure," Joe replied. "I didn't notice it when you first came to my office but I see it now. My grandmother was Catherine's maid of honor and every time I walked into her house, I saw a picture of Catherine and my grandmother when they were much younger. With the exception of your coloring, you look very much like Catherine way back then. In my mind, the DNA is just a formality."

"But Joe, it's so creepy. All those times we've vacationed down here. Catherine and my mother were actually living less than a mile apart. Why couldn't this have happened a few months ago, when my mother was still alive?"

Mike reached over and squeezed Laura's hand. "You have three beautiful children. Your mother lives in you and in them."

Laura took a deep breath. She began rubbing her arms, trying to smooth the goose bumps that were breaking out all over. She looked at Joe. "Will you stay with me?"

"If you want."

Mike got up and walked over to Laura. He gently massaged her shoulders. "You said you don't think you're ready for this, but I think you are. You've been ready since you found out that the Abbott Farmhouse was still standing. It's an incredible story."

Laura finally pushed her chair away from the table. She got up, hugged Mike and then kissed him goodbye. "Wish me luck."

Mike held Laura close. "You don't need luck," he whispered. "You'll know exactly what to do and say. It's one of the reasons why I love you."

Laura smiled. "Does that mean the offer's back on the table?"

"Maybe," Mike teased. "I've always wanted a seaside mansion." He kissed her again and then held her at arm's length. "An heiress. Guess I shoulda known. Must be in the genes. Your mother was such a classy lady."

"You say that 'cause she always took your side."

"I say that because she raised one hell of a daughter. You'd better go. You don't want to keep your grandmother waiting. I never met the woman but I guarantee she's going to feel the same way I do and the same way your mother did. You're going to make her very happy."

Chapter Twenty-Nine

July 6th

The ride from Joe's house to Whalehead was way too long and not long enough. Laura was looking forward to meeting Catherine Preston as much as she was dreading it. "I can't believe we're doing this," she said as Joe pulled out of his driveway.

"You and me both. This is the last thing I expected when Mike called me last night."

Laura sighed. "Tell me. I'm not complaining but why was I the only one to get sick?"

"Because you were on the second floor and it was pretty hot. If you'd been upstairs with everyone else, you would have been fine. It was much cooler. Not as much heat, not as much carbon monoxide."

"Thank Meg for that. She loves it cold. Everyone conked out right after dinner and I didn't want to carry the kids downstairs so I just covered them. They looked so peaceful."

"There might be a reason for that. Meg said she felt groggy after eating the soup and that you were the only one who didn't have any. We're looking into it. We think the soup might have been spiked. Guess Keith wanted to make sure you all slept to the very end."

"That's despicable. Catherine made that soup and by leaving the door open for Keith, I played right into his hands. I don't think we should mention this to her. She would feel awful."

"Agreed. Keith has been like a son to Catherine and Tad was her lifelong friend. Family is very important to her and she's been betrayed by people she trusted. It won't be easy."

Laura shrugged. "Just think, if my kids hadn't gone chasing their kite on her property, we wouldn't be doing this. It's so odd. Every year when we would come down here, my mother would go walking by the Sound so she could take pictures of Whalehead. Said it reminded her of the house she grew up in. Until yesterday, I figured she was talking about Greenview. Is it possible she was talking about Whalehead?"

"The scientific answer would be no. Memory at age two is not well developed."

"Well, I'm glad the screen on my phone isn't totally destroyed. I've got some nice pictures of my mother on it. I hope Catherine will want to see them. If only my mother were here. It would make this so much easier."

Joe nodded his agreement as he pulled through the iron gates marking the entrance to Whalehead. He drove slowly, giving Laura plenty of time to absorb the view. The long, straight road ended at a circular driveway. Joe turned to the right and drove almost three quarters of the way around before stopping at the front door. Catherine came rushing out.

"Joe! Thank God you're here. They tell me something happened at Gatekeeper but they won't tell me what. That's where Mrs. Hunter and her children are staying. What's going on?"

Joe put his arm around Catherine. "Don't worry. Everyone's fine."

Laura got out of the car and walked over to Catherine. She couldn't help but notice that despite Catherine's advanced years, she was a beautiful woman. Laura extended her hand. "Hello, I'm Laura Hunter. So nice to meet you."

Catherine slapped her hand over her heart. "Oh, my." She reached for Laura's hands and squeezed tightly.

"I was beginning to think we'd never meet." She peeked into the car. "Where are the children?"

"They're at Joe's with Judy and the boys. They're all well and they loved your soup."

"That's wonderful. Please. Come inside." She slid her arm through Laura's and then turned to Joe. "I have so many questions."

They stepped into the foyer. It was dark but welcoming. An arched doorway on the right led into a ballroom sized living room. A wide curved staircase sat some fifteen feet back. A wall of glass lined the back end of the house, its tiny paned windows providing a stunning view of the water.

"This way," Catherine said leading them down a windowed hallway on her left and into a book filled library. She offered Joe and Laura a beverage and not wanting to waste time, was relieved when they declined. "Sit," she said, gesturing to two wing backed chairs. She took her seat and then turned to Joe. "Please. You must tell me what's happened. Keith's in serious trouble, isn't he?"

"He is," Joe replied. "I'm very sorry. I know how much he means to you."

Catherine stiffened. "Meant to me. I'm afraid I've just realized something and I can't tell you how awful I feel." She walked over to the credenza, slid the drawer open and removed a book. She sat down, opened the book and then took out a folded piece of paper. "Keith wanted me to believe my daughter's governess wrote this shortly before her death sixty-five years ago." She handed the paper to Laura. "I realize now that it's a farce. A complete farce and I fell for it. Go ahead. Read it out loud so Joe can hear."

Laura complied. Knowing what really happened, she was shocked by the cruelty of its content. "Where did you get this?" she asked when she finished.

"Keith claimed to have found it with his grandfather's things. I should have known. Charming as Keith is, he can't be trusted. He was clever, aging the paper, copying Rosa's handwriting, writing the translation between the lines. That awful man wanted me to think that my little girl could have been saved had she not slipped out of her life jacket. 'Zippers', Keith wrote. He claimed she kept unzipping her life jacket but her jacket didn't have zippers, it had buckles; buckles that she couldn't have loosened by herself. It took me a while to realize that this had to be Keith's version and not my daughter's governess."

Wow, Laura mused. Catherine was more astute than she expected. "Why? Why would he do something like that?" she asked.

Catherine took a deep breath. "Several days ago, I made it known that I wanted Keith to be my heir. My lawyer went crazy. More than anyone, Henry Weinstein understood the bad blood between Charles and Keith's grandfather and he was determined that no Quigley would ever get a dime of Preston money. He came to me with doublespeak about some letter that he believed my daughter's governess wrote to her sister after the accident; a letter he accused Tad of secretly getting his hands on and using to his advantage. I won't bore you with all of Henry's insinuations, but I can tell you it was very upsetting."

"Did your lawyer know what was in the letter?"

"He thought he did. Whether he was right or not, he made such a stink over this letter that I had to know if it really existed. Frankly, I never expected Keith to find anything, but I asked him to look through his grandfather's things just in case. He understood how important this was to me and that the issue needed to be resolved before I could change my will.

"I hate to say this but Keith's ploy almost worked. When he read that letter to me, I was horrified but actually a little bit relieved. You see I've lived my entire life refusing to accept that my little girl had been killed. This letter gave me closure—closure and nightmares. Keith was brilliant. Not wanting to be tainted by what his grandfather did, he provided the perfect cover for him. That letter gave me every reason to forgive Tad but to be angry with my lawyer.

"The zipper wasn't Keith's only mistake. The handwriting was exactly like Rosa's, a woman who's been dead for sixty-five years. I had to wonder how Keith could have done that. Obviously he had to have a sample of her writing and there was only one way that could happen. My lawyer was right. Rosa must have written a letter to her sister after the explosion, a letter Tad got his hands on when I sent him to pick up Helga's things. Why he kept it all these years I'll never know, but that letter must be how Keith knew what Rosa's handwriting looked like. I feel so foolish. These past several weeks I've been warming up to Keith. Without Tad here to beat him down, he seemed to be coming into his own. I was proud of him. Blind, actually. Perhaps my lawyer was right. Only a fool would trust a Quigley."

Laura glanced at Joe. "But you and Tad were lifelong friends."

"More like partners in grief. We propped each other up. There was a lot of finger pointing after the accident; all kinds of gossip about Tad causing the explosion. I defended him by reminding everyone how much he loved Marney and how he would never do anything to hurt her. Thing is, Tad and I were the only ones who knew Marney going on the yacht that day was a last minute decision. The guilt. At times it was overwhelming. If I hadn't been so wrapped up in myself, Marney would never have gotten onto that yacht. To be honest, remaining friends with Tad was all about appearance. If I had let him go, tongues would never stop wagging. Besides, he was a fabulous caretaker. I needed him. If I had known then what I know now."

"We can all say that about something," Laura replied. "All my life, I believed my mother was born in Greenview and that she left after a tragic fire killed her father and brother; her mother and twin sister had predeceased them. I used to beg my mother to take me up there, to let me see where she grew up, where her family was buried. She never did and eventually I stopped asking.

"A few weeks ago, I agreed to mentor a young reporter who was determined to identify remains that had been discovered in Greenview under the foundation of a sixty-five year old hotel. I was stunned when he linked my family to those remains. Turns out there was no fire and the farmhouse where my mother grew up was still standing. It was a very dark day for me. My mother had recently passed away. I felt so empty. I wished I'd been more persistent."

Catherine leaned over and patted Laura's hands. "I'm so sorry."

"Thank you. On the plus side, I finally got to go to Greenview. Dave introduced me to my mother's neighbor and I learned things about my mother that I don't think she knew. Turns out, she was not born in Greenview but had been brought there when she was two by a woman who called herself Linda Ferina. September, 1945. Linda led everyone to believe she was my mother's mother. She disappeared a short time after they arrived in Greenview. We now believe her remains were the ones found under that hotel."

"That's terrible. Was she…was she murdered? Your own grandmother?"

"She was, but according to DNA she wasn't my grandmother. We were stymied. Then the other day, Dave found a letter in the dead letter file of the Greenview Post Office. The letter was written in German so it took a while for Dave to get it translated. This letter not only confirmed the Jane Doe was the woman who brought my mother to Greenview, it gave us every reason to believe that she was actually my mother's governess and that her name was Rosalinda Berman. In her letter, Rosa mentions a man named Tad and a little girl named Marney."

Catherine squinted. "What are saying? Are you aware that my daughter's name was Marney and that Rosa was her governess? This is crazy. My husband, Marney and Rosa were all killed when my husband's yacht exploded."

Laura hesitated. "I know that's what everyone thinks, but according to this letter, Rosa and Marney were not on the yacht when it exploded. Marney had gotten terribly seasick and your husband brought them back to shore."

"That's impossible. If Rosa and Marney weren't on the yacht when it exploded, I would have been the first person Rosa contacted."

"That's probably true but Rosa was terrified. She was convinced Tad was trying to kill her and Marney so she ran. Wound up in Greenview. Told the family who raised my mother that she was running from an abusive husband who had already tried to kill her and my mother. She didn't want anyone to find her. She wrote to her sister in the hope that she would let you know she and Marney were alive. Essentially, she used her sister to circumvent Tad. She changed her name to Linda Ferina and told everyone Marney's name was MaryAnne. They called my mother Mary when she lived in Greenview, but after she left she changed her name to Anne."

Catherine bristled. She stared at Laura. After Tad and Keith, she wasn't about to trust anyone. "This letter. I must see it."

"Of course," Laura replied. "Dave has the letter and is on his way down. Hopefully, you'll confirm that it's Rosa's handwriting."

Catherine was visibly agitated. Her lips were dry, her hands trembling. "I...I don't know what to think."

"I understand," Laura whispered. She pulled her chair next to Catherine and gently reached for her hand. "Maybe this will help." She turned Catherine's hand over and placed one of her mother's barrettes in the center of her palm.

Catherine gasped, staring at the barrette. She ran her finger over the face, the collar, the body. *How could this be*? she wondered. It was exactly like the one her husband had designed for their daughter. *Don't give in*, she told herself. *Not yet*. She couldn't stop the tears welling in her deep blue eyes. "Where did you get this?" she demanded.

"When I was in Greenview, my mother's neighbor gave this to me. There were two of them. Ethel Abbott, the woman who raised my mother, gave them to her when she learned she was dying of cancer. She asked her neighbor to give them to my mother when she turned twenty-one and to tell her the whole story. Unfortunately my mother ran away from Greenview when she was seventeen and never went back. Had Dave not been so determined to identify those remains, I would never know any of this."

Again Catherine ran her finger over the barrette. "I...I don't know," she replied. "It looks...it looks like Marney's but why should I believe you?"

"They came in a locked box," Laura added. "Rosewood. I have it at home. Looks like a tiny treasure chest. Red velvet interior."

Catherine's heart was pounding. She didn't know what to believe. She took a deep breath. "My daughter was wearing three of these the day she boarded the yacht. Three, but you only have two. What happened to the third one?"

Laura chose her words carefully. She was more convinced than ever that Catherine Preston was her grandmother. "In the letter Dave found, Rosa references all five barrettes. You're right. She originally had three but we believe she sent one with her first letter to her sister as proof that Marney was alive. My guess is if Tad kept that letter, he also kept that barrette. Oddly enough, the day Keith brought the kite over, my little girl pranced into the room wearing the barrettes. Keith's whole demeanor changed and I wasn't quite sure why until a little while ago. Obviously he realized those were the same barrettes that belonged to Marney."

"Keith," Catherine sighed, shaking her head. "I'm so sorry. I never should have sent him over. Can I tell you something? Meeting your children, the way they talked about their grandmother. I found myself envying her. I was sad to hear that she recently passed away, but I couldn't help but think how lucky she was to be so beloved by such wonderful children."

Laura felt oddly relieved. "They loved her very much and something tells me they'll be just as fond of you."

"Me?" Catherine asked. She hesitated. Her eyes widened. She brought her hand to her mouth. Suddenly it dawned on her. "They could be my great grandchildren. Please. Don't do this to me. If this is all a big hoax, I'll be so disappointed."

"I understand," Laura replied. "I'm sure you'll feel better once you see that letter. Last I heard, Dave had just turned onto Southern Shores. He should be here soon."

No one spoke for several seconds. Laura was concerned. Perhaps this was all too much for an old woman. She took a deep breath. "I don't mean to burden you further, but we spent hours searching for someone named Linda Ferina. We figured she was in her twenties in 1945. We had no luck. Does that name ring any bells to you?"

Catherine stared at Laura. Her jaw dropped open. "It…it…now that you mention it. My maiden name was

Ferarra but when I told Rosa, she thought I said Ferina. We had a good many chuckles over that. Linda Ferina. Rosa's full name was Rosalinda. Do you think that's why she chose that name?"

"Could be. It might have been her way of letting you know how important you were to her."

Sniffling, Catherine dabbed her eyes. "Forgive me. I guess it's all starting to sink in. Marney being alive all these years. I don't think I'll ever be able to forgive Tad, not so much for the explosion but for what happened afterward. He had to know that Marney was with Rosa. Why didn't he bring her home to me? That is the ultimate betrayal."

"He might not have realized she was alive. We believe Tad accosted Rosa at the cemetery where little Amelia Abbott had just been buried. You can imagine how terrified she must have been. This is just speculation, but we think that Rosa, in a desperate attempt to protect my mother, might have told Tad that my mother was the one buried in that tiny grave."

Catherine patted Laura's hand. "That's very kind and as godawful as that is I'd love to believe that. Please. I want to hear all about your mother."

Laura took a deep breath. "Well, she was a very brave woman. After Greenview, she put herself through college, met my father, got married and had me. She was my lifeline. My husband was killed in a car accident shortly after my youngest was born. She came to live with me. I don't know what I would have done without her and, to be honest, I'm still trying to figure that out. She was an incredible person. No matter how bad things got, she always put one foot in front of the other and kept right on going. Had she lived, she would have been sixty-seven this September. September the 6th."

Catherine smiled. "That's sounds like her. Even as a little girl, nothing kept her down. Can I tell you something?

When I first met your daughter, I was stunned by how much she reminded me of Marney. Frankly, that's why I wanted to meet you. I...I...can't believe it. It would be a dream come true if that little girl is my great granddaughter."

Laura sighed. "We'll know for sure once we do a DNA test. That shouldn't take too long."

The elephant in the room was breathing louder. Catherine wiped a tear from the corner of her eye. "I know your mother recently passed away. Was she ill?"

"No, at least not that we knew. Brain aneurysm. Very sudden."

"Do you have any pictures?"

Laura reached for her cell phone and began flipping through her pictures. "I have a really good one from last summer. My mother loved the Outer Banks. She was the one who got us started coming down here. Every year she would pick the house. Oddly enough she was fascinated by Whalehead. Said it reminded her of the house she grew up in."

Catherine smiled as she watched Laura search for that picture. "She was such a spitfire. Two years old and she acted as if she owned the place. Do you have any brothers or sisters?"

"No. My father passed away when I was three. My mother never remarried. She was young, beautiful, and had plenty of suitors but always said no one could hold a candle to my father."

"Not many women can say that, you know. She was blessed and that makes me happy."

Laura handed the phone to Catherine. "Sorry about the screen. I've got a lot more pictures and videos at home."

Catherine didn't move. She stared at the picture for several seconds. She blinked several times. She squinted but she could not take her eyes off the picture. "Did…did your mother like to walk, by the Sound, bright and early?"

"Yes, the earlier the better."

Catherine's hand was shaking as she brought it to her mouth. She stared at the picture for several seconds and then closed her eyes. "It's her. I'm sure it's her. Your mother was my Good Samaritan."

Laura was incredulous. "What do you mean?"

"Last summer, I decided it was time for me to get more exercise and I thought a daily walk by the Sound would be just the thing. Of course I was aware of all the gossip that flies around down here about the old lady and all her money so I always wore an old baseball cap and an ancient short set. I never told anyone I was going out. I felt like a teenager, sneaking out on her parents. I would go early so I could be back before my cook called me for breakfast. Such fun. There I was out on the trail, blending in with the tourists. That day I twisted my ankle. I'll never forget— it was the second Saturday in August."

Laura's eyes widened. "Our departure day. I remember. My mother loved to walk by the Sound and since it had rained the morning before, she hadn't gotten to go and was a bit antsy. She promised to be back so that we could be on the road no later than 7AM. It was after eight by the time she got back. She was very apologetic. Said someone got hurt on the trail and that she stayed to help."

Catherine sighed. "That was my fault, I'm afraid. We were the only two on the trail and it was still a little dark. I was heading back to my house and your mother was just getting started. There was something about the way she walked that distracted me and I wasn't watching where I was going. She saw me trip and came running up to me. She was so kind. She helped me over to a bench, loosened my sneaker and had me elevate my foot. Honestly, I thought she was a nurse. She was so calming. We chatted for a while. Then people started coming down. We said our goodbyes but when I got up, I couldn't walk. Your mother brought me back to Whalehead."

Catherine's eyes twinkled. "Can I tell you a secret? There are emergency phones all along that trail and I could have called for help but I didn't want to. I had a sense that your mother was in a hurry, but selfishly I paid it no mind. Arm and arm, we hobbled back to my house. We had every intention of exchanging phone numbers but Tad caught us sneaking into the house. Tad of all people. He was furious. I knew Tad wasn't well but had I not been in so much pain, I would have reamed him out. He dismissed your mother without even a word of thanks. I watched her leave and by the time I realized I didn't know her last name or where she was staying, she was too far away. I felt so sad. There was something about her. She was a lucky woman. She had you and your children. That reminds me. I haven't met your youngest."

Laura smiled. "You haven't met my youngest or my future husband."

"Mike," Catherine replied. "Your children mentioned him. He was the one who gave them that wonderful kite. They really seem to like him."

"They're all waiting for us. It's a little chilly out so if you want to grab a sweater, we can head over to Joe's house."

Catherine hesitated. Expecting to serve brunch, she had more than enough food and was tempted to invite everyone to Whalehead. *No,* she told herself. *It was time to make a new start.*

On the way to the car, Catherine grabbed Laura's arm. She leaned closer. "Can I tell you something? Sixty-five years ago, I thought I lost everything that mattered to me and not a day went by that your mother didn't live on in my dreams. To be perfectly honest, right now I'm afraid to blink. I guess we'll never know what she was like from two to seventeen."

"Two to twenty-five," Laura corrected. "That's when she married my father. From then on, we have a ton of pictures and videos."

"Twenty-five to sixty-seven. I'll take it. You have no idea how much this means to me."

"I think I do," Laura whispered.

Catherine squeezed Laura's arm. "Of course I would give anything to have her here but now, I'll no longer have to dream to see your mother. For the rest of my life, I'll see her in you and in your children. She always liked to surprise me and by some miracle, she's come back to me, in grand style I might add. Thanks to you, she's finally home."

THE END

About Margaret Groh

Margaret is a freelance writer and a former speech therapist. She and her Cardiologist husband married after his first year of medical school. She learned to expect the unexpected through residency, fellowship and many years of emergency night calls.

Margaret raised three wonderful children although when they were little, she sometimes listed her occupation as CEO, Chaos Unlimited. When her youngest went off to college, she volunteered to do taxes for the elderly and is now the local coordinator for the program in her home town.

Margaret received her BS and her MA from the College of New Jersey. She and her husband live in South Jersey.

Social Media

Website: https://margaretgroh.com/

Acknowledgements

To say this book has been in my head for a number of years would be an understatement. It began when I first toured *Whalehead,* a historic hunting club on the Outer Banks of North Carolina. A wicked thunderstorm was blowing in and I knew this would someday make the perfect setting for a suspense novel.

My protagonist came about as a collective response to my experiences with reporters, family secrets and an unshakeable belief that if you look hard enough, you can find a silver lining in most clouds.

While there are many people to thank for helping me along the way, I want to give a shout out to my good friend Charlotte, for all the years she patiently listened to my many book ideas and for her editorial expertise.

Oddly enough, this book started to come together after I mustered the courage to show my manuscript to my husband. He patiently went through not one version but two, each time making valuable suggestions.

My siblings and my children took over after that. Thanks to all who read my manuscript, commented honestly and encouraged me to keep going. One of my biggest surprises was all the support I received from my brother, Mike. A numbers person at heart, Mike took the time to outline the book, print it up and then share it with his wife, Debby. I knew if it made sense to Mike, it would make sense to my readers.

One of the greatest joys in writing this book came when I received the publication contract from Solstice Publishing. I will always cherish the reaction of my family and friends. They say a joy shared is twice the joy. So very true.

CPSIA information can be obtained
at www.ICGtesting.com
Printed in the USA
BVHW042010191218
535999BV00019B/371/P

9 781625 268440